I0690684

VOLUME FIVE

Airship 27 Productions

™

Bass Reeves Frontier Marshal Volume 5

"A Quack's Salvation" © 2022 Michael Panush
"The Ballad of the Tumbleweed Outlaw" © 2022 Thomas McNulty
"Wages of Gold" © 2022 Gary Phillips
"The Dead of Night" © 2022 Mel Odom

Published by Airship 27 Productions
www.airship27.com
www.airship27hangar.com

Cover illustration © 2022 Warren Montgomery
Interior illustrations ©2022 Rob Davis

Editor: Ron Fortier
Associate Editor: Jonathan Sweet
Marketing and Promotions Manager: Michael Vance
Production designer: Rob Davis

ISBN: 978-1-953589-33-0

Printed in the United States of America

10 9 8 7 6 5 4 3 2 1

BASS REEVES
FRONTIER MARSHAL
VOLUME 5

TABLE OF CONTENTS

A QUACK'S SALVATION

By Michael Panush

"Gentlemen, I ask you a simple question: what is the greatest treasure which Providence has delivered into the hands of all?"

I waited. No answer was forthcoming. No sound but the gentle crackle and spark of the campfire in this dismal dark clearing, and the nightly chorus of birds, frogs, and other forest creatures who called this wild section of Indian Territory home.

"I'll tell you." I offered a smile and doffed my fez. "It is our health. And what better way to honor Providence, or the Most High as I call the Good Lord, then by keeping and safeguarding our health with all manner of salubrious tonics?"

My potential customers stared back at me in silence somewhere between bemusement and total idiocy. A collection of half-a-dozen slack-jawed *goyish* sons of the soil who had cast civilization behind and sought their fortune in the lawless Territory. They sat in a half-circle around the fire, working chewing tobacco in their cheeks or puffing on cheroots as they watched. All of them bore weaponry of some kind—six-shooters holstered on their belts, rifles on their backs, or knives in their boots—and they struck me as the kind to use them with enthusiastic alacrity.

Gevalt—what a sour predicament. I've studied with the true masters of the grifter's trade in my time. Bunko Kings who sold non-existent railroad shares, worthless cures, and dubious psychic dousing rods to all manner of rubes, and learned their lessons well. Why, in my time I've courted and conned Captains of Industry and blue-blooded New York royalty alike.

And yet, there I was. Trapped in the Territory.

One rangy outlaw, a fellow with a knife scar that rendered his left eye white, sightless, and drooping, unleashed a long spray of tobacco into the fire. "Who the hell are you?" The liquid made the flame sizzle and steam.

I unleashed another bow as I darted back, to my waiting wagon. "Professor Alexander Ashe. Traveling purveyor of wonders."

I swirled my turquoise blue cape around me and gave the side of my

5

transport a rap. My wagon, the Ambulatory Arcanum, had a splendid galaxy of designs painted on the wood. Stars and moons swirled in the cosmic dust, mingled with Hebrew lettering and Talmudic designs. If my teachers at the Yeshiva, may they rot in the earth, had a glance at it, they'd probably share a long laugh. But for the *goyim*, it bespoke the kind of mysticism that they often attached to the Hebraic people—that, along with so much else, marked us as forever apart.

Perfect for fooling the rubes. Blinding the credulous with a little Old Testament magic.

And yet, these rubes were not fooled. It would take more than that.

I gave it another rap. "Milo—move your bones, *boychick*!"

Milo Ashe—Motl Asche, to use his real name—stumbled his way out of the back of the wagon, one of his beloved dime novels tucked under his arm. A nine-year-old *luftmensch*. He would live in those adventure stories if he could.

Now, at least, he did his job. Namely, standing by my side in a blue Norfolk suit that somewhat matched mine, and displaying his massive and startlingly blue eyes to the assemblage. As fine a prop as the wagon behind us.

I reached to the back of the wagon. "Tell them, Milo. Provide testimony."

He glanced at me and back at the assorted ruffians gathered by the fire. "Um—Uncle Alexander, are you certain—"

"Testimony, Milo—speak!" I opened the back, where a variety of crates waited.

He cleared his throat, his face going pale. "Well, when I was younger, I was once stricken by a terrible bout of rheumatism. Golly, I felt certain that death was at my door. Then, Uncle Alexander here unlocked the mysteries of the Kabbalah and the Talmud and prayed like the dickens. It was like enough to make the angels cry, and he bottled the results, which cured me like that." He attempted to snap his fingers, but didn't quite manage it.

I returned, bearing a bottle of Elohim Elixir—my favored product. The mud brown bottle with angel wings on the label, rested in my hands. I hoisted it up. "Gentlemen, you have heard from your own ears how effective the Tears of Angel can be at banishing maladies. Who will be the first to take a taste?"

Usually, I'd prepare my pitch with a little more salt. Perhaps a few limping members of the audience, who would cast aside their crutches upon a sip. But we were in a hurry, and hadn't time for such gilding.

The blind-eyed bad man came slowly to his feet. Another stream of tobacco went hissing down into the fire. He walked closer, as the others came to their feet. "So you travel around, professor, peddling that there concoction?"

"Indeed." I gripped the bottle with both hand and stepped back—in front of Milo.

The protective instinct of an uncle.

"What we gonna do with him, Abner?" A hirsute outlaw, his face almost entirely obscured by a bush of a black beard, called out in a high voice.

Abner's hand emerged, bearing a cruel Bowie knife. "So you got money in that wagon?"

"Not—not very much." Not nearly enough as I would like.

"Supposing we take it. Supposing we take every cent you're carrying and carve you up like a goddamn hog. That elixir gonna cure you?"

"Uncle?" Milo's voice went higher than usual—moving from a chirp to a whine.

I raised my hands. "Gentlemen, there's no need for this…"

"Uncle?" Milo repeated the question. "Uncle—someone approaches!"

The crowd of desperadoes went quiet, their eyes going to the edge of the clearing. I looked as well.

A horse, a lean roan mare, trotted to the clearing, bearing a broad-shouldered fellow in a cattleman's duster and weather-beaten Stetson. He slid from the saddle in a practiced motion, took hold of the horse's reins, and walked over to join us. Firelight revealed dark skin—a colored fellow. He wore a massive moustache, occupying his upper lip with the same confidence that the two heavy revolvers occupied the gunbelt below his coat. The flame glinted on a golden watchchain, the only bit of frippery emerging from his checkered waistcoat.

His eyes—half-closed and narrowing into a slight scowl—seemed like those of a hawk. They took in everything. Settling with a particular finality on me. My tongue swelled. I went silent—*verklempt*. An impossibility for me.

He touched the brim of his hat. "Howdy." A thunder's rumble of a voice.

"Marshal Reeves…" Abner stammered. "Didn't know you was riding the Territory."

"There's a lot you don't know." He nodded toward the knife. "Stow that."

Abner acquiesced without comment. "Who you going after now, Marshal?"

Reeves led his horse to a waiting tree and commenced tying the reins. "Ain't you. Now take your leave."

"Right." Abner motioned to the others. "Come on, fellows. We'll camp down somewhere else." They drifted away, eyes downcast, and slipped their way into the woods. In just a few moments, the clearing lay empty, apart from myself, my nephew, and this mysterious dusky gunslinger, who hobbled his horse and strode toward us.

Milo took my hand. "Who is he?" He whispered—but as usual, the boy miscalculated.

Reeves doffed his hat. "Bass Reeves, Deputy US Marshal." He opened his coat, letting the firelight shine on the star encircled in gold. "And you're..." He seemed annoyed to even announce my title. "Professor Alexander Ashe. Is that correct?"

"You have named me properly, sir." I still held the Elohim Elixir. This fellow had been seeking me. He certainly seemed fearsome. Strong as an ox, no doubt—but probably as foolish as one too. Perhaps I could distract him. "Can I ask you a simple question? What is the greatest treasure which Providence has delivered into the hands of all?"

"Uncle..." Milo grabbed my hand tightly. "Don't try and—"

"Hush!" I delivered a rapid cuffing to the boy. "Well, Mr. Reeves, I will tell you the answer. The greatest gift is our good health and—"

He crossed the clearing faster than I could imagine and pulled the jar of Elixir from my hand. I went silent as he worked out the cork and gave it a sniff. The glare from his eyes told me what he thought of the scent. "You were lately at the Big B Ranch, down Kansas way. Is that right?"

I tried my best to smile. "I'm a traveler, Mr. Reeves—I have ventured all over our great country."

"Marshal Reeves." His voice darkened. "You were selling your merchandise to Bartholomew Braddock. Called Bighead, on account of his oversized noggin. Is that correct, Mr. Ashe?"

"Professor Ashe." Though, in truth, it was an entirely honorary title. "And I perhaps made the acquaintance of Mr. Braddock. I didn't chance to call him 'Bighead,' though. That name seems entirely rude."

"You witnessed him bringing in cattle bearing other brands? Sending his hands out to rustle?"

It is a sin to bear false witness—so I chose to say nothing. Not least because I had indeed witnessed just such things. It was the reason Milo and I were currently trapped in the wilderness of Indian Territory. Like Moses and his Hebrews, fleeing from Pharaoh's army.

I made a slight humming noise, but said nothing more.

But Milo—idiot boy!—raised his hand like he was in a schoolhouse. "Um—I believe that we did, sir."

"Then you're coming back with me to Fort Smith." He pointed to me. "You're gonna tell Judge Parker just that and you'll swear to it and sign your name. You understand?" He rolled his eyes. "Professor?"

Judge Parker—Hanging Judge Parker. This Reeves fellow must be his agent. He seemed dangerous, but so was Bighead Braddock. I had no intention of placing myself in the midst of such behemoths.

"I have considered your offer, marshal, and I refuse. My nephew and I shall seek greener pastures and—"

Reeves upended the bottle of Elohim Elixir, right over the fire. The liquid spilled down. A flash of light and steam shot up, blasting the clearing with a profusion of color. Smoke sizzled out and the burning scent stung our nose. Reeves just poured, cool as could be.

"Wait—stop!" I had the feeling he'd dump out the entirety of my inventory if I didn't stop him. "I agree. We'll ride with you to Fort Smith."

"Good." He tossed the bottle my way and I struggled to catch it. Then Reeves walked to the edge of the clearing and stared out into the shadowed forest. Twilight had given way to night. "We'll camp here for tonight. Get a fresh start in the morning." He walked back to his horse, where his bedroll waited. "Don't try nothing."

"Oh, I wouldn't dream of it," I lied.

Because Marshal Reeves may be many things. A brute. A *schwartze*. But he was the law. *Goyish* law. And that meant I couldn't trust him. *Goyish* law had kept my family trapped in the Pale of Settlement, a miserable section of snow and cold on the Eastern European battlefield of Empire. It sent Cossacks riding through our villages, butchering to their hearts content, and had painted one such ruffian's blade in my father's blood.

I couldn't trust him. Particularly with Milo under my care. He and I took our bedrolls and blankets from the Ambulatory Arcanum and spread them by the fire, as I considered how I could outsmart Reeves and make good my escape.

I kept myself awake with the memories of prayers from my Yeshiva days. An oddity—the words had been repeated so often that the Hebrew slipped into nonsense, but the syllables remained, sewn into the fabric of my being. I mumbled them to myself, over and over again, as Milo curled himself near the fire and slipped into the Land of Nod in a matter of moments. The good Marshal Reeves was another story. He lay silently in his bedroll, gazing up at the stars. By and by, he rolled over. The prayers continued in my head.

Those *mamzer* rabbis at the Yeshiva would certainly be proud. Rote memorization and an adherence to the upright path. That was their goal. Hoping in turn to mold us into another generation of Jewish scholars, dust-covered and joyless—and they spared not the rod in their miserable quest. Thank the Most High I had escaped.

I would escape Reeves in the same way.

Enough time had passed. The marshal slumbered. I was certain of it.

"Milo." I whispered the word and gave his cheek a flick.

"Ah!" He sat up. "Uncle, what are we—"

"Hush!" I put a finger to my lips. "Do you want to wake that Cossack over there? Keep your mouth closed, *boychick*." I scrambled out of the bedroll and handed him his coat. "Come on. We're going to the wagon."

I made my way over as Milo blinked his eyes and slipped into the coat and put on his yarmulke. "What? But he just wants us to go to Fort Smith. For you to tell the truth." He summoned all the dignity that a child could muster. "It's what is right, uncle."

Our mule, Judah, waited in harness. I worked at the hobble and got it free. "No point. If you think the American government gives a damn about us—"

"I am an American," Milo replied. And indeed, he was. Born in New York and raised by my older brother before I had offered to make him my apprentice. The better to keep him out of the garment factories. "And this is—this is law-breaking."

"The law cares nothing for us." I scrambled to the coachman's seat of the Ambulatory Arcanum and patted the board next to me. "Now climb aboard. It's time for us to go."

"And where would that be?" Reeves' voice.

I froze, the reins grasped in my hand. Judah stared back at me, his ears perked up. "You—you heard us?"

He sat up. Moonlight shone on his pistol—aimed straight at me. "Wouldn't last long as a marshal if I weren't a light sleeper." He sprang up and approached, facing the wagon in vest and shirtsleeves with his revolver raised. "Come on down from there, professor. I can't rightly say I know what a Cossack is, but I'm fairly certain I ain't one. You come with me and you tell the truth, you'll get fair treatment. That's what the law of this land promises—even if it don't always deliver. That's my aim, though."

I shivered in my coat. That revolver yawned wide—the mouth of the lions in the den with Daniel. "Are you going to shoot me?"

"I'm considering it." He shrugged me. "If it would shut you up."

"Please." Milo spoke up. "Please, sir. He'll go with you. Uncle Alexander—Professor Ashe—he's a good person. A *mensch*." A word I had used, now and then. "He just, sometimes, makes bad decisions."

I moved to give Milo a quick cuffing—just as a shot rang out. It hummed past me and blasted into the back of the wagon. Judah snorted and stirred, jostling the Arcanum and Reeves' horse whickered from where it waited against the tree.

An ambuscade.

"Down!" Reeves shouted. "Bushwhacker!"

The Marshal sprang behind a fallen log by the fire and emerged bearing a repeating rifle. I hadn't seen him stash the long arm there. Reeves aimed in the direction of the gunshot and returned fire—three rapid shots, punctuated by him working the lever as if that rifle was some fifth limb. The shots burned through the air, the cracks echoing over the wood. No gunfire followed.

One thought burned my brain: Milo. I shoved him back, through the curtained partition, and sent him into the center of the wagon. Would the Ambulatory Arcanum provide him any protection? I could only hope.

Silence in the woods. Reeves kept the rifle trained at the forest—at some hidden gunman. I still held the reins, but ducked back. For the moment, Reeves held my would-be assassin at bay, but how long would that state of affairs continue?

"Reeves?" A rasp called from somewhere in the darkness and trees. "Is that you?"

"Who I am addressing?" Reeves called back.

"Prong, Mr. Marshal. Heck Prong."

Prong—I had heard the name whispered about Bighead Braddock's ranch. Even seen him pointed out, as he stood off by the edge of some corral gazing at the red sun over the prairie. I had inquired as to the terms of his employment to Braddock, and had received only a fond shake of the head. "Prong solves my problems, son," Braddock had explained. "Let's leave it at that." Now, I was the problem to be solved.

Reeves betrayed no fear. "Heard you raised Hell over in Nebraska. The Carlyle-Pike Range War."

"Carved me plenty of notches then, Reeves. I'd like to add a pair now." Prong hesitated. "Any chance of you stepping aside? Letting me do my job?"

"I've got to do mine, Prong." Reeves glanced at me and waved a hand up and down. Pantomiming the cracking of the reins. I nodded back. An escape seemed worthwhile. Reeves tensed himself, squaring his shoulders and sucking in air. "So I guess there's no more point in talking."

"Nah." Prong let out a laugh—dry as the dusty twigs in summer. "But that's all right. I prefer it this way."

Reeves rolled out from behind the log. He fired again—then kicked over the remains of the fire. Logs, charcoal, embers, and ash spilled into the air. They billowed wide, forming a bluish cloud. Hiding him from view. He darted to the wagon next, springing up as I cracked the reins. Judah went into a gallop, letting out his warbling cry as we ran pounded through the clearing and out toward a trail winding into the woods.

Gunshots hummed behind us. The wheels of the Arcanum rumbled and creaked, the whole wagon jostling and threatening to throw me from my perch. The same for Reeves. He had one hand on the seat, the other on his rifle, and his feet flailed as he sought purchase.

I sensed an opportunity.

Remove our captor and assassin in one fell swoop? The Most High but rarely delivers us such good fortune.

I pulled back my leg. "What the hell are you doing?" Reeves demanded.

In answer, I slammed it down and banged my loafer against his shoulder. His grip increased, so I jabbed him again. On the third time, I had some luck. Reeves slipped back and tumbled down. He crashed against the earth, rolling over before vanishing beneath the Ambulatory Arcanum.

Had he gone under the wheels? In the chaos of the night, I couldn't tell. Another rifle shot blasted out somewhere behind, and the shot cracked against the side of the Arcanum. Splinters flew. I ducked and cracked the reins, stirring Judah to new feats of speed. Night would cover us, and the waiting trees. Let Prong and Reeves fight it out. Hopefully, they'd devour each other.

I smiled to myself as I maneuvered Judah around a bend in the road. The trees thinned, giving way to some sparse grasslands and the waiting stony hills and mountains. We'd ride through and make good our escape.

"Fortune favors the bold." I murmured the words to myself. A Yiddish proverb? Probably not. But it fit my situation perfectly. I had been bold, and good fortune had come to Milo and myself. Now, we merely had to make good our escape from Indian Territory and the open road itself would be our sanctuary.

Morning found us on the road, away from the tangle of the forest and closer to the hill country. A splendid day had dawned. Bright sunshine on the prairie grass, the flowers adding a dash of color to the ancient hills. Up ahead, stony peaks stretched into the sunlight. I hummed an old synagogue tune as Milo emerged from the back of the wagon and joined me on the perch. He bore a canteen of water, which I snatched from his hand and consumed. Some beef jerky, kept in a pack in my coat, completed our morning repast.

I offered a fistful of jerky to Milo. "Chew slowly, my dear boy. Savor the tang."

"It's not Kosher, is it?"

"What is Kosher, Milo?" I gestured with the canteen, spilling a few drops in my motion. "Some gray-bearded rabbi murmurs a few words over the beast before the blade crosses its throat? Kosher means sanctified, and this jerky has been sanctified by our experience. Valiantly contending with death itself? There is no holier blessing in all of God's Kingdom."

He accepted the jerky sourly. "We didn't contend with death. We ran away."

"We survived, didn't we?"

"That was Mr. Reeves' doing." Milo looked exasperated, his face growing red as he fumbled for a triangular piece of jerky. "He drew his rifle, battled with the assassin, and allowed us to escape. And *you* kicked him off our wagon."

There is something particularly cruel about being called to account by a child. I considered cuffing him for his criticism, but my hand would not rise. Instead, shame sizzled in my guts. It was like when I was a boy and stole trinkets from the back of my father's wagon. He would seemingly know I had the *tchotchke* hidden in my pocket, and his cold glare was all that was needed to tell me I'd done wrong.

Now, I looked away. Unable to stare down a child.

"He was trying to protect us. To save our lives from that assassin in the brush."

"He is a lawman, attempting to get his bounty. A Cossack, serving a Tsar in Fort Smith."

Milo's voice went to a shrill squeak. "There's no Tsar in Fort Smith, Uncle Alexander. You know better."

I clutched the reins and stared ahead. We neared the edge of some large rocky slope, the gray burnished by sunlight. "Say what you want, *boychick*. You only have to look at Marshal Reeves to know that he's not like us." I

"There's no Tsar in Fort Smith, Uncle Alexander."

left the rest of it unsaid.

"So, he is different, and therefore, you hold him in low regard?" Milo stared away. "Well—that's just the same sort of thinking that drove you and everyone else out of the Old Country in the first place. And now you're spitting bigotry at a lawman—a hero of the west, for God's sake." His voice rose to a squeak. "Goddamn you!"

The swear sounded absurd, but it stabbed deep. I dropped the reins. "You watch your tongue. I brought you out here for your edification, you little *pisher*—not to adopt the rude manners of harsh language of the frontier and—and—and—" I trailed off. He was staring past me at the mountains. "What is it?"

"We seem to have reached a settlement, uncle."

Sure enough, the trail ended in a sort of outpost built outside a cave. It looked like a truly miserable excuse of what passed for civilization, with a collection of ragged tents and cabins set upon a gravel slope. Assorted Indians and outlaws relaxed about the camp, indulging in moonshine and games of chance. The cave itself looked like the capitol of this miserable empire, glimmering with torchlight from within and even emanating some tinkling, off-key piano music. A sign above the entrance, nestled in the stone, bore the name of the establishment: the Cave-Inn.

How charming.

"Well, it seems that the Most High smiles on us once more." I directed my wagon up to a hitching post set at the foot of the slope. "This appears to be some sort of boarding house carved out of the earth. We can eat a decent breakfast and maybe even get some rest. Once again, your uncle has succeeded in keeping you safe."

Milo turned away and said nothing. Becoming sullen.

"Come on." I let Judah trot to a halt and hopped down from my perch. "I'll get you breakfast. A real one. Maybe even a warm bed to sleep in. I owe your parents that, at least." I offered my hand. Milo accepted it—begrudgingly.

I helped him down. After unhitching Judah and setting him near the wagon, we trudged up the slope toward the shadowy entrance of the Cave-Inn.

"You don't think anyone will try and rob the wagon?" Milo asked.

"Fear of the supernatural symbols will keep them away." Besides, there wasn't much in the Ambulatory Arcanum worth stealing. A few bottles of Elohim Elixir? They were welcome to pilfer those. I had too many. "Now, let's see what delights are in store for us within."

Not many, as it turned out. The Cave-Inn offered a few ramshackle tables constructed of barrels and wooden planks, and a single counter in the back where one could procure coffin varnish. Further stone pathways led off to a little kitchen, which released foul smelling smoke. The clientele relaxed amongst chairs made from halved logs or crates, and gazed at Milo and I over their cups of coffin varnish. In the back, a little piano, which must have been placed here with great difficulty, jangled away under the efforts of an unskilled player.

Far from an earthly paradise.

However, it did present one diversion—a card game, taking place at the table in the center. Currently, about four players worked their way through a deck, with a good pot in the middle of the table. Bundles of rumpled bills, a smattering of change, and even a pearl-handled six-gun. All switching amongst the players as fortune ebbed and flowed.

I'm a good hand at cards. To be a good gambler requires a similar sort of skill as to be a salesman of patent-medicine: a willingness to let certain confounding truths vanish away and to give oneself permission to pretend wholeheartedly that a pair of twos is the greatest hand in the world. Reading the opposition—whether fellow gamblers or potential customers—is similarly vital.

Perhaps this sojourn wouldn't be a bust after all.

I drew some bills from my pocket and passed them to Milo. "Get yourself some breakfast. Fried eggs and fatback, perhaps. And a drink for me. Then bring them to the table and I'll dine as I play."

"You're going to gamble?"

I patted his head. "Have some faith in your uncle, *boychick*. I'm still feeling lucky."

"But Prong is still after us. We should depart—"

"One game, Milo. That's all I ask." I waved my hand. "Now go. I'd like something strong to ease my playing. A good whiskey, yes?"

He toddled off. A good little fellow. I'd be sure to buy him another dime novel when this was over, as a reward for services rendered.

Then I settled down at the table. "Gentlemen!" I examined the crowd. "A pleasure to you all on this cold and yet starkly beautiful morning. I am Professor Alexander Ashe, late of Poland." I let a little trace of the Old Country's accent drift into my words. "A stranger to your shores, but not to games of chance. May I heartily suggest you deal me in?"

Silence from the gentleman gamblers. Then one, who on closer inspection was no man at all, pushed up the brim of her hat and squinted at me.

"What are you playing with?"

I set a few bills down. "Enough to gain me admittance into your game?"

"Why not?" She had a darker hue to her skin. Some Indian blood, perhaps? Clearly, she was a rough sort, bearing a bandolier over her chest and a knife and pistol in her belt. Her tattered and stained waistcoat and men's trousers completed the look. A heron's feather protruded from hat, which topped rumpled chestnut-colored hair. "You got money to lose, I won't stop you from losing it."

There was something familiar about her, but I could not put my mind on it. I had seen that likeness before.

"Splendid!" I extended my hand. "Deal me in."

The cards came and we played. I did well enough—neatly winning the first hand as Milo returned bearing his breakfast and my drink. He settled next to me, jabbing his fork at a particularly noxious pile of eggs heated and scrambled on some hidden stove. My offering proved much better—a glass of amber whiskey. I gave it a sip as the dealer delivered our subsequent hand.

The feminine desperado cocked her head. "Quite a pair you are. Father and son, maybe? I can see the resemblance."

I nudged Milo. A chance to put his politeness on display would never go amiss. "Actually, ma'am, we are uncle and nephew." He bowed his head, scrambled eggs still clinging to his chin. "I am Milo Ashe."

"Ma'am, huh? Haven't been called that in a dog's age." She winked at Milo, making him flush. "A bit funny." She examined her cards as she leaned back in the makeshift seat. "The two of you, dressed alike, wandering around out here."

"Rather like a knight and his faithful squire?" I suggested.

"Like that mad Spaniard. Fellow likes to tilt at windmills and the little runt that follows him around." She shrugged. "Territory's no place for a child, professor. And ain't that an oddity, seemingly giving how whole generations have grown up in this godforsaken place with no one giving much of a damn." She touched the brim of her hat. "My mama's Cherokee. I know it well."

"And by what name may I call you, madam?"

Now, she did smile—revealing a single gold tooth gleaming under her lip. "Pearl Payne. Though they call me something different on the posters—Pistol Pearl."

Pistol Pearl Payne—the knowledge of where I had seen her previously came flooding back like a divine revelation. During our last visit to Mule's

Mound, Missouri—a singularly depressing stretch of mud—her Wanted poster hung prominently on telegraph poles and the walls of the local saloon. The Wanted poster bore a fearsome likeness, her mouth open in something like a lioness's roar, while a long list of her crimes stretched below her.

Bank robbery, train robbery, stage coach robbery—murder and mayhem running across a half-dozen states and territories. And now, there she was. Sitting across from me over a hand of playing cards. Like when King Solomon had conjured up Asmodeus. The fellows with her, perhaps a half-score of hard cases, must be her loyal outlaw band.

Her presence here made sense. Indian Territory—notoriously lawless—was the perfect hideout for those not wanting to be found. Only US Marshals like Bass Reeves would dare to cross it. In fact, that was why I had come here. Seeking refuge from Bighead Braddock along with numerous other lawmen and irate townsfolk angry at the quality of my merchandise.

After crossing the Atlantic Ocean in search of refuge, it was a small journey.

But now, with Pistol Pearl's fearsome gaze on me, salvation seemed far from assured. I shifted in my seat. Sweat made my collar sticky.

Milo looked from me to Payne. "Uncle, Pistol Pearl's an outlaw! I've read about her in the dime novels. She's a—a bandit queen!"

"*Gevalt*, Milo—shut up!" I gripped his shoulder and hissed the words. He went silent. "Never mind him. A *luftmensch*, I tell you—his head in the clouds. Half of what he says makes little sense to me."

Payne shrugged. "Never mind that. It's your time, professor. Call or raise."

I had nearly forgotten about the game. I glanced at my hand, pushed a silver dollar toward the center, and let the circuit continue. Payne stared back at me, smiling a little as her turn arrived. "I call." She let the cards fall.

A winning hand. All the pot went to her.

It appeared that the metaphor of the frying pan and the fire might sum up our predicament. We had escaped from the manhunter Reeves and the assassin Prong, only to find ourselves sharing company with, as Milo had said, an outlaw queen. She didn't appear to be hiding her identity—there was little need for it in Indian Territory—but that didn't mean she would keep our company in a friendly manner. I glanced at Milo. He had eaten about half of his eggs, the remainder congealing on the plate.

He'd have to finish the rest on the road.

"Well, I fear my luck has turned against me." I made a show of yawning and stretching. "Your poker skills, Ms. Payne, are equaled only by your beauty."

"Shucks, professor—you always this complimentary?" Payne chuckled.

"It presages my departure." I pushed back the chair. "The money I've lost will not be regained. Farewell, Ms. Payne. It is with pure sorrow that I must—"

A harsh, familiar voice called from the entrance. "Sit back down, Professor." The speech bore volume, but not rage. "Sit yourself down, slowly."

Milo grabbed my hand. Ice in his fingers. "Uncle—it's *him*."

Heck Prong. Our would-be killer.

Payne looked up from her hand and motioned to the empty chair next to her. "Up for a game, Heck?"

"Always."

He crossed the stone floor and the Cave-Inn had gone so quiet that the clicks of his boots echoed like thunder. Prong settled into the seat and stared at me as Payne sent some cards his way. It is not every day one can look one's would-be assassin in the eye. I would not recommend the experience. He had cold gray eyes, a gray broadcloth coat and a gray kerchief. Stubble of a grayish color clung tightly to his face and while he looked to have a rangy, youthful strength about him, the hair under his pearl bowler had transformed into gray strands.

On the whole, he resembled a corpse below the shroud more than a man.

A matchstick rested in the corner of his mouth, and it jabbed up and down as he examined the cards. Why hadn't he pulled the long-barreled revolver at his hip and planted a bullet in my back from the mouth of the cave? Confidence, no doubt, that I could not escape. Or maybe this wolf liked to watch the rabbit squirm in its jaws before biting down.

"How you been, professor?" He lazily eyed his hand. "Been a while since I saw you at the Big B."

"That it has." I kept my tone even. Milo shivered next to me, looking as if those eggs had disagreed with him and would soon emerge as vomit. "How is Mr. Braddock?"

"He's doing all right—but he fears the hair he lost due to your tonic won't ever return." Prong made a dry sort of chuckle. More like a raspy murmur than anything bespeaking merriment. "Ain't that the way? He wanted something to end the headaches, and you gave him something that took the hair off his noggin and made his head look even more like a giant egg. Draws attention—which is just what Mr. Braddock don't want."

"I heartily apologize. Perhaps he used the concoction incorrectly." Maybe I could still find salvation. "If I could merely speak with Mr.

Braddock, perhaps I could tell him how to apply the Angel Elixir. Hair growth is actually one of its many restorative powers. If I could merely speak with him."

"Yeah…" Prong shrugged. "I don't think you'll get the chance."

"Prong." Payne spoke for the first time. "I don't want any unpleasantness here."

"I don't care what you want." He tossed his cards on the table with a grunt. "I fold."

Silence as the game continued. There had to be something I could say. My fast words had saved me a thousand times. They had come to my aid again—for Milo's sake.

He raised a hand—weakly. As if he was a Yeshiva *Bucher* in a schoolhouse. Prong glared at him. "What?"

His voice went very quiet. "What became of Marshal Reeves?"

Prong smiled—or maybe he was just revealing his teeth. "Why do you care? He wanted to haul your uncle before Judge Parker."

"What became of him?" Milo repeated.

"We quarreled. He was in a weakened state, after being kicked out of a wagon." Prong grinned at me. "Thank you for that, professor. I proved victorious and he fled. I fired at him and he went into a river. If my bullets didn't end him, then the current did. Cold as Hell this time of year, and that river flows fast." He drew out the match and produced a cigar case from his coat. "Hell, maybe that marshal's badge gave him so much pride was what dragged him down."

Milo shuddered. He pulled his hand away from me and commenced shivering. Would the boy burst into tears? I had been catching him sobbing, now and then. Stricken with homesickness. Not manly, of course, but I never criticized him for it. I had cried do, after my father's passing, when my brother tossed me in the Yeshiva and went on his way.

But to weep over Reeves?

"Milo." I patted his shoulder. "Reeves was a lawman. A Cossack. A *schwa*—"

"Don't—don't say his name." Milo turned away.

"You admired the colored lawdog?" Prong asked. "Don't that beat all." He fixed his eyes on me and stood up. His hand had gone low—resting on the butt of his revolver. "All right. I'm tired of talking."

Payne stood as well. "Hold on, Prong. This is my place. If there's money to be made in bringing the professor back to Braddock, it ought to be me who earns it."

He shot her a glare. "I said I'm tired of talking. We can argue over what happens to their carcasses later. But they both earned a bullet and they'll get it now."

So that was it. The end—right here in this miserable stretch of Indian Territory. I sprang from the seat. "No!" My tongue had gone swollen and slow. *Gevalt*! Maybe I could save Milo, at least. What wrong had he done, besides trust his uncle? "The boy. Please." I stood in front of Milo. "He's of tender years. Let him go. He'll return to New York, to his family, and never bother Mr. Braddock again. I swear on the Most High, he'll present no trouble. Just let him walk out to the wagon."

Even Payne added her voice. "He's the size of a chigger, Prong. You oughtn't to hurt him."

But Prong just shrugged. "Hell, these Jews killed Christ, didn't they? Maybe they earned all the hurt they got coming to them. Besides, what does he got to look forward to?" He pulled the pistol and let it rest calmly at his side. "And I'm not swinging from a rope in Fort Smith on the word of anyone."

The Cossack who had slain my father, who had gutted him during an argument at a toll bridge somewhere on the Russian Frontier, had the same uncaring look when he glanced back at my brother and I, huddling in our peddler's wagon. He hadn't slain us—but he could have. For men like Prong, so detached from the rest of the world, taking even a young life matters little.

And I had placed Milo squarely in his sights.

My eyes went to my whiskey glass. Still full. "A final drink, if you please." I put my hand on Milo's shoulder. He shivered still, saddened over Reeves' apparent demise.

Prong shrugged as he leveled the gun.

I raised the glass—and hurled it as hard as I could in Prong's direction. A desperate gesture. Feeble, you might say. I hoped to bounce the shot glass against his forehead and send him reeling. Instead, the drink fell short and its contents erupted over Prong's shirt front. Whiskey splashed over his kerchief and chin. The acrid alcohol tang hung thick in the air.

No point in lingering. Instead, I grabbed hold of Milo's scrawny arm and hauled him toward the door. A few dollars and coins rested on the table. Grab them? No time. Those coins would be lost to the ages. One more disappointment in a journey full of them. Milo yelped as our feet pounded together against the stones. We reached the cave entrance and stumbled out into cold sunlight.

Behind us, a blast of gunfire. I risked a look over my shoulder. Prong had fired—but Payne had struck his arm, forcing the pistol into the table. The bullet had stirred nothing but sawdust. Prong planted an elbow in Payne's throat, banged the handle of his pistol against her closest underling, and hastened out to give chase.

We departed the Cave-Inn. "To the wagon!" I shouted the command to Milo. "We'll ride away. Leave this place in the dust." We started down the slope, passing the tents, benches, and their inhabitants, who watched the chase with a bemused disinterest.

It must be just another Sunday morning in Indian Territory.

Down the rocky slope we scrambled, leaving grooves in the gravel and covering our fine shoes in dust. The Ambulatory Arcanum loomed close. A few more steps and we'd be there.

But the rocks slipped under my shoe. My leg jutted forward, my arms flailing. I tumbled down, rolled over twice. My fez fell away and bounced out of my reach, just past my fingers. Dust all around, choking in the air, painting my dug, and clinging to my fine garments.

"*Gevalt!*" I sat up. Milo remained, standing close by—offering his hand. "No—you idiot—get to the wagon—get away!" I tried to shoo him, to push him. Anything to get him to safety.

Until a hand settled on my arm and pulled me up. Prong spun me around. "Professor." He muttered my title, then struck me with unbelievable force in the chin.

The world spun around me. I crashed hard into the side of a ragged tent, then slid down and fell into some stash of tools. Cloth bent on my feet as I once again landed on my back. A pickaxe and shovel rattled past me as the sky above burned white. I tried to stand, or even to speak—but the pain had other ideas.

"Don't hurt him!" Milo, the fearless *luftmensch*, standing up for my defense. A slap to his face and he joined me on the earth.

"Should've been simple." Prong muttered to himself as he opened the cylinder of his revolver. "Put a bullet in some Jew snake oil-peddler and his runt nephew. Like beating a pup to death with a length of stove wood. Be home in time for supper." He placed a bullet in the empty chamber. "But the pair of you make everything hard, don't you?" He gave the cylinder a spin—checking the action perhaps. "I'm gonna send your nephew to Hell before you, professor." He grabbed Milo's wrist and pulled him closer.

"Dear God—no!" I managed to sit up—but that was all I could do. I could not save Milo, any more than I could have saved my father. The

Most High delights in murdering what we love.

"No reason for it, except spite." He shrugged. "But that's always been reason enough for me."

"Prong!" A booming voice—shouting from the edge of the encampment. Prong went still.

Bass Reeves rode in, on the back of his roan. He looked a tad soggy, perhaps, but otherwise none the worse for wear, and certainly not a candidate for the World to Come. He slowed his horse, cantered past the Ambulatory Arcanum, and swung down from the saddle. His repeating rifle rested in one hand, aimed casually at Prong.

"Huh." Prong looked surprised—an impossibility, I had imagined.

"Next time you kill a man, Prong, you ought to make sure that you put a hole through him." He opened his duster, revealing the gap in the cloth. "And not his coat."

"Marshal Reeves!" Milo beamed at him. "You're all right—you're okay."

He smiled at the boy—a rather strange sight. "Ain't the first time I've been shot at. Won't be the last either." He walked closer, keeping the rifle trained on Prong. "But I'm tired and it's Sunday. How about you let them go, Prong? I'm sure Braddock's paying you a pretty penny for their hides. Is it really worth dying over?"

He increased his grip on Milo's shoulder—making the boy wince. "Seems to me like I'm holding the cards. Drop that repeater or I'll put a hole through the whelp's back."

Reeves stared back as my heart pounded again. I crawled closer to the marshal. "Please—sir—I beg of you—do it." Now, the words tumbled out of me, all tainted by lamentable truth. "I cannot allow any harm to befall Milo. I'll accompany you to Fort Smith. I'll testify. I'll say whatever you like. But do not let him hurt the boy."

Milo merely stared back, his eyes big and luminous. "You'll protect me, sir. You protect the innocent."

Trusting his dime novels like they were holy scripture.

Reeves took a step closer, until he towered above me. He let the rifle fall into the dirt.

"Pistols too." Prong uttered the command coldly.

"You want me to draw them?" Reeves asked. "Lay them down in the dirt?"

"Goddamn, you must think I'm as dumb as you." Prong sneered. "Keep them holstered. Undo your gun belt and let that fall into the dust. Slow-like."

"You'll protect me, sir. You protect the innocent."

"Whatever you say." Reeves shrugged. He worked out the belt buckle carefully.

"See, this is why I always got you beat." Prong tapped his gun barrel on Milo's shoulder. "You read them dime novels they got about you—or about your kind—and you think the words on the page matter. That there's some truth in them. Ain't any more real than the piss the professor here peddles. Pure hokum. But you go on thinking you're some kind of white knight. It makes you weak." He gave another of his mirthless smiles. "Me? I know exactly what I am. I'm a killer. I take money and I kill people. That's all there is to it."

By now, Reeves had the belt out and dangling in his hand. "Not a smart one, though."

"What's that?"

"You sent me in the river, Prong." He let his belt dangle low. "Soaked me to my skin. You think I'd disarm, if the guns weren't already useless?"

With that, Reeves swung his arm out—using the gun-belt and its heavy contents like a giant flail. They lashed out and struck Prong about the head. He made a choking noise as Reeves grabbed his arm and twisted to the side. The pistol lowered in his hand—aiming at the earth, instead of Milo's back.

"Go to your uncle, boy!" Reeves' boot slammed out, driving into Prong's knee. "Go!"

Prong gasped and folded, his fingers loosening—until Reeves bashed him again with the gun-belt. Those six-guns had real weight to them, and they bloodied Prong's nose and sent him to the earth. He dropped his pistol and Reeves kicked it aside.

Another chance to escape. I would take it. Milo scrambled to my side and I joined him. We ran to the Ambulatory Arcanum and he went to the coachman's seat while I untied Judah and readied him to the run. The mule had the chance only to let out a confused grunt before I had him running before us. The wagon twisted about, the wheels crunching over the gravel. Our salvation was at hand.

"Professor." Reeves' voice. He rode closer, back on his horse. Right next to me this time. "You going somewhere?"

I gripped the reins. "Making good our escape, with time you so nobly bought us, my good marshal. Now, the open road beckons! Why don't you ride behind us and—"

"I'm fine where I am." He moved his horse to a canter, making the pace of the wagon. We left the settlement in an odd convoy and headed down the trail. "And you can slow your pace. Prong won't be after us for a bit."

I judged my options. Reeves was in command now—but he had dispatched Prong. Perhaps I could outwit and outrun him yet again?

Before I could crack the reins, he leveled a six-gun straight at me. "Or, you can walk behind me, hands tied up. Nursing a bullet wound."

"Hah! You've overplayed your hand, sir. You just told Prong that the tumble into the stream rendered all of your firearms wet and useless and—"

Reeves fired the pistol straight into the side of the wagon. Leaving a bullet hole directly in the center of a painted moon. Milo gasped at the noise and I shared his fearful outburst. By now, we had left the encampment and rode along a dusty road winding upward. No cover on the sides but a few patches of scrub brush and stone. No escape.

"My pistols and repeater got wet from the river." He holstered the pistol. "They'll dry eventually. But this one and its brother was right in my saddle bag. Works just fine." He looked down the trail and then at Milo. "You all right there, son?"

"Yes, sir." Milo stared at his shoes.

"Did I scare you with the gunshot? I apologize, if I did. Or back in the camp, with Prong. Did that worry you?"

"No, sir—I wasn't frightened."

"You lie far worse than your uncle." Reeves shrugged. "That's all right. Lying's a skill best not practiced." He faced me. "I would've figured you'd leave the boy. Run off to save your own skin. But you stayed and risked it all, for him. You care for your nephew. That's no lie."

"And you risked your life to protect his," I replied.

Milo bobbed his head. "Of course, Marshal Reeves would do that. He is a hero."

"Well?" Reeves asked. "How about it, Ashe? You want to ride alongside a hero for a spell? At least until we get to Fort Smith?"

"Have I a choice in the matter?"

"Not at all." A sly grin.

I glanced at Milo, who nodded expectantly. Eager for me to agree. I shrugged. "*Kenahora*, this will all be over with soon." A little blessing against the gaze of the Evil Eye, though I doubted it would do much good.

Milo, on the other hand, seemed entirely satisfied with his lot in life. Why wouldn't he be? For now, he got to ride alongside a legend.

We rode together in silence as the terrain took a turn toward the steep and rocky. The trail wound past jagged mounds of stone, the higher peaks reaching above us. The air grew colder, and our breath and the breath of our horses came as mist. Cold sunlight gleamed. Not an easy trail, but Reeves' knew it well, and kept us to the easier path—even though the Ambulatory Arcanum rattled and clanked, its contents of Elohim Elixir perhaps endangered by the difficult journey. Companionable silence reigned amongst us.

At least the sunlight meant that Reeves was able to dry and clean his weaponry—laying them out on flat stones and attending to them with practiced care as we took a break after an hour's ride. We all needed the respite.

We consumed some hardtack and jerky, washed down with cold water. Reeves taking his sip before reassembling his rifle. Milo wrapped himself in an old buffalo blanket I had purchased in Missouri and watched Reeves work.

"Excuse me?" Once again, he raised his hand—a child in the schoolhouse. "Excuse me, sir? Is that a—a Winchester?"

Reeves glanced back at him. "Milo, let the fellow work!" If I had a dunce box, perhaps I'd order him into it. I settled for giving him a stern finger-wagging instead. "Our savior needs his concentration, not questions from a brain addled by frontier romances and—"

"It's all right." Reeves silenced me with a raised hand. "I don't mind it." He worked the lever of the gun, carefully examining the action. "You are correct, Milo. Winchester 1873. It can use the pistol cartridges. Means I don't got to carry extra ammunition. Out here, miles from a town, you've got to be careful you ain't unprepared."

Milo nodded solemnly at this wisdom. "That's very smart."

"Why, Mr. Reeves must be a veritable Aristotle of the gunslingers." I put a trace of sarcasm into my words. "A Plato of the Plains. A Socrates of—"

He glared at me—and the words died on my tongue. "Being a Deputy Marshal is honest work. You can't say the same."

Flummoxed. Tongue-tied. *Verklempt.* Why could Reeves cut to my very heart with just a look and a word?

"But it's dangerous work?" Milo asked. "Working as a Marshal?"

"Yeah." He walked back to his roan and replaced the rifle in its scabbard. "You and your uncle got yourselves a fine look at that." He looked away and returned to his revolvers—which had been similarly disassembled and placed on a flat stone by the trail's edge. "But it's what I'm good at. Hunting folks—it's what I know. That, and being hunted." He hesitated. "You been in America long, Milo? You and your uncle?"

"Well, I was born here, sir," Milo explained. "Though I have arrived out West only recently. My uncle, though—he's from the Old Country."

"Then you're strangers to America—the America out here." He finished with the pistols and tucked them into the holsters at his side. "You'll learn soon enough that this is a violent country. Maybe it'll change. Maybe it won't. But for me, the lash, the blade, and bullet have always been close. If that ain't your way, then maybe you don't belong."

A question of my own came to mind. "Do you like it, Marshal Reeves?"

He paused. "Hell, I don't know. You like what you do?"

I glanced at Milo, who had descended from the coachman's seat of the Ambulatory Arcanum and now stood alongside Judah. He petted Judah, and the mule lowered his head to receive scratches about the ears, which the lad readily supplied. A gentle boy. A *luftmensch*. Behind him, the Arcanum squatted like a painted beast. Loaded with lies, which I peddled at every little town from here to the Arizona Territory and beyond. Would my parents have wanted such a life for myself? Would the Most High?

Maybe that was how we came to be in our present position. Being escorted to face justice in Fort Smith in the company of a killer.

I removed my fez—a replacement for the one lost near the Cave-Inn. "My job—the professorship—is what I must do to provide for Milo and for myself. But I would be lying if I told you there wasn't a certain thrill involved."

"Maybe that's my answer too." Reeves drew one pistol out and loaded it. "But I got me a ranch. Got me a family. The Deputy work—that's money for them." He smiled suddenly—a rarity below his massive moustache. "Hell, when this is over, maybe you two can come visit. I'll cook you something special." He hesitated. "Wait—you Jewish folks can't eat every sort of vittles, can you?"

I nodded. "We have to maintain the dietary restrictions of—"

Milo interrupted me. "We'll eat whatever you serve. The care for your cooking is blessing enough. We would be honored." He winked at me.

The very words, more or less, that I used whenever I devoured bacon or other *treyf*. The little *pisher*. He was learning.

Reeves had finished the second revolver. He holstered it and patted the butt. "Then I wouldn't mind hosting you. Providing you keep your mouth shut, professor." He returned to his roan with a click of his tongue. "All right. Let's get moving."

We resumed our journey. Milo joined me on the coachman's seat as the trail leveled out, crossing a sort of hillock before going to further stony lights. I glanced at my nephew. "You admire our marshal, don't you?"

He nodded. "He's a hero, sir. And he's honest."

Honest. I have been given many names, a few of which by own hand. 'Professor,' for instance. And 'Ashe'—I had transformed it from the much more unwieldy and Eastern European-sound Asche—which always made it sound as if I was clearing my throat. But honest? Upright? Those words simply did not apply. I glanced at Reeves as he walked his horse ahead of us, taking lead down the stony trail with a sure gaze and easy tread. He pulled himself into the saddle. If I had his strength and skill with a firearm, could I afford the luxury of honesty?

It was a foolish thought. One might as well wish one were back in Eden as imagine a different future. I would continue to take the Ambulatory Arcanum back and forth across the country, playing the part of the Jew swindler to keep fine garments on my back and to give Milo the comfort and dime novel delights he enjoyed.

But perhaps, this once, I could follow Reeves' example. I could end this little adventure with telling the truth. And who would end up on the hook? Not I.

Bartholomew 'Bighead' Braddock who already had a quite unreasonable distaste for me, would face the hangman's justice. "If you want to know what God thinks of money, look at the people he gives it to." That was my father's favored proverb. He was foolish, but in this instance, he spoke the truth.

Braddock deserved everything he got, and I would be proud to give it to him.

And if Judge Parker decided that other difficulties might be worth keeping me in Fort Smith, such as outstanding warrants or proclamations that I had cheated others with my products, well, I would merely present Milo and have him flash his enormous blue eyes to gain the judge's sympathy, then seek escape at the first opportunity.

I had learned to trust my ingenuity.

Reeves stopped, his horse clopping to a halt. We had neared a mass of outcropping—jagged pillars stretching up and flanking the trail. He raised a fist, and I pulled on the reins as well. Judah made a distraught bray, but ceased walking. The Arcanum rolled to a halt.

Milo perked up. "What's happening?"

"Shadows ain't right." Reeves reached for the rifle in his scabbard—but lately cleaned. Would it serve its purpose now? "Professor, you keep the boy back in the wagon. Ain't no call for him to see this."

"No need, Marshal!" A woman's voice, in a harsh twang. Pearl Payne—Pistol Pearl herself—emerged from behind a fallen boulder. Gray dust covered her form, making her heron's feather droop. She had a coach gun aimed straight at Reeves. "We don't want trouble. Do we, boys?"

A quartet of other gunslingers emerged from the dust flanking the road. All a-bristle with rifle, shotgun, and pistol. Pistol Pearl's gang. One carried a string of ponies, small horses ideal for scrambling up narrow mountain passes. They closed in, tromping around the Arcanum and glaring at Milo and myself. One hirsute fellow, bearing a long beard to match his massive mutton chops, snapped his teeth in Milo's direction. Perhaps attempting to frighten the lad.

Milo stuck his tongue out at him.

"Ought to give that damn whelp a beating!" He snarled right back.

"Easy there, Hiram." Payne pointed to him. "We're all being friendly here."

"Friendly." Reeves had his rifle raised—but not aimed at anything in particular. "Is that a fact?"

"Long as you care to be friendly, marshal." Payne smiled. The sunlight shone off her single gold tooth. "A lot of paper on me. Big old reward. You wouldn't be trying to collect it, would you?"

He shook his head. "I'm a marshal—not a bounty hunter. I got one task right now and it's bringing Professor Ashe back. That's all."

"And I also have no intention of collecting the bounty." I gave her my best smile.

"I wasn't worried about you, professor," Payne replied.

"Just so that you're aware, Ms. Payne."

"Yeah." She shrugged. "Well, maybe we can guide you." Payne waved a hand further up the trail. "We know these mountains pretty well. Beat you, didn't we? Even though you had a head start. So how about we take you through the pass. Put you on the road to Fort Smith. Just being hospitable, is all."

"You would do that for us, ma'am?" Milo asked. "Thank you."

He believed her. I would like to think that riding by my side had increased his skepticism, but that was not the case. He was still a boy—still as trusting as a pup.

Payne looked away. "No trouble. But Reeves? If we're guiding you, I'd appreciate it if we could take hold of your shooting irons. Just to be certain."

I leaned forward on the bench. Dropping my voice to a whisper. "Draw. Draw on them, marshal."

He stared back at me, and his dark eyes closed slowly—then opened. He spun the rifle about, extending the butt toward Payne.

"Thank you kindly." She accepted the rifle and tucked it under her arm. "The pistols too."

Reeves pulled them free and handed them over.

"All right." Payne whistled. A piebald pony cantered over to join her and she swung into the saddle. "Come on, then. You'll be safe in Fort Smith in no time."

We resumed the journey. This time, Payne's gang surrounded us. Her quartet of bandits rode about us on their ponies—keeping their distance, but preventing any escape. Payne took lead, occasionally glancing back at us. If I was a dunce, I would consider them our guardians. Outriders, trotting alongside us for purposes of defense.

But I knew better.

I leaned toward Reeves. He had slowed his mare, matching the pace of my wagon. "What are you doing? *Gevalt*—don't you realize that this nefarious band is taking us to our doom?"

He glared back. "What? You want to get into a gunfight right now?"

Milo stared between us. "They're taking us to our doom?" Speaking far too loudly.

We both shushed him. His eyes flashed and he looked around at the outlaws. Realizing the truth too late.

Reeves resumed. "They outnumber us—and had us dead to rights. I'm not an idiot. Didn't buy your elixir, did I?"

"But you allowed yourself to be disarmed." I gripped the reins tightly. "You fool! Now we are entirely within our power. Some great marshal—some legendary gunslinger you turned out to—"

He reached down and patted his saddle bag. "I ain't disarmed."

My worry vanished. The other pair of revolvers—the set he had drawn on me that very morning. Pearl Payne hadn't taken those. "Ah—genius!" I rubbed my hands together. "Draw on them now! We shall shoot our way to—"

"No." He silenced me with a glare. "Not with them all around. Not with your nephew so close. I won't see him endangered." He looked over at Milo. "You just keep close to your uncle. You don't got to worry none. I aim to get us out of this."

He nodded—reassured. "I'm not worried, Mr. Reeves." A bit of a lie in his words perhaps.

"All right." He took hold of the reins. "I know what it's like, you see. To be small. To be powerless, and at the mercy of cruel men. I won't let it happen to anyone else." Then he increased his horse's pace and rode a little ahead. Leaving Milo and I to our thoughts.

I patted Milo's shoulder. "I, also, would never let any danger come to you, *boychick*. But you know that, don't you?"

He looked away. "Certainly, uncle."

This time, not even bothering to hide the lie.

And why would he? If I hadn't taken us from New York—fleeing, really, with death and my enemies close behind—and sought refuge in the west, we wouldn't be here. Nor would we if I hadn't chosen to stop by the Big B Ranch and attempted to grift Bighead Braddock. Or if I had accepted Reeves' earlier request to accompany him back to Fort Smith. Why, there were a thousand junctures that I should have taken and choices I should have made, all of which would have placed Milo and I away from this godforsaken peak and the present danger.

The guilt hit hard. I faced the road.

Could I do anything yet to set matters to right? For once, I resolved to try.

The trail ended on a wide plateau. A rather picturesque locale—a square of gray stone, surrounded on four sides by jagged, sheer slopes leading down to rocky canyons. Swathed in mist and with a trace of frost upon the stones, it looked like some celestial kingdom where the Most High and his seraphim held court. Instead, it was an earthlier power that ruled here. Bartholomew 'Bighead' Braddock, standing at the center of the plateau before a roaring bonfire, his thumbs hooked in his belt.

He had certainly earned his nickname. A spectacularly large head rested atop his shoulder, with no neck to speak of. He sported a broad-brimmed hat of dark silk, which seemed small given his mammoth skull. And—just as Prong had said—all his hair had fallen out, making his head resemble that of a giant infant, swollen to an impossible size.

An unfortunate side effect of Elohim Elixir, perhaps.

A bolo tie of silver and turquoise emerged somewhere below his substantial chin, and he wore a black broadcloth suit of an expensive cut. He drew out his watch, squinted at the time, and returned it to his pocket with a grunt. "Well, Professor Ashe. Once again, our paths cross. You lit out of my ranch so goddamn fast; I thought the devil was on your tail. Be good to finally give you a proper goodbye."

I slid down from the seat of the Ambulatory Arcanum after our odd little convoy entered the plateau. A large private coach rested behind Braddock, perched near the edge of the plateau. The horses had been unhitched and grazed restlessly at a patch of grass further along. Leaning against that coach, a cigarillo smoldering in his teeth, was Heck Prong. His rifle leaned against the intricately carved stagecoach door, close to his hands.

The Angel of Death had followed us here.

Braddock drew closer. "Mr. Prong, it seems that fortune has smiled on us. Our quarry has been delivered. And in a timely fashion too."

"Yes, sir, Mr. Braddock." Prong puffed out smoke and snatched up the rifle. "And we got that colored marshal to boot." He swung up the rifle, aiming at Reeves. "Get on down from that saddle, boy. And the little Jew—you come down here too."

"Why not?" Braddock asked. "Let me look all my enemies in the eye." He stared at me as I helped Milo down. Reeves dismounted as well—but stayed close to his saddle. A good thing as well. The pistols waited there, hidden in his saddle bags still. "Nothing to say, professor? Ain't that an oddity!" He slapped his knee. "When we last met, you were about as loquacious as they come. Ain't that right, Mr. Prong?"

"Yes, sir, Mr. Braddock."

"By God, your verbosity knew no bounds. The words spilled forth like water from a rushing stream. And yet now, you are silent." He walked closer, navigating about the fire and standing next to me—allowing me to stare at his substantial head. "I find it curious. Why are you so quiet, professor?"

I stared back, trying to be calm. Buy time. Wait for an opportunity—and pray to the Most High that one would arrive. Let Reeves get hold of his pistols, and put an end to Prong and Braddock both.

"Well?" Braddock demanded.

"Perhaps I have nothing to say."

"Nothing to say?" Braddock chuckled. "Don't that just beat all?"

"Mr. Braddock?" Payne approached, her four banditos clustered behind her like schoolchildren behind their teacher. She pointed to Reeves, Milo and me. "We've done as you asked. Captured the snake oil man and his nephew and brought you before you. The marshal—I don't know. I figured

He stared at me as I helped Milo down.

you'd know what to do with him."

"That I do." Prong let his cigarillo fall to the stony ground and gave it a stomp.

"Now, you promised a reward?" Payne let out a little chuckle—a weak one. "Once I get it, we'll be on our way."

"A reward, eh?" Braddock faced her as Prong stalked closer. "Well, darling, you ought to have followed this Israelite's example—ask for the lion's share of the money up front."

Prong's rifle swung out, driving straight into Payne's gut. She gasped at the blow and stumbled back—before sinking weakly to her knees. A kick from Prong's boot sent her straight to the stones.

"Miss Payne!" Milo cried out, and I took hold of his shoulder to keep him from running to help. A *luftmensch* indeed—he would help even our betrayers.

"Any of you boys want to try something?" Prong swung the rifle up, aiming straight at her gang. They had frozen. The bearded fellow made the mistake of twitching, and Prong's Bowie knife sliced out from the holster on his boot, carving a line across the outlaw's arm and up to his shoulder. He wailed and sank down—joining his mistress on the earth.

Wild dogs they might be, but the wolf had them cowed.

"Have them toss their guns over the side," Braddock suggested. "The marshal too—if they haven't disarmed him already."

"You heard him." Prong swung his rifle about. "Either your irons go—or you do."

They went, one after the other. Even Payne managed to send her coach gun—along with Reeves' pistols and repeater—over the side.

Reeves watched them descend, his eyes impassive.

He still had those pistols. But Prong was smart—cruel, but smart. He must know that saddle bags often contained firearms. Would he search them? If he did, and found Reeves' revolvers, we were truly doomed.

Braddock stomped closer to Payne. "You think I'd give payment to some half-blood Cherokee?" Braddock sneered. "Some Indian heathen, stinking of whiskey and the soil? I got better uses for my money." He glanced at Reeves, and his features changed. A smile appeared, a pearl-white gash on the huge canvas of his face. "Such as you, Marshal Reeves—how you'd like to walk away from here?"

Reeves stared back. "I'd be pleased as punch. As long as Professor and Milo Ashe went with me."

"They ain't ever leaving this rock." He wiggled his fingers at Reeves.

"But you can. With money in your pocket. How'd you like that? Go home with a nice fat billfold. Spend it on the card house, if you want. Live high on the hog. How'd you like that?"

"You trying to bribe a deputy marshal, Mr. Braddock?"

"You catch on quick, boy." He patted his pockets. "I run one of the biggest outfits in the Territories. You know I got the cash."

The cold stare from Reeves was answer enough. He added to it. "I ain't for sale."

Milo smiled suddenly. He nodded his head. Proof of the miracle of this legendary lawman, right before him. If only it could help us.

Braddock's good humor—short lived as it was—faded. "Insolence." He turned away. "Just pure insolence. You see what happens, Mr. Prong? You give them government office and a fancy coat, stick some six-guns on them, and insolence is the result." His eyes went to me. "Not like your people, professor. You've learned how to please the gentile, haven't you?"

I had kept quiet—an aberration, as Braddock had said. Considering what to do. My best option—perhaps the only option—was a distraction. One that would allow Reeves a chance to retrieve his shooting irons and cover our escape. We still had the Ambulatory Arcanum and Reeves' wagon. Getting them around on the mountain road might prove tricky, but just running on foot down the mountain would be preferable to certain death up here.

But how to distract Braddock? Plead for my life, perhaps? I'd done that plenty of times, with Milo helping. It usually worked on motherly innkeepers with soft hearts when it came time for the bill, and good farmers who were taught to Love Thy Neighbor in their bibles. For a man without a conscience like Braddock, it would not do.

No. I would have to sell to him. A good salesman knows his customer. And I knew what Braddock wanted.

"Mr. Braddock?" I kept my tone light and casual—suitable for a parlor conversation, not when I had a rifle aimed at me. "May I pose a question?"

"I don't see why not. What could the harm be, at this juncture?"

"Precisely." I walked closer—leaving Milo. He took a step after me, but I shook my head—and nodded toward Reeves. The boy did as he was asked. Hurrying to Reeves's side. If the carnage began in earnest, the lawman would do a better job protecting him than I ever could. I faced Braddock. "Tell me—when you applied the Elohim Elixir—"

"You mean the damn snake oil you sold me? For a steep price, I should add?"

"The very one, sir." I held out my hand, mimicking shaking the bottle. "Did you simply pour the liquid on your head?"

"Yeah." He grunted. "That's what I was supposed to do, wasn't I?"

Payne let out a groan from where she lay on the ground. "What the hell are you getting at, professor?"

"Merely this." I took my two fingers and spun in the air, making constant circles. "The problem is now clear to me, along with the solution. You are not to simply pour the Elohim Elixir upon your skull. That created the unfortunate side effect which has presently pained you. Removing all of your hair and making your skull look…" I decided against going further. "Instead, you must massage the Elohim Elixir. Little circles, sir. Inscribing Kabalistic sigils into the flesh." A trace of mysticism, I hoped, would not go amiss. "That will unlock the substance's rejuvenating abilities."

Silence followed my proclamation. Braddock's face shifted, making him look as if he in the throes of constipation.

"That's the biggest load of hogwash I ever heard!" Prong waved to me. "Hokum, Mr. Braddock. Purest hokum. He's trying to save his hide with lies, at the very end."

I'd need more than that. An expert testimony. "No lies at all, Mr. Braddock. Milo, isn't that right?"

He peeked out from behind Reeves. "Yes, sir. You have to massage the Elixir. Kabbalistic sigils. That's the ticket, sir."

"Getting his runt to back up his lies." Prong shook his head. "Ought to be ashamed."

Braddock cocked his massive head. He had to be rolling the matter over in his head. "Well, now that I know how to use the Elixir, why shouldn't I just kill all three of you and apply it myself. Seems like you got damn-near a lifetime supply in that gaudy wagon of yours."

Reeves answered that. "Only the professor knows the proper hand gestures. You try it, liable to make your whole head set to boiling."

I nodded my agreement. "And consider this—what can the harm be?" I clapped my hands. "If you feel that I've misled you, then you can have Mr. Prong execute Milo and myself right here. It will only be a stay of execution. But if it works, your headache will have vanished, your hair will soon return, and your health as a whole shall come rushing back. In short, the rewards far outweigh the risk."

A classic grifter's tactic—talk the customer through the transaction, showing them how little they have to lose and how much they have to gain.

Time to deploy another stratagem. "Or, if you don't wish to waste a few more minutes, you can simply send Milo, Marshal Reeves, and myself to the World to Come, and return to your life of headaches and hairlessness. Which would you prefer?"

A quiet followed my request. Braddock traced thumb and forefinger over the peninsula of his large, hairless chin. "You have the stuff—the Elixir—"

"Elohim Elixir, sir," I corrected.

"The Elohim Elixir. You have that in the wagon?"

"I could easily get you a bottle, sir. It would be but a matter of moments."

Prong drew closer to me. He had the rifle at his side and brandished his blade, still crimsoned with the wounded outlaw's blood. "You oughtn't to listen to him, sir. This one's a snake. Worse than that fellow got to Adam and Eve. He's planned something."

"And what could that be, Mr. Prong?" I replied. "Do you suppose I have a Gatling gun stashed in the wagon?"

"Let him get his medicine, Prong." Braddock had settled on a rocky outcropping and already cast off his bowler. He rested a hand on his forehead. "You keep your rifle on the marshal." His coat slid open, revealing a pearl-handled revolver—a millionaire's weapon—in a little rig affixed to his coat. "I'll watch him."

Another firearm to consider. *Gevalt.*

"Have him send the boy." Prong sneered. "It oughtn't be to no trouble—if there's no gambit the professor's planning, of course."

There was indeed no gambit—none that I had in mind. Perhaps inspiration would have presented itself. Perhaps the Most High would send a grand idea into my mind, like he requested Moses to raise his staff and part the Red Sea. But no inspiration arrived—and now it was in Milo's hands.

He emerged from behind Reeves's hands, shuddering a little—his hands in his pockets. This wasn't the *luftmensch's* world.

Braddock shrugged. "Go on, son." He waved to Milo. "Go on and get the bottle."

He looked to me. I nodded. "You fetch it, Motl."

A slip of the tongue. But that was his true name. The one his father and mother had given him, and what would be inscribed in the Book of Life and—when the time came—the Book of Death. He looked at me and nodded. Perhaps it gave him strength. Then he walked around to the back of the wagon, pausing to give Judah's head a pet. The mule emitted a pleased bray. Milo continued about and went to the back. He hopped inside.

We heard rustling within. All stayed quiet. The bearded outlaw let out a little whimper and Prong glowered at him—silencing the fellow for good. Reeves stared up at the sky, his hands in his pockets. Preserving his strength.

Footsteps on the stone heralded Milo's return. He emerged around the wagon, bearing a bottle of Elohim Elixir.

"Ought to be careful with that." Reeves spoke up and Milo froze. He listened to Reeves like the old prophets listened to the voice of God. "I saw myself how dangerous it can be. First night we met." His eyes flicked to the fire. "You remember."

"Yes, sir."

And I did too. When Reeves had—in a rage—dumped my bottle into the campfire and created a shimmering conflagration.

We had a campfire right here as well.

Milo approached it. He worked at the cork, gritted his teeth, and finally drew it free. Then he looked back at me, his face drained of color. As nervous as I was when I faced the Yeshiva masters—knowing that pure punishment would come my way unless I could make them believe my lies. "Uncle?"

"I'll take it." I offered my hand.

"No." Braddock held out his. "You bring it here. I like your uncle, right where he is." He stamped his boot on the stone. "Bring it here, boy. Now!"

The lad took a deep breath, took his step—and stumbled.

He tipped over the bottle, causing a long stream—almost the entirety of the container's contents—to tumble down into the fire.

Instantly, the flashing, blazing conflagration reared to life. A thousand colors leapt up from the campfire, dancing and flickering their way over the plateau. They cast a wild whirl of shadows across the stones, and even Prong looked away from the sudden burst of light. The force sent Milo stumbling back—falling straight onto the stones and rolling over. A ragdoll in my nephew's dusty and rumpled Norfolk jacket.

I forgot the guns aimed at me. I ran to his side.

Movement behind me. Reeves, going for the guns in his saddle bags.

"Goddamn it!" Braddock shouted as the explosion thundered above us all. He dove into his coat, fumbling for his pistol. "Prong—shoot the marshal!"

I reached Milo, grabbing his arm and scooping him up—just as Prong aimed his rifle at Reeves. It thundered—the boom almost lost in the echo of the Elohim Elixir's explosion. Milo's eyes shot open. Had Reeves met his end?

I spun around to see. Prong's rifle had fired into the dirt, the dust settling—because Payne had tackled him, gripping the rifle and pulling it to the side. They tumbled back, both cursing and shouting and then Payne screamed and stumbled back—blood and bite marks on her face. Prong had bit her. He raised his rifle at Reeves.

But the marshal had already drawn his pistols. He held it up, arm extended, body poised. It seemed like a cloud-covered sky, the storm just beginning to rage—the lightning soon to come crackling its way down across the mantle of clouds, for that was where lightning belonged. And those pistols belonged in Reeves' hands, expertly aimed at his target.

He fired, fanning the gun—sending four rapid shots blazing into Prong. One went wide, striking the stone and casting up a hail of dust—but the other three sunk home. Prong stumbled back, falling toward the wagon. The rifle fell from his hands as he settled on the stagecoach's step.

Braddock had drawn by then. He leveled his pistol at me and Milo.

Reeves shot him too. Braddock let out a squawk and fell backwards from his seat, his big head bouncing against the stony ground.

"Reeves..." Prong gasped. He stood from the step, dropping his rifle—but his hand went to the pistol on his belt. "Pistol's empty and mine's plumb full. Got you—even you can't be fast enough to—"

Reeves reached for the second six-gun in his saddle bags.

They drew together. Prong cleared holster, just as Reeves had his second pistol out. They fired in tandem.

Prong fell back, right into the heart of the fancy stagecoach. He slammed back, his limbs flailing—banging against the wall. The force made the coach rock slightly on its wheels. Dust rose up about the spokes and the entire conveyance shifted hard to the side. Gravity—or perhaps the hand of the Most High—did the rest. The stagecoach rolled back a few paces, its rear poking over the edge of the cliff and its two wheels jutting upward into the air.

Then it was over the side—tumbling down and falling out of view. Bearing Prong with it. From somewhere down below, we heard the crash.

Reeves set both pistols in his holster. He hurried across the gravel and reached me and Milo—just as I had gotten the boy on his feet.

He bore bruises on his cheek and blood from somewhere on his forehead. But he stood all right, and accepted the monogrammed handkerchief I pressed into his hand. "Mr. Prong—is he—." He stammered out the words.

"You don't got to concern yourself with Prong no more." Reeves offered his canteen. "How are you feeling?"

"I'm—I'm all right. Dizzy." He grinned. "I want no elixir to cure me."

"I'll see that you get some soup in you once we return back to civilization." I grinned at Reeves. "Now, with Braddock sent to the World to Come to face the judgment of the Lord, there is no need for me to testify and—"

"Reeves!" Payne's voice. "Braddock's making a run for it!"

Reeves spun about, aiming his pistol—just as Braddock had pulled himself onto the back of one of his coach horses. He cracked his heels against the flanks of the big animal and sent it galloping down the mountain trail. For a moment, Reeves trailed horse and rider with his pistol—before letting his hand slide off the hammer. Evidently, he was too far and there would be no point in wasting a bullet.

I helped Milo back to the wagon. "Well, Marshal Reeves, perhaps you could give chase. Then, you could meet Milo and I in Fort Smith and—"

He gave me a withering stare. That was answer enough.

Payne had come to her feet, her hand pressed to her cheek. Blood trickled through her fingers. "And what about us, Reeves?" Her bandits once again gathered behind her. Children, hiding behind their mother's skirt. "You've got the drop on us now, I suspect."

"I told you before." He walked back to his roan and pulled himself into the saddle. "I'm no bounty hunter. I came here to do a job and I've nearly done it." He took the reins and cantered close to the Ambulatory Arcanum. I helped Milo up to the seat next to me and took my place as well. "Ain't that right, professor?"

Milo stared at me—turning his luminous blue eyes in my direction. "Uncle?"

I managed a smile. "Of course."

"Then let's be on our way." He leaned from the saddle and glared at me. "And no more distractions."

Reeves had saved us both. It was the least I could do. We started off down the mountain.

Fort Smith proved as noisy and crowded as I remembered. Wagons and horses cluttered the streets, so that the entire settlement seemed lost under a constant haze of dust. New structures rose up, their skeletal frames sprouting besides the bank, general store, and courthouse. Usually,

I would be happy to visit such a bustling metropolis. More citizens meant more customers. Milo and I would set up the Ambulatory Arcanum on a promising street corner, I would pay a blind fiddler to scratch out a tune, and begin pitching Elohim Elixir to all.

But Reeves had other ideas.

I soon found myself in a particularly unpleasant situation. Seated across the desk of the local US Marshal, at the corner of his office. Other marshals lingered about, working on cigarillos and papers. The outlaws on the Wanted posters gleamed down at me from the far wall, as Judge Isaac Parker—the Hanging Judge, as he had been named—sat across from me and fixed me with a stern gaze. His white beard and cold eyes reminded me of the rabbis of my youth, who seemed to know my every sin just by looking.

He pushed a number of papers before me. "I present you with a statement showing that you witnessed stolen cattle being brought into the Big B Ranch, the brands being changed by Braddock's ranch hands—at his command. You take some time to read them, if you'd like."

I perused the document. "I find the prose workmanlike, sir. If I might add a flourish of my own, perhaps—"

"You may not." He supplied a quill and ink. "Sign on the bottom. If you can't write your signature, an X shall suffice."

"I assure you, my penmanship is exquisite." I dipped the quill and signed. "Now, that this chore is done, may my nephew and I take our leave? Surely, you would not stop our business from proceeding on its path across this nation and seeking new markets—"

"You shall remain in Fort Smith for as long as need be." He sniffed. "Otherwise, I'll see what other warrants might be outstanding against you."

"Oh, I'm certain that any charges pressed against me are mere misunderstandings. If I had just the opportunity to explain—"

He settled back in his chair and pressed the stem of a pipe into his mouth. "I am done speaking with you. You may go."

I had no desire to spend more time in the company of this ornery oldster. I doffed my fez and walked out. Back in the streets, I breathed the dusty air. I suppose it had gone as well as could be expected.

A moment later Reeves and Milo came around from the corner, the lad enjoying a stick of rock candy. "Uncle Alexander—Marshal Reeves bought me a sweet from the general store!" He darted over to me and I gave him a quick embrace.

Reeves had gone to his roan mare and undid the knot by the hitching post. "A token of my gratitude." He shrugged. "You're staying in town, I take it?"

"Indeed. Until further notice." I watched as Reeves mounted up. "Where are you off to?"

"Back to the Territory. Judge Parker had the warrant for Braddock all ready to go. Thanks to you, it's finished. Now, I'm to bring him back." He leaned in the saddle for just a moment—his hands resting on the horn. Fatigue in his limbs.

"You must?" Milo asked. "Back into all that danger?"

He shrugged. "It's what I do." He tugged at the reins and his roan trotted down the main street, as he hummed a little jaunty tune to accompany the clatter of his horse's hooves.

THE END

A Quack's Salvation Explanation

Bass Reeves is truly one of the great Western figures, with a backstory and adventures that should put him on par with household names like Wyatt Earp and Wild Bill Hickok. I remember hearing about him on a history podcast about the real Lone Ranger—a connection that seems tenuous to me, but is still a good way of getting Reeves more attention—and then seeing him make appearances here and there in the following years: Wild West podcasts, a mention in a conversation amongst modern US Marshals on the TV Show Justified, an important role in HBO's Watchmen—but that was the limit of it. The Reeves story had everything—a unique location in Indian Territory, a badass gunslinger, and a connection to one of the darkest periods of American history—and each tidbit I encountered made me more interested.

So when Ron Fortier contacted me to write a story starring Reeves, I instantly agreed. I wanted a unique take and I also knew that getting in Reeves' head, with his skills and experiences, was probably an impossibility. I decided that the best route was the classic set-up of a buddy comedy. Pairing up the laconic, heroic Reeves with a chatterbox ne'er-do-well seemed like a surefire recipe for entertainment. That brought up another question: who would be the dastardly rogue that would contrast the best with Reeves?

I turned again to a historical figure, this time from Turn of the Century New York. Abraham Hochman was a Jewish immigrant who became a major fortune teller, offering palmistry, astrology, and other such practices to his fellow tenement-dwelling Jews on the Lower East Side in the 1890s. Such charlatans have always fascinated me, and I created a fictionalized version of Hochman—Professor Alexander Ashe—who became the subject of several short stories. While it was a lot of fun writing from the perspective of an unrepentant scumbag like Ashe, I couldn't sympathize with him alone, and so I gave him his young nephew Milo. He treats the kid as a living prop and yet genuinely loves him, and this depth makes him more than just another swindler. It makes him—I hope—interesting.

Reeves and Ashe seemed a natural partnership. I wanted to tell a story that was a character study of a hustling con man with a heart, explore how the Jewish experience—one of persecution in the Old Country, but overall acceptance in America—contrasts with the deep, and completely American injustice facing someone like Reeves, and create a rip-roaring and entertaining Western Buddy Comedy as well. I hope I succeeded.

MICHAEL PANUSH - has distinguished himself as one of Sacramento's most promising young writers. His books with Curiosity Quills include *The Stein and Candle Detective Agency, Volume 1: American Nightmares, Volume 2: Cold Wars*, and *Volume 3: Red Reunion*, all featuring a pair of occult detectives in the 1950s, *Dinosaur Jazz*— where *The Great Gatsby* meets *Jurassic Park* — a story about a Lost World battling against the forces of modernization; *El Mosaico, Volume 1: Scarred Souls, Volume 2: The Road to Hellfire*, and *El Mosaico, Volume 3: Hellfire*, a Western about a bounty hunter whose body was assembled from the remains of dead Civil War soldiers and brought to life by mad science; and Dead Man's Drive, a 1950s urban fantasy about a hot rod-riding zombie.

With Airship 27, he created the Clay Shamus—a story of a golem detective. His latest novel from Pro Se Press is *Ape's Honor: A Novel of Victoria's Ape*, the story of a gorilla lord in Victorian England. His short fiction has been published in Towers of Metropolis and George Chance: The Green Ghost from Airship 27.

Follow him on Twitter at @Michael_Panush and on the web at https://michaelpanush.com/

THE BALLAD OF THE TUMBLEWEED OUTLAW

Thomas McNulty

The sandy-haired boy named Corbin lived with his step-father on the outskirts of town where they had a garden of fresh vegetables. The soil was good out there a mile from the saloons and brothels, and they had enough extra vegetables to sell which helped pay the taxes. The old man's name was Rum Doggy, or so they said, and he was part negro and part Apache. Corbin was of undetermined lineage, having been saved from a wagon train massacre when Rum Doggy was young and full of vigor. Rum Doggy, they said, had a reputation that rivaled Wild Bill Hickok, but those days were long past him. The morning when Corbin found Rum Doggy slumped over the kitchen table may have been the saddest in his life. He knew the old man was dead the second he looked at him, and Corbin's first reaction was to miss the melodious sound of the old man's voice. That old man sang sad songs about working the cotton fields down south before the war, and he had taught Corbin everything he knew about being a man. Now Rum Doggy was dead.

Grief was something Corbin had never been prepared to handle. Now here it was slapping him in the face as Rum Doggy's body began to attract flies at the old wooden table. Corbin set to the task of burying him. He took a shovel from the barn and meandered around the farm trying to choose a good spot to bury him. The soft, spring earth turned over easily as Corbin spent nearly two hours digging a six-foot hole. Corbin was lanky but muscular enough and in good shape. Being lazy wasn't part of his disposition. He removed his shirt and when he did so he recalled how the doves at the Crystal Palace liked to talk about him. Those girls were kind-hearted and skilled in all things a man enjoyed, and thanks to Rum Doggy he'd been educated in the ways of the flesh at an early age. Rum Doggy had made certain that Corbin was familiar with a woman's body

46

having told him, "It's like a treasure map to gold, except you get pleasure instead of treasure." Once again, he was assailed by grief as he pondered losing the man that had raised him as if he were his own.

When the grave was deep enough, Corbin fetched Rum Doggy's body from the kitchen. The smell had started to fill the air and fat black horseflies were crawling all over Rum Doggy's cotton shirt. Some of the flies were buzzing around the thick locks of the old man's gray hair. Waving his arms to scare away the flies, Corbin lifted the old man and carried his body outside. He held the old man's body in his arms the way a man carried his bride into the bedroom, and Corbin felt awful holding the old man like that. Rum Doggy's head lolled back with his eyes open, and a fly emerged from between his lips before buzzing away.

Corbin tried to climb down into the grave but he slipped and tumbled into a haphazard heap. It took him a full ten minutes to disentangle himself from the body, straighten out Rum Doggy in a respectable manner, and climb out of the grave.

He looked down at Rum Doggy and his emotions got the better of him. A few tears rolled down his cheeks as he looked down at the body, and Corbin had never been so confused before. When he started to shovel dirt onto the body, he realized he should have covered Rum Doggy with a blanket. Corbin had no desire to climb into that grave again, so he shoveled extra hard, tossing mounds of dirt over Rum Doggy's face. With the old man's face finally covered, he was able to manage filling in the grave.

He was irritated. He mourned Rum Doggy, but he was thinking the damn old fool should have had better manners than to go and die on him.

Corbin washed the sweat and dirt off himself in the nearby creek. He let the sun dry his shirt, and soon thereafter he realized he didn't know what to do next. The idea of working the farm by himself wasn't appealing. He had never been alone before. In fact, the solitude was already making him nervous. Rum Doggy and Corbin would have been at the chores already, and the old man would have had a story to tell as they worked. Rum Doggy's stories made the time go faster. He had survived the battles around Atlanta, and once he was free he'd traveled west and become a bounty hunter, a profession that Rum Doggy had excelled at. Rum Doggy was fast with a gun, and he'd taught Corbin how to shoot, although he was never a good shot.

Corbin also had a bad temper, and in this regard Rum Doggy had warned him to cool down. "A man with a hot temper has got the odds stacked against him right from the start." Corbin, however, was soon to learn that keeping his temper in check was easier said than done.

He strapped on the gunbelt and went to town. The town of Voyager's End was more of a settlement than a town. A ramshackle collection of saloons, brothels, and feed and grain stores catering to the farming community, Voyager's End prospered on the site of a now defunct Overland Stage line and switching station. The settlement was named by a Pony Express rider who referred to it as his voyage's end on the day he quit riding for the Pony Express. He was plum tired of being attacked by the Aniyunwiya, or Cherokee Indians, who made several attempts to puncture his hide with arrowheads. While Voyager's End stuck as a name, that mail rider remains an anonymous and forgotten corpse buried in Boot Hill, done in by too much grain alcohol from a local still.

It was Thursday, and that was the day Rum Doggy and Corbin normally came to town for supplies. Corbin had already made up his mind to spend some time in a crib with one of the doves, but he needed money. He set straight for the bank where Rum Doggy had a savings account of indeterminate wealth.

The bank clerk was a buck-tooth effeminate boy named Jessup who slicked his hair back with grease and smelled like his starched shirt. Corbin never liked him much but there was no choice in the matter. Jessup was polite and Corbin asked for a withdrawal of twenty-dollars, the amount Rum Doggy would withdraw about every eight weeks to pay for his supplies. Rum Doggy paid cash and didn't believe in operating on credit. The vegetables they sold reimbursed them for their expenses, so that each month they made a tad more than they spent. Corbin wasn't certain how much money Rum Doggy had stashed in the bank, and when the thought struck him he asked Jessup what the balance was. Jessup had just handed Corbin his cash, and he raised an eyebrow.

"Mister Rum Doggy has got two-hundred and forty-seven dollars and eighteen cents in his account right now. You can tell him that's his balance after your withdrawal."

"I reckon I'll take it all then." Corbin said. The amount was astronomical to him.

"Normally Rum Doggy hisownself makes his withdrawals and deposits." Jessup said. "We'll need his signature if he's closing his account."

"That ain't gonna happen. I buried Rum Doggy this morning. I found him dead at the table before he could even have breakfast." Corbin was genuinely sorrowful with his explanation.

Jessup looked quite amazed, and then after a moment's contemplation, he looked perturbed.

"I've made a mistake then," Jessup intoned, "and you'll have to give me the twenty dollars back. This is Rum Doggy's account, and not yours."

Corbin was astounded. "That's plain foolishness. I'm his son. Give me the money."

"No, you are not his son. You're an orphan he raised. You'll have to make a claim and see a judge about getting this money. Now please give me that twenty dollars."

"No, I won't!" Jessup was indignant. Corbin watched Jessup's nostril's flare and his brow furrowed with disgust. "If you don't give me that twenty dollars I'll have to report you to the law!"

Corbin's anger was beginning to rise; it swelled to life in his chest and made his pulse race. "There isn't any law here in Voyager's End," Corbin said, trying to keep his voice calm.

At that moment a door in the rear of the bank opened and the manager, George Brown, stepped out. "What's all the commotion out here!" He demanded. He cast a wary glance at Corbin.

"Rum Doggy has died," Jessup said quickly, "I gave Corbin here twenty dollars before I knew it, and now he wants all of Rum Doggy's money. I explained that he can't have it!"

Corbin wanted to slap Jessup. The bank manager appraised Corbin and said, "Jessup here is right. You can't have the money. I'm willing to let you keep that twenty dollars to hold you over until a judge can sort this all out. Now, Corbin, you best skedaddle. We don't want our good customers coming in here and getting upset over things."

"Good customers?" Corbin's mind was piecing together the sneering inflection in the banker's tone in conjunction with his blunt statement. "Rum Doggy was a good customer, wasn't he?"

"He was." Brown said, "But you're not. You're nothing, really. Just a stray dog that helped the old man out. Now skedaddle!"

Corbin's anger was like a hot flame that scorched the earth and turned everything to ash. He felt small and useless, and he had never felt so humiliated in all of his life. He wouldn't recall drawing his gun from the holster and pointing it at Jessup, but he did, and George Brown stood there in shock with his mouth open.

"Good Lord! You're robbing us!"

"Yes, I am! Now empty that cash drawer!"

Jessup, however, who fancied himself a well-dressed man like he saw in the Sears Roebuck catalog, and as heroic as the Pinkerton men he read about in the nickel magazines, decided to lift a silver derringer he kept in the drawer for just such eventualities. He lips curled in disgust as he pointed the derringer at Corbin.

"You ain't nothin' but a pig farmer's welp! I got you!" Jessup looked downright pleased.

Corbin shot Jessup in the head. The sound of the gunshot thundered in the small room, much louder than Corbin had expected. Acrid gunsmoke filled the air. In the same instant that Jessup's head exploded, the bank manager squealed, "Oh God, no!" and dropped to his knees shaking. Corbin was astounded to see Jessup's head split open like a dropped pumpkin, brains and skull fragments splattering the wall five feet behind him. Jessup's body dropped from view.

Corbin ambled around and pointed his gun at the shaking bank manager. The gun in his hand made him feel immensely powerful, and it was a new feeling that Corbin enjoyed immensely.

"Why, you son-of-a-bitch! Stay put!"

Corbin found a sack and filled it with greenbacks. He had no idea how much money he was stealing at this point, and he didn't care. He glanced down at Jessup's bloody body. The little bastard looked downright shocked with his head all busted open. Serves him right, Corbin thought.

"Damn you, Mister Brown! You never should have treated me poorly!"

The banker was still on his knees with his hands raised, shaking and nearly crying. "Don't shoot me! Please!"

"Aw shaddup!"

George Brown blinked and Corbin was gone. Not being a brave man at all, the bank manager had wet himself when Corbin had shot Jessup. The sight of Jessup getting killed was too much to think about. Corbin was gone, and still Brown stayed in place, his urine dripping through his trousers and staining the floor. God almighty, help me! It was over, and he was alive; of that he felt relief, but his shock and fear had crippled him. It finally dawned on him that he couldn't allow people to see him in such a pathetic state. No, that wouldn't do at all. He had to pull himself together, and then he had to let people know that he'd tried to stop Corbin from killing Jessup and robbing the bank. First, he had to change his clothes.

One thing at a time. Later, when he had told everyone what had happened, he would send a telegraph message to the U. S. Marshal's office. This was a matter for the law now, and he hoped whoever they sent after Corbin was tough enough to handle the job.

Nothing had gone right all day. U. S. Deputy Marshal Bass Reeves had trailed Dirty Lonnie Blake across a rolling green prairie and into the rocky foothills of a desolate place known as Vulture's Hollow. Blake wasn't alone. He was accompanied by Phil Gorton, Clark Strachen and Jayhawker Johnny Dolan. Reeves had encountered these men before, although he'd never had the pleasure of arresting them. They were heavily armed and wanted to kill him. Reeves was alone. He felt even lonelier when he'd realized he'd lost sight of Jayhawker Johnny. He figured they were going to flank him and give him lead poisoning.

Being flanked and outnumbered wasn't the worst of it.

There was no sign of the female hostage thought to be with them. The stage driver was dead, and so was the shotgun rider. Craning his neck, he glanced down from his perch in the rocks and saw the driver's body lying in the dust, a pool of crimson spreading from beneath his shattered head. Dirty Lonnie Blake's gang, having already robbed two banks, had waylaid a stagecoach with exceptional brutality. Reeves saw a woman's fancy purse lying in the dust, but there was no sign of her.

A bullet clipped the boulder next to Reeves, splaying shards of sandstone and dust into his eyes. Dirty Lonnie Blake's voice boomed in the air.

"You're gonna die, you black-skinned devil! That lawman's star on your vest don't mean nothin' to us. We're gonna roast your carcass over a fire and feed you to the wolves!"

"Wolves won't like how I taste, you mangy bastard!" Reeves said, trying to sound authoritative. "Now you scoundrels need to let me know what happened to the woman that was on this stage, and then give yourselves up, otherwise I'll have to kill all of you!"

A phlegmy laugh echoed up from the switchback. Reeves was trying desperately to pinpoint each man's location, but to no avail. They had scattered and took positions in the maze of switchbacks, mule trails and jumbled boulders. The merciless sun beat down at him, and he was drenched with sweat.

"You hear that Johnny? This lawman wants us to surrender!"

"We gonna do to him what they done to his emancipator!"

Jayhawker Johnny's voice drifted out from the rocks and echoed across the sunbaked foothills. Reeves couldn't pinpoint him, but he was moving high on his right. That left Phil Gorton and Clark Strachen to worry about. They were trying to box him in to finish him off. He had to move.

Bass Reeves didn't like retreating, but he had no choice. Those buzzards would cut him to pieces at the first opportunity. He scrambled down the trail slowly but methodically. He needed a workable plan and he didn't have one. All he had was his gun and his determination to set things right.

They were in the foothills of Mount Magazine, Arkansas and the early June heat had slowed the horses. Reeves knew the place well having hunted more than wild turkeys in the thick forest and jagged hills.

Reeves had been in Fort Smith when he received word that Dirty Lonnie Blake was in the area. Lawmen were in short supply, and it fell to Reeves to chase after them. Blake was wanted for robbing multiple banks, killing two guards during one of the robberies, and his gang were all complicit in these deeds. Only hours before he set out after Dirty Lonnie Blake and his gang, another telegram had arrived and he had one of his fellow deputies read it to him as Reeves couldn't read or write. It informed him to be on the look-out for a boy named Corbin who had killed a clerk named Jessup Watkins when he robbed the bank in Voyager's End.

Reeves was only vaguely familiar with Voyager's End. There were no additional details regarding the killer named Corbin, and the description was limited to the word "boy." Not much to go on. Still, bad men often flocked together the way ducks scuttle about in a pond, and if he was lucky this Corbin kid might try and join up with Dirty Lonnie and company. Hell, he was already outnumbered. Tracking down another one didn't matter.

Grudgingly, Reeves backtracked, moving away from the outlaws. The landscape protected him. This wild Arkansas country offered ample opportunities for a man to hide. The rolling hills and canyons were often impenetrable, with poor visibility made worse by the tall trees, cliffs and scrub. Reeves knew that he could easily hide from these men, but that's not what he came here for.

When he was about three miles distant, he surveyed the area looking for a good defensive position. He found a high ridge with clusters of birch and flowering green brush where he could hobble his horse. He would go without a fire that night. He had to hunker down and put together a workable plan.

His immediate concern was determining Dirty Lonnie's next move. He was a bold if not foolish rascal, and it wasn't beyond him to come after Reeves out of spite. This was a real possibility that Reeves now had to plan on. If Dirty Lonnie, Gorton, Strachen and Jayhawker Johnny decided to come after him, they would have the advantage of numbers.

Still, Bass Reeves accepted each assignment and he accepted the responsibility that came with wearing a lawman's star. He would not relent, and he refused to give in to fear. Being outnumbered was, to his way of thinking, simply a challenge that he had to overcome.

Of his adversaries, Jayhawker Johnny was the fastest with a gun. He'd heard that Dirty Lonnie was moderately fast, but a lot of men were faster. It was Jayhawker Johnny who relied more on his reputation as being a mean and ugly bastard to give men reason to fear him. Phil Gorton was nothing special; a saddle tramp and dangerous because of the company he kept and his willingness to fight. Clark Strachen was probably a coward; he was a man that liked to surround himself with tougher men and go along with whatever they had planned.

The other possibility was that all of them would vamoose, at which point Reeves would be obligated to give chase. Either way, a gunfight would happen one way or another. Bass Reeves was a realistic and practical man, which in part accounted for his success and longevity as a lawman. He took nothing for granted except his willingness to engage these owlhoots in a dance of death.

He decided his best option was to pick away at them, wear them down slowly either by wounding them or killing them outright. Dirty Lonnie and the boys certainly had no intention of surrendering.

Reeves took inventory late that afternoon. He had biscuits and hardtack in his saddlebag, extra cartridges, a '73 Winchester and his trusty Colt .45 single-action Army revolver in his holster. Bass Reeves was practical, indeed, and he'd survived numerous gunfights because he followed one simple rule—remember that it only takes one bullet to kill a man. To that end, he made certain that his aim was true. The ten or so men that he'd been forced to kill in his career to that point would attest that his aim was true, that is, if they weren't already moldering in their graves. Still, this was no time to get cocky. He was facing capable men that didn't like him one little bit.

Reeves waited until twilight before emerging from his hideaway. He removed his spurs, and with his rifle in hand, he slipped through the foliage like a silent, fast-moving wraith. He needed to know if these scoundrels had decided to come after him, or if Dirty Lonnie had sent any of the others to ambush him.

Half a mile from camp and he thought he heard a horse nicker. The question was answered. They had come gunning for him. That was fine, Reeves thought. The day hadn't started out good, and it probably wouldn't end good. At the very least, he intended on letting these boys know they were in for a fight.

Bass Reeves was sweating under the hot June sun as he eased his way along an old deer trail. Those boys had nearly flanked him earlier, but he had a good idea how to handle them now. Yet a tingling at the back of his head, like a second sense that pervaded his mind, set him to thinking, and soon he stopped in his tracks. He couldn't place the anomaly at first, but something was out of order.

Bass Reeves had experienced this before, and once he accepted that something was awry, it was a matter of identifying the problem, and then surviving whatever happened next. No, he thought to himself, this damn day hadn't started out good at all.

He listened, and there it was again. A horse nickering, down on his right. There was nothing there. The ground dropped away treacherously, and then rose into a steep hill which made the area at the hill's base an impenetrable valley buttressed by a cliffside covered in brush, trees and grass. Accessibility was limited and far too dangerous for the average man to attempt. Yet someone was down there.

Reeves wondered if that Corbin kid had wandered into the wild valley and found himself disoriented. Such things happened to even experienced travelers.

He waited on the trail but no ambushers came lurking along the path. He wanted to satisfy his curiosity as to who it was that had hunkered down in that green and inhospitable crevice and so Reeves set out while the light was still good. The sun was dropping fast and what he could see of the horizon was rose colored.

After a few minutes he was surprised to find wagon tracks indented on the soft forest path. There would be only enough room for a wagon to follow this path as it dipped low and slung deeper into the valley.

He could hear an occasional horse stomp a hoof or nicker, but nothing else. That is, until he was twenty-five feet from their camp when the cold iron end of an old flintlock rifle was placed gently against his right ear. Then a voice said calmly.

"American, do not move."

The accent might have been French, or possibly Hungarian, not that it mattered. The man smelled of odd, exotic scents and spices. Reeves had a glimpse of the man's long black hair in his peripheral vision. A gypsy. Reeves had encountered them before. They were harmless unless irritated, and this man was irritated.

"We move, yes."

The rifle probed his ear so he started walking downhill, slowly. Reeves held onto his horse's reins, stepping slowly down the trail. The camp was tight and well organized. The canvas topped Morgan wagon was about twenty feet from the cliffside. Two horses were hobbled behind it and chewing grass. A middle-aged white female was reclining against a wagon wheel with her leg bandaged. Remarkably, Reeves recognized her. Serena Cross, a prostitute from Little Rock.

The man holding the rifle to his head said, "I am Shandor. You sit here."

His Winchester was taken from his hand and his Colt lifted from his holster.

Reeves had a good look now at the man with the flintlock. Shandor was about forty, strong looking, and suspicious. Shandor gestured to his companions.

"This is my brother Danior and my cousin Yoska. You see my wife Mirela, and our daughter Nuri. This woman is…"

"Serena Cross."

For Bass Reeves, the Wild West was suddenly very crowded. He was astounded at this turn of events.

"You know her?" Shandor was perplexed.

"I'm a U. S. Deputy Marshal. I'm after Dirty Lonnie Blake and his gang. I think they're camped about three miles from here." Reeves nodded toward Serena. "This woman is wanted for questioning in Batesville for allegedly attacking a saloon owner with a knife."

"There's no allegation." Serena said. "I cut the bastard good. He owed me money."

Serena looked tired.

Shandor came around from behind Reeves and looked at the marshal's badge on his vest. "A lawman? You are alone?"

"I am."

"Then you're a fool!" Shandor exclaimed. His brother Danior and cousin Yoska nodded their heads in agreement. The two women remained standing at the rear of the wagon staring at Reeves as if they had never seen another human being before.

"How did you end up here with a hurt leg?" Reeves asked Serena.

"I was on that stage Dirty Lonnie highjacked. He shot the drivers and killed a passenger named Mahoney. That's how I got hurt. A bullet clipped my leg. My companion is still with them."

"Your companion?"

"A fine boy named Corbin."

"He's a hostage?"

Reeves held onto his horse's reins, stepping slowly ...

"No, I think he joined them, the damn fool!"

"How did you get hooked up with him?"

Serena laughed. "How do you think? Boys like that drift my way like tumbleweed. I gave him what he wanted, and I got paid good, too."

"That boy Corbin is wanted for murder. He robbed a bank and killed the clerk."

"I'm not giving the money back that he gave me!"

"We have other problems. Dirty Lonnie and his men are probably hunting for me."

"Well, lawman!" Shandor nearly shouted. "This is not our problem." Shandor barked at his brother and cousin in a foreign tongue, and they gave the beleaguered Deputy Marshal his rifle and Colt. "You can go! We have seen enough of American law and lawmen before. No good will come to us if we stay together!"

Reeves didn't like it, but he admitted that separating was undoubtedly the better idea. Other than the flintlock rifle and some knives, these gypsies didn't appear to be well-armed.

"Tell me what Corbin looks like."

"He's got sandy colored hair and blue eyes. Lean but strong. Damn shame if he gets his neck broken by a noose."

"He brought it on himself."

"They left me to die." Serena said bitterly. "Last night after having some fun, they left me on the trail. Shandor here found me and saved me from being eaten by wild animals!"

"Go!" Shandor said, although he had stopped waving his flintlock once he learned that Reeves was a lawman.

Reeves gave Shandor a long look. "Shandor, you need to be careful out here. Dirty Lonnie and his men will cut you to pieces. Serena, you need to turn yourself in once you come to a town that has a sheriff."

At this Serena let out girlish giggle. "Bass, you are a fine lookin' man, but Shandor here is right—you're a damn fool!"

Reeves was disgruntled but kept his poker face on. He leveled what he hoped was a firm look at each of them. "I don't have time to stick around jawing with you people, so keep in mind what I've said. That's the only thing I can do for any of you on this fine day."

Pulling himself into the saddle, he set his horse into a canter and made a point of not looking at them again. He'd catch up with Serena again one day, of that he was sure. His immediate concern was locating the murderous group that roamed the hillsides, and to bring them to justice without getting himself killed.

Meeting the gypsies in such a remote location as Vulture's Hollow was an unfortunate circumstance. All the same, stranger things had happened. The problem was, Reeves thought, those gypsies can't be trusted. They weren't bad men, not like Dirty Lonnie and his gang were bad men, but the gypsies were a secular, secretive group. No, he didn't trust them one bit, and the best thing would be for them to move on as quickly as possible.

The sooner they were all out of Vulture's Hollow, the better off they'd all be.

Handling Dirty Lonnie Blake and his gang was trouble enough, and adding Corbin to the mix might be the same as pouring kerosene on a fire. It was five against one. Of course, Bass reminded himself, I could always pull out and request assistance. He rejected the thought as soon as it crossed his mind. Bass Reeves often preferred working alone. Once he thought a problem through, he liked the sense of accomplishment that came with a resolution. Hell, he'd been shot at before. He was alive today, he thought, because of his unswerving willingness to shoot back.

He made camp on the crest of a small hill and surrounded by pine, aspen and birch. Bass Reeves hadn't had a good day and he was glad when the sun dipped below the treeline and cast the landscape into a shadowy twilight. Alert for unusual sounds, he decided to simply hunker down a bit and watch his backtrail. His enemies were out there, that was for damn certain. He couldn't let his guard down for a moment.

No fire tonight, he thought. He wasn't going to take any chances until he had a better idea where those scoundrels had gone. He drank water from his canteen and appeased his hunger with beef-jerky and some cold biscuits from his saddlebags. His stomach grumbled with a desire for a bloody steak. That would have to wait.

He had his horse hobbled nearby where he let it contentedly munch at the grass. His saddle and horse blankets served as a makeshift bed. With his Winchester propped against a tree and his Colt in hand, Reeves hunkered down, stretched out his legs with his hat pulled low over his eyes. He dozed a bit and briefly dreamed about his childhood in Texas when his family were slaves.

When he awoke he'd been dreaming about his years spent living with the Cherokee, good years where he'd learned to live off the land and fend for himself. A sound coupled with his innate sense for danger had awakened him. He lay still without moving. It was pitch black so there was no danger that he was being observed. Still, something or someone was nearby. He listened for the sound of his own horse but heard nothing, which meant the horse was sleeping. He would have heard any effort to un-hobble the horse. Whatever had awakened him had been something else.

He bent his knees and pushed up into a crouched position. His back hurt slightly from having laid down on a rock. He stretched his aching muscles and holstered his Colt. The sound had come from straight ahead, and down in a hollow. Then he heard it again. The muffled sound of voices. He found his rifle in the dark and set off through the brush. When Reeves had made his camp, he'd taken the time to memorize the set-up for precisely this reason. The Cherokee had taught him how to move in the darkness, how to find his way when it was too dark to see, all of which were survival skills most men lacked.

He didn't intend to wander far from camp. He came out of the trees on a ridge-line where the dark forest was a jagged line of blackness etched against the star-sprinkled horizon that swept over him with startling clarity. The clear, calm night made it easier for him to discern distances and even some vague animal trails. His position on the hillside offered a splendid view, no matter the darkness.

His eyes probed the jagged treeline and he felt his pulse quicken when he spotted the small, yellow blaze of their campfire. No doubt about it, it was Dirty Lonnie and the boys. Even at this great distance he recognized Dirty Lonnie's silhouette. Other figures moved around the campfire. Perplexed, Reeves moved closer.

They were less than a mile away, squatting down near the very trail he'd followed up this hill. Reeves deduced they had been attempting to follow him. That fact didn't bother Reeves at all. He made no effort to conceal his tracks. He was confident he could evade pursuit in the darkness of any forest. His Cherokee friend, Atohi, had guided him on the path of the night world, and while Bass Reeves seldom spoke of his years living with the Indians, he nevertheless held dear all of the knowledge he'd acquired from that life-changing experience.

If Atohi had been present at that moment, he would have laughed at the stupidity of Dirty Lonnie Blake and his gang. They were spending the night in a vulnerable position. They were noisy and their fire burned strong making it easy to locate them. They sounded drunk. Reeves calculated the option of confronting them now and taking prisoners. He harbored no misconceptions about the task. They would rather die than be taken prisoner, and taking any of them alive was probably a fantasy. All the same, a lawman was obligated to try.

A thought nagged at Reeves as he studied the camp. There had been no loud sounds in the forest, and yet it appeared that others had joined up with the outlaws.

His immediate problem was the rugged terrain. Although they were only a half mile away, he would have to bring any prisoners back to camp on foot. He couldn't chance riding his horse because of the potential for noise. He would have to go in on foot, probably engage in a shootout, and walk any prisoners to his camp in the darkness. Either that, or stay put with the prisoners at their camp until sunup.

He internally debated whether to proceed or wait till daylight. In the end Reeves made up his up his mind and started down the hill.

He had every advantage now, and that was a sight better than his circumstances the day before. At the very least, Reeves told himself, I'll get a better look at the people in camp. Knowledge is power. Bass Reeves was a careful, meticulous lawman. He wouldn't attack them blindly, but for Reeves, gathering as much information about his enemies was akin to an assault, at least mentally. Everything that he learned was put to good use. He already survived one difficult day, and he didn't want another bad day.

Reeves had removed the spurs from his cowhide boots and moved carefully along the pine-needle path. He enjoyed the cool night air and the mossy smell of the earth. Alert for any unusual signs, he nearly reveled in the night bird songs and low hoots of the owls high in the trees. Chipmunks and other small voles scampered across the path, their crackling presence a welcome sound. He wondered sometimes about the Cherokee boys he'd known all those years ago, and he wondered what had become of Atohi. Years had passed since he'd heard anything of him, and he grudgingly accepted he might be long dead. So many of the tribes had been decimated from either the white man's bullets or from disease.

Gone as well were the slaves he'd known as a child, and while he had his freedom for many years now, the great struggles he'd witnessed in his life never ceased.

He pressed on, brushing aside his memories and concentrating on closing the gap to Blake's camp.

He stopped when he heard a woman's voice.

He cursed under his breath.

That sounded like Serena Cross. Peering into the flickering light of Dirty Lonnie's camp, his heart sank when he saw the women from the gypsy camp tied up near their wagon. Of all the damn poor luck! Somehow the outlaws had gone after the gypsies and taken them prisoner.

He hadn't heard any gunfire, and he thought Shandor and his group were capable of at least fighting back. Whatever had happened, they were all somehow with Dirty Lonnie Blake. He wondered if any of the gypsies had been killed.

Undaunted, Bass Reeves proceeded across a dark swale until he was on a rise between several birch trees. He could see the flames of the campfire licking at the night breeze and tossing grotesque shadows across the clearing where they had made their camp. It was a poor site for a camp, too. Reeves had his pick of which direction he could come at them. With a few extra men he could have easily overcome any resistance.

Then he saw Mirela and Nuri. They had been stripped naked and stood near the horses and the wagon with their hands tied behind their backs. Their ashen features and wide eyes revealed their shock at being held captive. Dirty Lonnie and the others were busy passing around whiskey bottles, getting themselves worked up for a night of fun with the unwilling ladies. Reeves had arrived before any true debauchery had befallen the ladies, but he would need to revise his thinking and act quickly.

He heard Serena's voice giggling from behind a nearby clump of greenery. "Come on, boy! You can do it! Come on!"

That Serena is always eager to lend a hand, thought Reeves. She was doing what she had to do to survive.

His gaze probed the camp's perimeter and he saw Shandor hog-tied off to the side. He was lucky to be alive. Danior and Yoska were nowhere to be seen. He wondered if they were dead, or if they had escaped? He picked out Dirty Lonnie, Phil Gorton and Clark Strachen. A few seconds later he spied Jayhawker Johnny Dolan which meant that Serena was giving the Corbin boy an education. Somehow, that was all right with Reeves. After all, the Corbin boy was a murderer and he was going to hang. Best that he have this last night of fun with a woman before Reeves hauled his sorry ass to jail for a quick trial and a quick hanging.

Bass Reeves was disgruntled, however by this unfortunate turn of events. He was now forced to save the two women from a certain gang rape and still somehow bring in five wanted men. Yesterday's problems were moderate compared to his current predicament.

He watched the camp, secure in the knowledge they had no idea they were being observed. Atohi had told him once that a black man like Reeves had the advantage at night because he couldn't be seen. Reeves had laughed at that idea, although he learned it was true. From his vantage point, Reeves might easily lift his rifle and take out Dirty Lonnie and Gorton with two swift shots, but that would be murder. No one need ever know. He could shoot them as easily as shooting ducks in a pond. But it was murder, plain and simple.

Bass Reeves was no murderer, although he had killed his fair share of outlaws, and no doubt he was about to kill more. Just as he made up his mind to shoot Dirty Lonnie with the intention of only wounding him, a shot blasted into the camp from the right, and from high up. The slug tore up the dirt near Dirty Lonnie and the camp erupted with activity.

Two rifles, Reeves thought, and both sounded like old flintlocks.

Dirty Lonnie was firing his Colt up into the trees, and Gorton and Strachen had grabbed rifles and were firing wildly into the darkness. The gun muzzles spit hot lead in every direction while Reeves watched with astonishment as Dirty Lonnie Blake cussed with vigor as another gunshot sounded from their left.

Reeves didn't need to see them to know it was undoubtedly Danior and Yoska taking shots at the drunk and confused outlaws. The sound of gunfire had roused the hog-tied Shandor from his stupor and he began wriggling about trying to get free of the ropes.

Reeves heard Jawhawker Johnny scream at Dirty Lonnie, "I told you we should have hunted them all down!"

Dodging branches, Reeves eased down the hill and made for Shandor. He held his fire hoping to keep his presence unknown for as long as possible. Blake and the others had disappeared from view, but they appeared to be chasing the shooter on the right.

He came up to Shandor, pulled a small but sharp blade from his belt-sheath, and slashed the ropes.

"Keep quiet!" Reeves said, "Get your women free." He handed Shandor the rifle and went looking for Serena and the boy. He found them just as Corbin was buckling his pants. Serena lay on the grass in a decidedly un-ladylike position. Reeves took his Colt and slammed it across Corbin's head before he had a chance to realize what was happening. The boy went down, groaning.

"Get your clothes on, Serena, we need to get out of here."

"Bass Reeves! You're as crazy as they get!"

"Shut up and get moving!"

Reeves grabbed Corbin's shirt and cut a section into a long scarf and used it to tie Corbin's hands behind his back with the boy on his knees and blood pouring down his face.

"You might have killed him!"

Reeves hauled Corbin to his feet. "Let's move!"

Shandor had cut his wife and daughter free and helped them dress. Reeves ignored them and went to the makeshift corral and cut the ropes holding the horses. A blast from his Colt sent the horses scampering in panic. Dirty Lonnie yelled, "Get the horses! Don't let the horses get away!"

The outlaws were in disarray, scrambling for cover and chasing the horses.

Corbin was bleeding profusely on the head and stumbling as he walked. Shandor came up next to him and said to Reeves, "Let me kill this pig!"

"Not now! We'll straighten this out later. Let's move!"

Reeves shoved Serena forward and yanked Corbin by the shoulder and pushed him uphill after her.

Danior and Yoska were waiting for them at the top of the hill. Shandor called out to them and they came forward eager to reunite with their family. Mirela and Nuri hugged them all, weeping. Reeves was anxious to move on, and blurted, "All right, we need to keep moving. Those men won't stop now and I'm not much on sentiment."

They followed Reeves into the forest, and Reeves told Shandor, Danior and Yoska to watch their backtrail. Shandor was in no condition to help, the emotional impact of being held prisoner and nearly meeting his maker too much for him. Shandor clung to the women, and they helped each other along the trail. Reeves wouldn't let Corbin slow them down. When the kid faltered, Reeves pushed him hard and hissed in his ear, "You better keep walking, kid, or I'll cut your liver out right here and cook it for breakfast!" The intensity in the black man's eyes and hard tone of his voice propelled the doomed youth through the brush, over another hill, and deeper into the forest, his mind reeling from the change in his circumstances in such a short time.

In the distance, they could still hear Dirty Lonnie and the others cursing, screaming and shooting. Reeves couldn't imagine what those fools were shooting at, but the sporadic gunfire at least let them know they were putting distance between themselves and the outlaw gang.

"Keep moving!" Reeves rasped harshly. "They may decide to come after us once they gather their horses."

When they reached the camp, Reeves insisted everyone sit tight and remain quiet. He was concentrating on listening for Dirty Lonnie Blake and his gang to come crashing after them. Yet the forest was oddly silent. Reeves was thinking if they were lucky, Dirty Lonnie and the boys would be occupied chasing their horses for some time.

They waited fifteen minutes and then Reeves went to secure Corbin with the wrist-irons from his backpack. He turned Corbin around and cut loose his makeshift bonds when the boy spun wildly and head-butted Reeves, sending him sprawling. Corbin dashed down the trail.

Cursing, Reeves pulled himself to his feet and started after Corbin when the panicky kid came rushing at him again, slamming a fist at the lawman's head. Reeves deflected the blow and sent a hard punch at Corbin's jaw which rattled the boy's teeth and nearly crossed his eyes. But Corbin wasn't finished. An injured wolf is among the dangerous species every outdoorsman learns to avoid. Reeves recognized the kid's fury stemmed from his awareness of his fate should he be captured and forced to stand trial. His life was at stake and he fought desperately to overpower Bass Reeves.

Reeves side-stepped and rammed a hard punch into Corbin's ribs. He heard the boy gasp in pain. Reeves hit him again, then swung a left at his eyes. His knuckles tore a bloody gash over Corbin's right eye, the blood staining his grimacing face like a red tattoo.

He didn't want to shoot the kid; at least not unless he had too. Reeves sent a fast right that he followed with two left jabs before delivering a haymaker punch that caught Corbin on the left temple, knocking him unconscious.

Reeves stood over Corbin's inert form with his fists balled and dripping crimson. He sucked in air like a tired bull. Eventually his eyes settled on Shandor, Danior and Yoska who had watched the fight calmly. Danior and Yoska still held their rifles.

"You might have helped me!" Reeves rasped.

Danior shook his head. "No. This is not our fight."

Reeves felt a tight knot in his chest as his pulse flared, the anger he felt a long way from abating.

"I just saved your carcasses! I saved your women, and now you sit back and say it's not your fight!" Reeves stepped toward Danior, his fists still balled. Danior raised his rifle and in his peripheral vision he saw Yoska do the same. "You dirty gypsy sons-of-bitches!"

Shandor, who was sitting on a fallen tree stump with the two women, shook his head sadly. "Let it be, lawman. Danior and Yoska would have freed us in time. You need to understand our ways. We prefer to do things for ourselves."

At this, Serena Cross let out a tired cackle. She giggled to herself, apparently quite amused by the ongoing spectacle that she'd been drawn into. Reeves tossed a hard look at her and she pressed her lips together and looked away.

It was growing lighter by the minute, and Reeves thought his best action now was to take Corbin to jail, and come back for Dirty Lonnie Blake with a posse. The circumstances had changed rapidly, and he'd only escaped serious injury himself by a hair's breadth. Lingering in Vulture's Hollow was a decidedly unhealthy activity. Bass Reeves knew when to retreat, although he didn't like it one bit.

"Get on the trail!" Reeves hissed at Shandor. "I've had enough of you." Turning to Serena, Reeves cocked a thumb and said, "You sit tight over there. You're going back with me, but we need to wait a bit while these fools get moving."

Serena made a pouty face, but then her eyes shifted to the prostate form of Corbin. "The poor tumbleweed boy." She said. "Are they gonna hang him, Bass?"

"He killed a bank clerk."

Shandor organized his bedraggled group and they started down the trail without another word. Reeves studied the pink tints in the sky. He was glad to see the gypsies move on, and by God that was the last time he'd help that ungrateful bunch! The sun wasn't fully visible yet, but once it broke the treeline the air would grow stifling hot. Good. The heat would slow everything, and everyone, down. With their horses scattered, Dirty Lonnie Blake and his gang would be hard-pressed to follow them. At least that was what Reeves hoped.

Reeves had only his own horse, but he thought he knew the country better than Dirty Lonnie. He began going over the route from the valley in his mind's eye. He'd put Serena on the horse and walk Corbin in front of him. Keep Corbin tired from walking. He would lead them three miles through the forest and out of the valley. Down near the creek there was an old hunter's shack. They would rest there for a few minutes and water the horse. Then they would cut south and pick up the main trail to Voyager's End where Corbin had sealed his fate when he killed the bank clerk. All we have to do is get there, Reeves thought.

The sky was only a tad lighter, but Reeves was anxious to get moving. He told Serena to get on his horse. Reeves took his Winchester and poked Corbin.

"Let it be, lawman."

"Get up, kid. You've been awake for fifteen minutes and playing possum."

Corbin opened his eyes and glared at Bass Reeves. "You are an evil man! My head hurts something fierce from you hitting me!"

"Time to go. You keep flapping your lips and I'll hit you again."

"Where are we going?"

"I'm taking you in for the murder of a bank clerk named Jessup Watkins."

"Jessup got what he deserved! He was keeping my money from me!"

"The judge can sort it out."

"They'll hang me! I ain't done nothin' wrong."

"Sure, kid, and a skunk doesn't smell. Now get up or I'm going to fatten your lip."

Corbin saw the look in the lawman's eyes and struggled to his feet. "You gonna bandage my head?"

"No."

"You're a cold-hearted bastard, ain't you?"

"Yep. Now start walking."

"I never should have joined with those stagecoach robbers! I'd be long gone from this territory if I'd kept moving!"

"I would have caught up with you eventually," Reeves said, "or someone like me."

Corbin shuffled along and Reeves pulled the reins, leading his horse. He noticed that Serena had a smug look on her face as she straddled the saddle. She's a real goddamn princess, Reeves thought. She was also a pain-in-the-ass. In fact, this entire venture had gone crazy from the start, and the sooner he had Corbin in jail, the better off he'd be. Then he could concentrate on apprehending Dirty Lonnie Blake and his owlhoot friends and be done with all of them.

This venture had been problematic from the beginning, and Reeves had to grudgingly admit he'd taken on a bit more than he could chew. All the same, now that Corbin was hog-tied he itched to be after Dirty Lonnie Blake and the others.

As they walked he studied Corbin. He was slender and wiry and way too young. Reeves had seen his type before. Young boys without a good upbringing and lacking in a formal education almost always became lawbreakers. It was downright heartbreaking and there was no need for it. Yet there was something else in Corbin's demeanor that bothered Reeves. It was the cold, emotionless look in his eyes. He had seen that look before, too, especially in the eyes of men convicted of murder. Jessup got what he deserved! When Corbin had said those words, a chill had run through

Bass Reeves. Corbin's eyes were like ice, soulless, and it was no different than the look a snake had in its dark eyes just before striking.

They had gone about two miles without speaking when Serena complained she had to relieve herself. Reeves pulled on the reins and stopped the horse.

"Corbin, you stand right there. Serena get down and go over by those bushes."

Serena slid out of the saddle and hitched up her dress, glancing at Reeves. "You all keep your eyes in a decent place!"

Corbin sneered and chuckled. "Ain't she something to say that, marshal."

"Shut up, kid."

Serena went behind the bushes and Reeves cast a glance her way to make certain she didn't wander too far. Corbin chose that moment to spin and charge like a bull at Reeves. With his head down, he slammed into Reeves with tremendous force, knocking the wind from his lungs. With his hands tied, Corbin couldn't do much, but he took advantage of Reeves being knocked into the dirt and did his best to kick his head in.

Reeves took a boot in the jaw and pain lanced through him. He rolled, avoiding the next kick, and he jumped to his feet with his Colt in his hand, his head throbbing with pain. His jaw was numb from the kick but his blood was boiling in his veins. He cocked the Colt's hammer with his thumb and resisted the urge to blow Corbin to hell.

Corbin stopped in his tracks. His face was flushed and his mouth was curved into a contemptuous sneer.

Reeves stretched out his arm, pointing the Colt at Corbin's chest. "You filthy little viper!"

"I almost had you, old man! You ain't nothin'! Next time I'll get you!"

"There won't be a next time. I'll send your rotten soul straight to hell if you so much as blink without my permission!"

Corbin spat into the dust. "My hands are tied and I almost got you! It's a long way to town! Think about that! I hope Dirty Lonnie and Jayhawker Johnny and the others are gonna gut you like a rabbit and roast you over a fire!"

Reeves stepped up and slapped his gun hard across Corbin's head and ripping another bloody wound on his skull. Corbin yelled in pain and dropped to his knees.

"That isn't fair, Bass!" Serena yelled, straightening out her skirt as she emerged from the bushes. "That boy should be treated fair and square. Isn't that what the law says?"

Reeves had never struck a woman in his life, and this was the closest he'd come to striking one, but he held back. No, damn it all, he thought, this has not been a good couple of days.

"I'm tying him to the saddle with his belly down. You'll walk with me."

"Aw, damn it, Bass, that ain't right neither! I gotta keep my strength for the boys in town!"

Reeves yanked Corbin to his feet, forced him into the saddle. Once Corbin was over the saddle he tied his wrists with the lasso and strung it under the horse to Corbin's ankles. He'd cut the fool loose when they got to town. Reeves wasn't taking any more chances. Corbin could wet himself for all he cared, but he wasn't getting cut loose until they were in front of the sheriff's office.

Keeping his eyes on the trail ahead of them, Reeves told Serena to hold the horse's reins as they walked. He wanted his hands on his Winchester. Dirty Lonnie and the boys might be in disarray, but that didn't mean they'd forgotten about him. Bass Reeves had learned from experience that bad men hold grudges.

"Bass, I want you to know I'm not all bad." Serena said, her lip turned down in a pout.

"No, I don't suppose you are." Reeves said, casting a glance her way. "All the same, you attacked a saloon owner with a knife. Cut him up badly according to the report I read. You'll answer for that."

"It was the circumstances, Bass. Honest it was...being on the run, and then with the stagecoach being robbed, well...I had to survive! You understand that, don't you Bass?"

"I understand."

"This boy here can't be all bad. I'm sort of sweet on him."

"He's a killer, plain and simple."

Reeves thought Serena was working really hard to make her pout look sympathetic. He wouldn't have any of that nonsense.

"Don't you think I'm pretty, Bass?"

"I think a blue jay is pretty. You're no blue jay. You're a plump whore with a big mouth and a bad temper."

That was enough to send Serena into a fit. "You go to hell, Bass! Next time you're off the trail doing your particulars, I hope you wipe your ass with a cactus!"

"Shut up and keep walking."

They made good time, moving downhill until they came to a fast-running creek. It was a good place to water the horse; secluded and out of view. Corbin was awake, turning his head back and forth trying to get a better view. The riverbank was studded with cattails and willows, and the trees offered shade which helped make the stifling morning heat a tad more bearable.

The problem was the horse. Reeves knew his horse, and in the past he had relied on his horse to survive. A good horse never let a man down. The horse was nervous, his ears flicking back and forth, his nostrils flaring. Occasionally, the horse clawed the earth with an iron-shod hoof.

"That's just a damn shame." Reeves said out loud.

Serena, who had gone to soak her swollen ankles in the cool creek water, bunched her skirt around her knees and tried unsuccessfully to get the lawman's attention, craned her neck around to ponder the figure of Bass Reeves.

"What's a damn shame?"

Corbin, still draped over the saddle and trussed up like a pig at a church picnic, sneered at Reeves. "I'll tell you what's a shame! It's the fact that you have me tied up! My arms are goin' numb! Cut me loose!"

Reeves ignored both Serena and Corbin. Nope, it wasn't going to be another good day at all, Reeves thought to himself. They were being followed, and his horse sensed trouble. It might be a mule or an Indian, but what most likely made his horse nervous was the scent of men on their backtrail. Desperate men had an odor, just like dead men have an odor. That odor distinguished them from all of the other wildlife in the area, and a horse would pick up that scent first.

Four humiliated and desperate men had come looking for Bass Reeves after all.

There was nothing left to do, he thought glumly, except get to it.

"It's a damn shame we're about to have company." Reeves grabbed Serena by the elbow and yanked her to her feet. "Get over by those trees and don't move!"

"Bass, I don't have my shoes on!"

Reeves shoved Serena and sent her stumbling away from the creek. There wasn't time for anything else. A rifle blast made his horse snort and chomp at the bit, and Reeves was diving for cover. Another second and it would have been too late.

A barrage of gunfire commenced to rip up the greenery. The air was filled with the hot, hard snap of cartridges detonating, acrid gunsmoke filling the air. His horse whinnied excitedly and turned a full circle. He heard Serena screech but he was too busy rolling sideways to look her way as he crab-crawled into the underbrush.

Reeves jacked a round into his Winchester's breech but there was nothing to shoot at. Dirty Lonnie and his men were uphill, positioned out of view in a strand of thick maples and stunted pine trees.

Slogging a path through the brush, Reeves was content to leave Serena and Corbin while he circumnavigated the area with the hope of drawing a bead on some of Dirty Lonnie's men, maybe even Dirty Lonnie himself.

Hoping to draw them out, Reeves brought the rifle to his shoulder and sighted down the barrel and aiming at a clump of wildflowers where he prayed an ambusher had taken up position. It was the only location visible to him from his crouched angle that seemed like a logical hiding place. He squeezed the trigger and cracked off a round.

A man cursed and yowled in pain. For a split second, Reeves thought his shot had struck and killed a man. In another moment, a peel of raucous laughter dashed his hopes as a voice boomed from the top of the forested hill: "Haw haw, Reeves! You clipped my boot! You'll have to do better than that you stinking pile of manure!"

Reeves winged another rifle shot uphill out of pure obstinacy. It was a waste of ammunition, but it felt good to be shooting.

More laughter boomed in his direction.

"Come on, lawman! Emancipate me from my earthly body, haw haw!"

"I'll do that, Lonnie! You might as well surrender now!"

Reeves was studying every branch and every leaf in view for the slightest hint of movement, and he wasn't quite sure how far uphill Dirty Lonnie was hiding. He couldn't gauge the distance properly because of the echoing and the constant murmur of the creek rushing along behind him.

A sudden whooping sound followed by the galloping crash of hoofbeats forced him to rear up and glance over to his right. His heart thudded anxiously as he saw Clark Strachen toss Corbin a six-shooter after cutting him loose from his horse. Corbin untangled himself and whooped like an Indian, raising the Colt above his head and screaming, "I'm gonna kill myself a lawman!"

They hadn't seen him yet, but Strachen was looking around, and then his eyes fell on Reeves. Both men fired simultaneously. Strachen's bullet nearly creased Reeves' skull, but the lawman's bullet had found its mark. Corbin scrambled for cover as Strachen looked down in horror at the blossoming red stain on his plaid shirt; and then is eyes rolled back in their sockets and he fell flat on his face. He was dead when he hit the ground, but the sound of his nose shattering as his face smacked the earth made Reeves grimace.

With Strachen dead, that left Dirty Lonnie Blake, Phil Gorton, Jayhawker Johnny Dolan, and, of course, Corbin.

Naturally, the kid had high-tailed it for cover. Reeves noted that his horse had also run off, and he still had no idea where the other men were hiding. What did matter for Bass Reeves at that moment was the singular fact that his experiences and instincts worked in tandem; propelled him to his feet and sent him running for cover elsewhere as another barrage of rifle fire ripped up the space that he'd occupied only seconds before.

Two slugs came dangerously close to his hip, and a third slug whispered against his leg, tearing at his trousers and leaving a thin but harmless bloody crease on his leg. Reeves didn't realize the slug had winged him until he burst through the brush and sprinted into a closely-knit grouping of birch trees where he crouched with his rifle ready. A fly buzzed in his face and he swatted it away. Realizing his leg stung, he glanced downward and saw the glistening blood and frayed edges of his trousers which he had only purchased a month earlier. He cursed under his breath.

"Bass! Bass! I've been shot!"

Serena's voice came wafting through the smell of gunsmoke.

"Stay put!"

He made his way around the trees and edged through another row of wild brush. He could hear the creek rumbling nearby. When he found the shoreline, he changed direction and started toward Serena, keeping low. Dirty Lonnie and the boys were keeping a safe distance no matter how confident they sounded. At some point, those owlhoots would get their courage up and rush at him.

He found Serena sitting with her back to a tree. A bullet had mangled the meaty part of her shoulder. She was sobbing, her hand held over the wound, blood speckled across her fingers.

"Oh, Bass! I've been hit!"

"Keep your voice down. Let me take a look."

The bullet had missed the bone completely and torn through her flesh. It was superficial flesh wound, but bleeding profusely. Reeves untied the bandanna around his neck.

"I've got to stop the bleeding."

He wrapped the bandanna around her shoulder and yanked it into a knot. Serena squealed in pain. "Ow, Bass! That hurts!"

"You're lucky it isn't worse. Now I want you to stay here and don't move until I come back for you."

"Oh, Bass, I'm all shot up! First my leg and now my arm!"

"Try and keep quiet and don't move!"

"What happens if you don't come back?"

"That'll be your problem."

He didn't say it out loud, but Reeves was thinking, "I'm surrounded by a bunch of damn fools!"

Reeves thumbed cartridges into the Winchester while still crouching next to Serena. Hunched low, he made his way to the right, doing his best to keep out of view. He knew they'd seen him when one of the boys bellowed, "There he is! He's a lot easier to see in the daylight!" A rifle boomed and Reeves was running hell-bent-for leather as bullets thumped into the ground near him or caromed into the forest.

A man whooped and Reeves turned in time to see Phil Gorton's long, greasy hair blowing in the breeze as he ran from cover, flung his rifle to his shoulder and triggered a shot. The bullet spanged off a boulder and ricocheted into the brush.

Reeves fired once, and Gorton screamed as the slug whammed into his side. Reeves saw Gorton's shirt puff out before he fell out of view. He's wounded, Reeves thought, but not dead.

A boot scuffed against a rock, and Reeves spun around just as Dirty Lonnie thumbed his rifle and fired. A sharp pain tore into Reeves, and he tumbled sideways. He rolled when he hit the ground, and then sprang upwards as quickly as he could lift himself, firing his rifle rapidly three times, but Dirty Lonnie had vanished.

The echo of his shots hung in the air, and Reeves set himself in a crouch, his eyes sweeping left and right searching for a target. Dirty Lonnie and the others had the advantage of the high ground, but Reeves had the advantage of being stubborn enough to hold his ground.

A glance down at his shirt confirmed another superficial wound. Reeves shrugged it off. He'd clean the wound later. At that moment he was interested in blowing someone's head off, and Phil Gorton had been the closest to him when the shooting began.

A movement caught his eye, and Reeves crept forward, his rifle leading the way, a cartridge already resting snugly in the breech. Up ahead, and positioned between two boulders on the hillside that were framed by young birch trees, Reeves saw Dirty Lonnie scramble out of view; but the other man he saw was Phil Gorton who looked over his shoulder and saw Reeves

A glance down confirmed another superficial wound.

advancing. A splash of red on Gorton's shirt revealed his wound, but it hadn't slowed him down, nor had it improved his unfriendly disposition.

Unleashing a mad guffaw, Gorton pulled back his lips in a sneer, flashing his crooked yellow teeth, and shouting, "Come on you smooth talkin' devil! You are gonna die today! Do you hear me, man? We ain't goin' to no jail, but sure as hell you all is gonna die!"

Gorton fired a wild shot from his Colt and followed Dirty Lonnie over the ridge. Disgruntled, Reeves called after the fleeing outlaw, "You're a master of eloquence, Phil, but you talk too damn much! I put one bullet in you already today, and I do have a hankering to put another slug in you before lunch!"

Without waiting for an answer, Reeves cut to his left, nearly tripping over some thick brambles as he looked for another vantage point. He found what might have been an animal trail and pushed his way uphill. He made steady progress, but he was ever alert. Jayhawker Johnny Dolan hadn't shown his face yet, and Corbin was no doubt lurking nearby and waiting for an opportunity to ambush him.

He had ascended halfway up the hill when he turned a sharp corner and surprised Phil Gorton coming downhill in front of him. Gorton bellowed in rage and sprang forward, flailing his fists, knocking the rifle from Reeves' hands. Gorton barreled into him and a fist cracked against Reeves' jaw. Reeves heard his rifle clattering away down the ravine as black dots swam before his eyes and Gorton wrapped his burly arms around him in a bear hug.

Reeves felt the breath being crushed from his lungs, and his anger surged hotly in his veins. Reeves was only an inch taller than Gorton, but far stronger. Planting his feet firmly in place, Reeves flexed his sinews and jolted sideways, tumbling off the trail with Gorton still hanging onto him.

They crashed through the sapling and thick bushes, and Reeves twisted at the last moment so that Gorton took the full impact when they hit the ground. The sound they made when they struck the earth was like that of a grain sack tossed over a cliff. Gorton's head cracked loudly on a rock. His eyes rolled in their sockets, showing the whites. Reeves was certain that Gorton was dying, but then the outlaw surprised him and sucked in a breath and coughed blood as his eyes rotated to their normal positions. Reeves slapped Gorton's arms aside, and pushed up, pulling his Colt from the holster.

"Don't get up, you son-of-a-bitch!"

Gorton's eyes were wide with shock and disbelief at what had happened.

Gorton's mouth was open reminding Reeves of a small bird waiting for the worm.

"Ahhhhmmm…" Gorton blustered, wheezed and coughed more blood. "Ahmm…gonna kill…you…"

"That's fine." Reeves said. "Meanwhile, you can lay here and wait for the buzzards."

Reeves stripped the gunbelt from Gorton whose chest was rising and falling rapidly as he sucked air into his lungs. The bullet wound didn't look fatal, but that fall appeared to have busted him up. Reeves knew he'd be sore himself for several days, but Gorton had taken the brunt of the impact. He estimated they'd dropped thirty-five feet.

Reeves tossed Gorton's gunbelt into the brush, and started making his way uphill, leaving Gorton gasping for air. It took him ten minutes of climbing to crest the hill, and as he expected there was no sign of Dirty Lonnie, Jayhawker Johnny or Corbin.

Reeves stayed down three feet from the hill's crest, which was a large granite boulder. A quick glance on the other side indicated the outlaws had vamoosed, or, more likely, had found a new place to hide. A sound behind him had Reeves spinning, his gun ready.

To his amazement, Phil Gorton was clambering up the hill. The man looked like death warmed over with his bloody shirt and his unkempt greasy hair framing his sullen, thin face. His mouth was open and he was gasping, wheezing, and spitting wads of yellow mucus as he lumbered toward Reeves. Gorton had pulled a small, bone-handled knife from a sheath on his belt. His rheumy, watery eyes stared dolefully at Reeves as he advanced.

Reeves had to admire the man's gumption, but it was about to get him killed.

"Now, Phil, you listen to me. You might have been better off dying on that switchback instead causing yourself all this effort."

"Ahmmm…hurt. You hurt…me…"

Bass Reeves raised his gun and set the sight on Phil Gorton's chest.

"Phil, drop that knife."

Two more steps, shambling along like a dead man walking. A line of drool stretched from Gorton's lower lip. Bass Reeves took a long breath. Hell of a day this had turned out to be.

"Phil, you're a no-good dishonest man and I want you to know that I sincerely hope your soul rests in peace, you damn fool."

The Colt bucked in his hand and the slug punched a neat hole through

Phil Gorton's breastbone, blowing a bigger hole out of his back followed by a geyser of gore, and spinning Gorton so fiercely that his legs tangled and he dropped in a bloody heap, twitching as he died.

"Amen." Reeves said, turning away.

The beleaguered deputy marshal had enough of backwoods idiot robbers, horse thieves and scoundrels trying to kill him, and while he didn't take pleasure in killing bad men, he certainly didn't lose sleep over them. The last few days set him to thinking about retirement. Hunting down Dirty Lonnie Blake and his gang had gone sour once he'd arrived at Vulture's Hollow, and then his encounter with those infernal traveling gypsies had darkened his mood. Then Corbin and Serena had complicated matters all to hell, and what Bass Reeves wanted at that moment was a cool glass of beer in some calm, law-abiding saloon.

A sound caught his attention, and his gaze swiveled right. They had circled downhill and come close to the area where Serena was sitting. He wasn't worried about her, not given her proclivity at handling men, but he didn't want them flanking him. Reeves started to back away, moving as quietly as a church mouse, or so he believed, just as a flurry of bullets chewed into the bark of a tree three feet on his left.

Dirty Lonnie appeared from behind a thick maple, snarling. "There's still three of us, you damnable bastard!"

"I can count just fine!" Reeves hollered, thumbing the hammer on his Colt. He fired swiftly and Dirty Lonnie dodged out of view. At that instant, he caught sight of Jayhawker Johnny Dolan, but his back was to him as he slogged his way through the trees. There was still no sign of Corbin, but Reeves decided to hell with it. He'd get Jayhawker Johnny later. He knew where Dirty Lonnie was, so he started huffing his way straight at the treeline where Dirty Lonnie was still screaming and cursing. When he saw Reeves running straight at him, Dirty Lonnie's eyes went wide, and he fumbled with his rifle as he began thumbing cartridges into the receiver.

"You went and made me angry, Bass! This is all your fault!" Reeves thought Dirty Lonnie was starting to sound desperate.

Every muscle in his body ached by this point, but Reeves was now possessed with a singular focus that spelled trouble for Dirty Lonnie as the lawman ran forward. Reeves heard Dirty Lonnie say, "I'm gonna skin your hide!" But Dirty Lonnie dropped a cartridge, cursed, and swung the rifle toward Reeves who was twenty feet away. Reeves had been counting as Dirty Lonnie reloaded. Dirty Lonnie had managed to reload only two bullets.

With his right arm extended, Reeves slowed his pace just enough to sight the Colt's barrel on Dirty Lonnie and snap the trigger.

All it takes is one bullet! He thought to himself.

Dirty Lonnie's jaw was shattered as the bullet tore through bone, ricocheted upwards and ripped a bloody swath that turned his left ear into a shredded mass of red cauliflower. He screamed, dashed a shot off that went high. Dropping the rifle, Dirty Lonnie fell to his knees with his hands to his face trying to staunch the blood. The sound he made was horrific; a plaintive wail combined with a choking sound.

Reeves came up close to him, wary of his surroundings. Dirty Lonnie was finished. The steady pulsebeat of blood pumping from his shattered jaw meant he had only a minute or two left.

"You would have been better off hanging." Reeves said unsympathetically. "What a .45 slug does to a man is something that gives a physician a nightmare."

Dirty Lonnie's bloody hands fell limply to his side and he toppled over, his unseeing eyes still wide with shock.

Bass Reeves punched out the spent brass from his Colt and reloaded. He made certain he had all six chambers loaded. He only needed two more of those bullets, but Bass Reeves left nothing to chance.

He heard the metallic rasp of a Winchester being ratcheted and then Jayhawker Johnny Dolan was standing forty-five feet away, half concealed by the trees.

"Bass, I'll hand it to yah! You're tougher than any of us thought! Taking on Dirty Lonnie like that was a sight to see!"

"Give it up, Johnny! You can't beat me and you know it."

"Brave words, Bass. Real brave words, but you won't find me rolling over for you that easily, no sir! Not one bit!"

A shrill voice rang out. "Kill him! Kill him!" Corbin had emerged from the tree on the left, and Reeves cursed under his breath for allowing himself to be flanked. Jayhawker Johnny let loose with a smarmy laugh. "Let the dance begin!"

Jayhawker Johnny's rifle boomed but the shot went high, at least a foot over Reeves' head; and Corbin began firing wildly with his Colt.

Corbin's shots whizzed through the air, plunked into trees, and Reeves was forced to crouch low as the area around him turned into a hornet's nest of buzzing lead.

Reeves snapped a shot off at Corbin who screamed although he hadn't been hit. Reeves took the opportunity to retreat deeper into the foliage.

Jayhawker Johnny was fast with a six-shooter, and Reeves had to take him down quickly if he could. Jayhawker Johnny was the real threat. Once Johnny put down that rifle, Reeves would have his hands full if the outlaw got close to him.

Jayhawker Johnny was enjoying himself. He dodged in and out of the trees, firing his Winchester at will, apparently content to simply keep Reeves running for cover.

This was no longer about bringing lawbreakers to justice; this was about staying alive, and Jayhawker Johnny's reputation as a mean-spirited, murderous and resourceful criminal was well known to Bass Reeves. He'd faced and conquered many outlaws in his career, but few of them gave him reason to believe he might soon meet his maker. Jayhawker Johnny gave lawmen reason to ponder their mortality.

A trickle of sweat dropped off his nose as he paused to catch his breath behind a thick maple. Except Jayhawker Johnny had anticipated his move and position himself so he had just a fraction of the lawman's body centered in the buckhorn sights of his Winchester. When the rifle boomed, Reeves felt the lead nip his arm, forcing him to spin crazily away from the tree, tumble foolishly through the chokecherry brush, and crawl through the mud as Jayhawker Johnny's wicked laughter rang out.

"You sure can move, Bass! I've never been so entertained watching someone try to outrun a bullet!"

Reeves clamped his mouth shut and concentrated on his next move. There was really no choice. He was slowly being cut to pieces, and not knowing what Corbin was doing put him in a bad place. He had to cross that creek, circle around and get cover on the high ground west of Jayhawker Johnny's current position. He would be vulnerable for a span of at least thirty seconds when he entered the water, just enough time to give Jayhawker Johnny time to draw a bead on him with his rifle.

He ran. His boots hit the cold water and sent a shock up his legs. Two, three, four, five long splashing strides and his left boot was raised onto the shore, and his right boot was dragging out of the sand when Jayhawker Johnny let loose with three quick shots that nearly took his ear off. Stinging from the lead that clipped him, Reeves cursed loudly. Characteristically, he felt no fear as he touched the bloody and tender crease where the bullet had clipped his ear.

Hunched down in the wild brush across the creek, he thought back to his youth spent with the Indians of the Five Civilized Nations, and everything he had learned from them. The landscape was an ally. He was facing dangerous men, but foolish men. Their arrogance was their weakness. Jayhawker Johnny believed himself superior with a six-shooter, and as good as he was, Reeves knew he could beat him.

Let the earth provide you answers, Atohi had said to him one day long ago. Use the trees and brush. Follow the mark of the sun as the shadows point the way.

Another bullet came whistling in from the opposite hillside and nipping the bark of a nearby ash tree. Reeves never flinched. Jayhawker Johnny was guessing at his location. Then two more bullets came crashing through the underbrush, closer this time and making his ears ring. Jayhawker Johnny was chortling with pleasure, taunting him.

"You're as tough as a turkey buzzard, and that's a fact!"

Reeves began the meticulous process of edging away, moving upstream, careful not to step on any branches or jostle any leafy twigs.

"You hear me, Bass? My mama cooked a fine turkey buzzard in her day! That's what's gonna happen to you! This Corbin boy and I are gonna cut you into bacon strips and fill the skillet!"

The creek curved like a snake, sharply angling east, and it was here that Reeves decided to recross and come around Jayhawker Johnny. Moving swiftly but with the agility he'd learned from Atohi, Reeves crossed the creek again. Once on the shore he temporarily holstered his Colt in order to concentrate on the task at hand.

He arrived at the hillside which was thicker with trees than the area where Jayhawker Johnny was uselessly firing his rifle. The gunfire was echoing through the valley, mingled with the humorless laughter of Jayhawker Johnny.

Behind him and downslope, the creek glimmered in the sun with deceptive tranquility. A life and death tableau was being played out in the deep crevices and rocky trails of Vulture's Hollow.

The continuous rifle fire helped Reeves pinpoint Jayhawker Johnny's location. Keep shooting, Reeves thought, I'm almost behind you.

In fact, Reeves had crossed the creek and ascended the hill and less than ten minutes, during which Jayhawker Johnny had reloaded the rifle and wasted his ammunition.

Changing direction, he crested the hill from the opposite side, and there was Jayhawker Johnny downslope thirty feet, winging his rifle left and right in his effort to catch Reeves with a lucky shot.

Reeves stopped and pulled his Colt from his holster, his thumb poised over the hammer.

"It's over, Johnny."

At the sound of the lawman's voice, the outlaw panicked, dropped his rifle and clawed his gun free of his holster as he spun wildly, trying fire from a crouched position.

The *click* of his Colt's hammer was unnaturally loud as Reeves fingered the trigger. The sound of the roaring .45 slug that took Jayhawker Johnny in the chest was even louder.

"Oh, Bass…" The outlaw dropped to his knees. "Bass…I'm…hit."

"You were fast, I'll give you that." Reeves said, but his words fell on deaf ears as Jayhawker Johnny plopped forward, a growing stain of blood flooding his shirt as his body twitched its last.

Reeves turned his attention to the hillside and surrounding area. That Corbin kid couldn't have gone far, and if he had any semblance of intelligence, he'd try a find the horse.

Reeves had an idea where his horse went, so again, he started slowly downhill.

He caught sight of the horse down near the creek, and Corbin was doing his best to climb into the saddle. The horse, being accustomed to and trained by Bass Reeves, spun about neighing, denying Corbin a solid foothold in the stirrups.

Keeping his gun in hand but held down at his side as he walked, Reeves started after Corbin. After a few seconds, Corbin saw Reeves, raised his gun and fired. Reeves knew the shot would miss by the way the kid held it in his hand. The muzzle was pointed too low, a common mistake among people unaccustomed to handling a six-shooter.

Reeves called out, "I don't want to kill you, kid."

"Go to hell!" Corbin's face was red with anger and frustration. The second shot plunked into the dirt, but a little closer, and since Reeves hadn't slowed his gait, Corbin's features changed from anger to perplexity. "Stay away! You're not arresting me!"

Reeves closed the gap and Corbin suddenly looked frightened. Ignoring the horse, he was forced to give Bass Reeves his full attention. Corbin raised the gun and pointed it at Reeves. The kid's hand was shaking. He'd been through a lot the last few days, and when all was said and done, he was still just a dumb farm boy. Reeves felt sorry for him, but his resolve was unchanged.

Serena, having determined it was safe to come out of hiding, limped out of the brush. "Bass, you can let the boy go with me. I promise he'll never hurt anyone again. Isn't that right, Corbin?"

"What the hell is this?" Corbin said, confused and looking back and forth at Reeves and then Serena. "You're nothin' but a whore! You're nothin' to me! I'm getting on this horse and riding off!"

Serena was shocked. "Why, I'm trying to help you!"

The gun waved back and forth, first on Reeves and then on Serena. "I'm gonna shoot you both if this lawman doesn't drop his gun!"

"I'm obligated to offer you a chance to surrender." Reeves said, keeping his voice calm.

It was in Corbin's eyes; that ice-cold glimmer of malice that Bass Reeves had seen hundreds of times before. It was a look that meant death, and Reeves saw the tension build like a wave in Corbin's features. His legs stiffened and he changed his footing, almost imperceptibly as a natural reaction to setting himself firmly before shooting, and just as the wavering gun steadied, Reeves had the hammer of his Colt cocked while it was still at his side. His wrist flicked the gun upward; a highly skilled move Reeves had practiced for years. The gun boomed and the bullet shattered Corbin's skull before he could blink.

Serena screamed.

She threw her hands to her face in shock. Corbin toppled into the dirt. Bass Reeves holstered his gun. Serena took her hands away from her face and looked at Corbin.

"Oh, my God! Bass, look what you did to that boy's beautiful face! Oh, Bass, you ruined him! You ruined him!"

Reeves went and fetched his horse. He climbed into the saddle, but kept his eyes on the perfectly smooth water tumbling south as the sun reflected off the rippling current. That was a better sight than the one down on his right where Serena was sobbing uncontrollably. He let her sob a moment. It was all she had left. When she was finished, she wiped her eyes and tried to pull herself together.

Bass Looked at Corbin's body, and uphill at Jayhawker Johnny's body. The other bodies would have been lying out in the hot sun a solid thirty minutes or more.

Sometimes a man answered to a higher power than the one that came with the tin star pinned to his vest. He had to bury the bodies. It seemed immoral to leave them laying out in the open for the buzzards and wolves to pick at. There was no sense doing any extra work with this group by hauling their corpses to town.

"Serena, I'm riding to that hunter's shack along the creekside to get a shovel. Sit tight until I get back."

"You're…you're leaving me…with these bodies?"

"They won't hurt you any."

He rode to the hunter's shack and retrieved a shovel. It had been a long morning, and it was going to be a longer afternoon. When he returned, Serena was sitting on a rock looking miserable. Reeves set himself to the grim work, never knowing it was Corbin's act of burying Rum Doggy that had set these circumstances in motion. When the grave digging was completed he sat on a rock and took a long swallow of water from his canteen. He was drenched in sweat and exhausted. The graves were shallow, but that didn't bother Reeves at all. Bass Reeves never harbored any sympathy for lawbreakers.

Reeves gathered the horses as well, roped them together. It was time to go.

A few minutes later, Serena came and stood next to Corbin's grave. She looked genuinely sad. "I guess being with me was the only good thing that ever happened to that poor boy."

He had Serena sit up on one of the outlaw's horses and instructed her to hang on as best she could with her good arm. When they were astride their horses the sun was beginning to slink low in the west, but there was still plenty of sunlight. Reeves thought they could ride ten miles at least, and get away from this stinking place. A warm breeze came up and made a whispering sound in the trees; the dust spun up off the graves and Reeves spurred his horse, eager to be on his way. With her bloody shoulder and bandaged leg, Serena made for a pathetic, mournful figure.

A few weeks later, Serena would stand before a judge and answer to the assault charges by the saloon keeper she'd cut up, and months later Reeves would hear that she'd returned to her vagabond lifestyle, all the while telling stories about the sandy-haired killer that had captured her heart. She was good at telling the story, and of course she embellished the tale for her rapt and devoted customers. Unknown to Reeves, the story took on a life of its own and was repeated around campfires on distant trail drives, or in the smoky confines of cantinas and hard-scrabble saloons between Dodge City and San Antonio.

So it was that Bass Reeves became part of a local song made up by a drunken balladeer in the brothels of Voyager's End; and the song was sung with raucous glee for years thereafter:

Corbin the orphan was a wicked lad
His eyes were blue but his soul was sad,

The day he shot a good man dead
His life became a tragedy or so they said;
He was hunted down by ole Bass Reeves
A lawman tall like a sturdy oak tree;
Fast with a gun and always brave,
Bass buried the boy in a shallow grave!
Corbin the orphan had met his end
Because his soul was evil and wouldn't bend!

THE END

About The Tumbleweed Outlaw

Airship 27's dedication to the New Pulp literary movement encompasses numerous genres, including Westerns. Naturally, having published ten Westerns it's clear I'm biased. Sure, I love detective stories, science fiction, supernatural tales and fantasy, but Westerns are special. Westerns are America's best genre.

When I read the Airship 27 series, Bass Reeves: Frontier Marshal, I knew I wanted to write a Bass Reeves story. I might not have considered this if not for those anthologies. I'm a writer who plays in "The Mythic West" so it's important to mention that the native American character, Atohi, is a figment of my imagination. It is true, however, that Bass Reeves spent his fascinating youth in the company of Native Americans, and all of the reports I've read cite those relationships as being positive. I may return to Reeves and Atohi in a future tale that is already percolating, but the ballad of Corbin the orphan was one of those plot devices that kept my imagination boiling as the paragraphs flew from my fingertips.

I'm not an expert on Bass Reeves at all, however, Reeves comes across as a capable, tough man. I have gilded the lily when it comes to his prowess with a gun, but I suspect that my interpretation of his survival skills is close to the truth. His reputation speaks volumes as to his capabilities.

Bass Reeves, like Wyatt Earp, will forever capture the fancy of writers looking for material. I find it gratifying that his legend is being reimagined and rediscovered by a new generation of writers and readers. A tip of the Stetson to Ron Fortier and Rob Davis for creating a series of popular books where writers and readers can indulge themselves in fanciful tales of the Wild West. Saddle up and let's ride!

THOMAS McNULTY—was born in Chicago and is a graduate of the famed writing program at Columbia College. His celebrity interviews, articles, essays, book reviews, film reviews and Hollywood and literary profiles have appeared in numerous magazines including American Cowboy, Filmfax, The Big Reel, Classic Images, Films of the Golden Age, Kung-Fu Magazine, Mystery News, Comic Effect, Scary Monsters, The Strand Magazine On-Line and The Golden Gazette among others.

His non-fiction includes a critically acclaimed biography of *Errol Flynn* and *Werewolves! A Study of Lycanthropes in Film, Folklore and Literature*. Tom's first western adventure novel *Trail of the Burned Man* was followed by *Wind Rider, Death Rides a Palomino, Showdown at Snakebite Creek, Gunfight at Crippled Horse, Coffin for an Outlaw,* and *The Gunsmoke Serenade*.

He also wrote *The Adventures of Captain Graves* for Airship 27 Productions. For more information, visit Tom's blog: "Dispatches from the Last Outlaw"

WAGES OF GOLD
by Gary Phillips

Bass Reeves guided his horse between rows stacked high with drying horizontal stalks of sugarcane. Workers were busy putting these stalks onto wooden carts to be taken inside a large open air stone structure. This was the mill where the cane would be heated, ground under a massive stone wheel pulled by a mule, and pulped to produce its sweet residue. The resulting particular aroma was palpable. Reeves cleared the row and continued toward the main house, a Greco-Roman designed mansion overlooking the Peachdale plantation. As he neared the house, an older man who'd been sweeping the porch under the portico came down the steps as the deputy marshal dismounted.

"I'll take care of your steed, suh," the man said, taking the reigns in his calloused hands.

"Thank you," Reeves replied.

The other man, dark as Reeves, regarded the Peacemaker on the lawman's hip. "That's a peculiar way you have your gun holstered. Don't that slow you down?"

Reeves chuckled in his throat. For whatever reason, he preferred a reverse draw, the handle of his six-shooter facing outward instead of the customary fashion. "So far I ain't come up short doing it this way."

"No, Mr. Reeves, I guess you haven't."

Reeves cocked his head slightly.

"Oh yes, we all knows who you are." He smiled broadly, a front tooth missing.

"Pleased to meet you." He stuck out his hand.

The other man was momentarily taken aback. Visitors to Peachdale didn't fraternize with the help. He then shook Reeves' hand. He even clasped his other hand on the marshal's as well. "Yes, suh, great pleasure indeed," he enthused. "They calls me Portifoy."

"Good to meet you too, Portifoy."

One of the double doors opened and out stepped a sturdily-built woman in a white apron. Her hair was wrapped in colorful silk and she also wore a peach-colored eyepatch that contrasted pleasantly with her medium-hued skin. "Stop you're jawjackin' you old rascal. Mr. O'Ferguson is waiting."

He waved a hand at her. "Hush. You jus' trying to impress our guest."

87

"And you about to press my last good nerve. Git back to work."

It was clear to Reeves from their light-hearted tone, this was their usual banter.

"Work?" Portifoy snorted, "now that's something you ain't familiar with."

"Come on in, marshal, 'fore you get contaminated with this one's foolishness."

Portifoy was leading the horse away. "I'll get her brushed down good and fed and watered for ya."

"I appreciate that." Reeves took off his hat as he stepped inside. The woman shut the door behind him. Like other plantations he'd been in, going back to his days as an enslaved child, there was a grand staircase, white marble floors and the sweep of plush drapes. He hadn't been impressed then and wasn't now. He made sure though to keep his face neutral.

"This way, marshal." She started off along a hallway.

"Yes, ma'am." On her heels he passed through the hallway, walking past the entrance to the study and continuing, noticed the various paintings along the walls. Rather than the usual portraits of vaunted stern-jawed, steely-eyed ancestors, Reeves cocked an eyebrow at what he saw. Nude woman reclined on loveseats, their privates barely hidden by cloth clutched to ample bosoms. There was one of a man with the lower legs of a goat playing a flute while people laughed and danced around him. Toward the end of the passageway he paused to regard one portraying a black woman in regal attire on a throne being fanned by a muscular bare-chested white man.

"Mr. O'Ferguson has broad tastes," the woman said proudly.

"Indeed."

On they went. They reached the kitchen where a slim girl—who couldn't be more than sixteen, Reeves estimated—was stirring the contents in a large pot. She stood before one of the fanciest wood-burning stoves he'd ever seen.

"Try this, Elmira," the younger woman said.

Elmira slipped a hand around the other's waist and tasted the offered sample from a long-handled wooden spoon the girl held aloft, a stew of some sort. "I'd say two more pinches of salt and just a bit more cayenne." She patted the younger one's backside and took her hand away.

"Come on, time's a-wastin.'" She exited a side door, Reeves following. Walking across an expanse of lawn their destination was a large rectangular hothouse, its windows steamed from the humidity within. Atop this was a smaller structure in the shape of a five-pointed star. "Hope y'all don't mind the heat of the conservatory. Presently I'll have Mary May bring in the sandwiches."

"Sure," he said, taking in the odd-looking greenhouse.

She opened the door for him and stepped aside. "In you go."

He nodded and entered a jungle. Vines thick as well-fed anacondas from which purple, yellow and flaming red flowers erupted crawled up the glass walls and smothered the glass ceiling. Explosions of African violets, moth orchids, cape primroses and all other sorts of hot house flowers abounded. Some were in elevated trays which in turn were mostly engulfed in greenery that sprouted from earthen containers or from the ground itself.

"Over here, Marshal Reeves," a woman's voice said from somewhere within.

He followed it to what was essentially a clearing in the contained tropics. There were rough-hewn tiles for flooring, a couch, several club chairs, and a table and matching chairs for dining. There was a freestanding grandfather clock and even a sideboard upon which were decanters of whisky and such, glasses, and a metal pitcher wet from condensation. Off to the side was a music stand with a plush red velvet adorned chair. An Indian woman Reeves took to be Seminole sat before the stand, a mandolin leaning nearby. She wore fine clothes and smiled upon seeing him.

"How are you today?" She said in Maskoki, a main Seminole dialect.

"Not so bad," he answered in the same language. He fanned himself with his hat, already beginning to sweat. "You?"

"Could be better, could be worse."

"Heaven knows that's right." Tyree O'Ferguson said, lounging on the couch. He was a light brown haired bearded man, clad in trousers and shirt, no jacket and no shoes. There was a splayed open book face down on the floor near him. A tumbler with amber in it was near him as well. From what Reeves understood from Judge Isaac Parker, the O'Ferguson money had initially come from the father and his uncles being war profiteers. Selling reprocessed wool uniforms and cardboard shoes to both sides in the Civil War. Items that soon fell apart given the mud and blood the soldiers had to wade through each day. Some dying literally in tatters.

O'Ferguson rose to a sitting position, gesturing toward a chair. "Sit a spell why don't you, Marshal? Feel free to take that coat of yours off and pour yourself something 'fore you do." He scratched at his beard which had streaks of grey in it.

His southern accent was evident but so too was his years away at college back east, Reeves assessed. "Thank you, kindly." He removed his jacket, draping it on the back of a chair. The front and back of his shirt was wet. He went to the sideboard. There was also a bowl containing a melting chunk of ice and an ice pick stuck in it as well.

Mary May, the one who'd been cooking, came in with a tray of sandwiches. There was a clutch of hand-rolled cigars in a tin cup on the tray as well. She sat these on the table. "Got your favorite, Mr. O'Ferguson, beef tongue."

"Oh my," he said energetically. He got up, his superior height fully on display. Must be at least three inches taller than he was, Reeves estimated. He loped over to the tray as the younger woman departed. He picked up the tray and took it over to the woman on the plush chair to push it toward her.

"My dear."

"You trying to get me fat?" Nonetheless she took a sandwich half.

"Store up for the winter."

Reeves decided he better keep his wits, forgoing the notion of having a bracer of cognac over ice. Though such would have been ideal in this heat. Reluctantly he poured water into a glass, clipped off some ice and plunked it in the liquid. Back at the table he fetched a cigar and lit it. He then sat in one of the comfortable chairs, puffing away. O'Ferguson poured a healthy amount of amber into his tumbler from one of the decanters, and he too lit a cigar. He sat close to Reeves, blowing a stream toward the lush canopy.

"I hear tell you know this rapscallion Two Knives."

"I know of him. Fellas I've posse'd with have ridden with him one way or the other over the years," Reeves acknowledged.

"He was an Indian version of a deputy marshal like you, a Light Horseman they call them, is that right?"

"Once he was, yes."

"Before he..." The plantation owner circled his hand holding the cigar in the air, searching for the right words, "...became this heap big chief, huh?"

Reeves shrugged, concluding to be frank with this odd white man. "Those I know tell me it's more complicated than that. But yeah, he's a leader. Always was."

O'Ferguson drew in deep and held the smoke in his mouth for several seconds, the ticking of the grandfather clock the only sound. Eventually he let the bluish cloud stream out. "What do you think about going up against him?"

"I don't rightly cotton to it."

His eyes steady on him he asked, "Afraid of him?"

Reeves returned the gaze. "I'd be a fool not to admit I get the crawlies in my gut from time to time. It ain't stilled my hand yet though."

"You consider him a colleague then?"

"Like you and the judge?"

O'Ferguson chuckled. "Good one, marshal. I guess a man like you has to go into any situation with his eyes open. The judge and I have a collusion of interests so in that way, we have need to palaver to get matters straight." He smiled. "If I'm not being too obtuse."

Reeves tapped ash from the end of his cigar. "Judge Parker asked me to come see you. I know this is not under his authority; the task you want done. But I also know you're paying a reward of a thousand for this thingamabob you want back. And I ain't the first one you've enticed about going after it."

"Correct you are. In fact the previous individual to go after the mask didn't come back. He'd been an Army scout and tracker. The one before him got scared off. That's why I doubled the reward. It's two thousand now."

"You did?"

"Oh yes, he did," the woman at the music stand said. She picked up the mandolin and began a melodic plucking at its strings.

On the ride to Peachdale, Reeves had considered this conversation would go something like how it was going now. He'd told himself he'd hear the man out as a favor to the judge, tempting as it was about the money he was offering. But now, hot damn, he almost blurted. Man would have to be addled to at least not consider this matter. The money would go a long way what with his and Nellie's offspring sprouting like weeds and the ranch always needing this or that to be taken care of.

It wasn't hard for O'Fergusin to read Reeves' expression. "What do you know about the Aztecs, marshal?"

"They believed in human sacrifice didn't they?"

"Yes, well, I suppose for a God-fearing man like yourself, you'd find such acts barbarous." He sat forward, eagerness animating his face. "A few hundred years ago they were the rulers, the architects in many ways of modern Mexico. Dripping in gold and silver raiment, or so the fairy tales tell us. Had themselves all sorts of deities. One for the crops, one for the rain and so on. Human fate was not theirs to control. The gods created the

Aztecs to fight for them, worship them and keep them fed. The sun, the source of all life, was kept alive by the blood sacrifice."

"That's something all right," Reeves allowed, smoking away.

O'Ferguson laughed, clapping his hands together. "It wouldn't surprise you to learn that these here Aztecs sought to conquer others. Raids and skirmishes back and forth. At some point in a battle with the Mayans, also an advanced bunch, a peace was reached. To show good will, tokens of this accord were exchanged. In this case the firstborn sons of the kings were exchanged as way to solidify the compact."

Reeves listened closely.

"Each son brought with him a tribute, a thingamabob. The Mayan one was apparently a clay urn etched with their deities and history and filled with gold coins. "But," he started, shaking a finger, "the Aztecs always knew how to put on the dog. They sent their son with a fancy statuette of Xiuhtecuhtli. About yay big." He held his hands a little over a foot apart.

"That's a mouthful. He supposed to be one of their gods?"

"Oh yes." Twin campfires lit behind his eyes. "The lord of volcanoes and the representation of life after death. Old God they also called him."

"Is that so, Mr. O'Ferguson?'

"I haven't lost my mind."

"Not yet," the woman said. She began playing a tune, quietly but assuredly on the mandolin.

"This figurines of however you say that name is what you want back. Because it's made of gold?"

"Encrusted with jewels in fact."

"The others who went after the mask, did they know this?"

O'Ferguson had the cigar in his hand and shook the wet end toward the lawman. "I appreciate your frankness, Marshal. But you see I'm forced to tell the truth and must relay on the upstanding character of those I implore to hasten the artifact's return. You see this saddle pard of your saddle pards sees the figurine as a symbol by which he will rally the simple-minded and superstitious. Like he gets the words direct from Xiuhtecuhtli. here on Earth."

"Raise an army you mean?"

"Not sure. But the last telegram I received from Preston Nettles indicated such."

"The former scout?"

"Indeed, my good marshal, yes. The telegraph originated in Crawford's Crossing. You know of that town?"

The mandolin's melodic tune filled the momentary silence as Reeves took his time answering. "I do. But how do you know the scout didn't get a'hold of the statue and run off with it? 'Cause from how you make it sound, the damn thing is worth a King's ransom and then some. Down in Mexico right now living the life of luxury, mebbe? His toughest problem being which butt cheek to scratch first."

"I don't directly," O'Ferguson admitted.

Reeves remained silent.

"So what say you regarding this matter?"

"If'n I take this on, I get the two thousand and the two others I'm considering to get in on this hoedown get five hundred a'piece. Against an advance."

"That there's supposed to come out your end, Marshal."

"Normally, yes. But this Aztec business is far from usual. The job is a hell of a tall order you present. Some up front money will help me secure who I'm figurin' on."

"I'll get somebody else, but you can be certain I'll let the judge know my displeasure."

Reeves got up, reaching for his hat and coat. "Ain't the first time there's been complaints about me." He turned to the woman who was still playing. "Ma'am," he said, hat on and touching the brim. He turned to leave. He got four steps away.

"Okay, you made your point, Marshal," O'Ferguson said to his back. "I'll meet your price."

Reeves turned his face to the side and said, "I'll be in touch."

The large Indian man stepped onto the wooden planks leading into Mayberry's general store and dry goods. He was six feet four inches, broad chested and slim hipped. In a scabbard hanging from his belt was a sheathed big-bladed knife but no gun. The three white men in front of the store glared at him. One of them had been whittling on a piece of wood, the shavings down around his boot and some curlicues on it as well. He had his chair raised backward against the wall, the rear two legs resting on the porch. One of the other men was leaning on a wooden barrel and the third had his arms folded, his back against the outer wall as well. He'd been talking to the one at the barrel about the price of hogs. They got tight-lipped at seeing the Cherokee gentleman. He glanced toward them then stepped inside.

Past a display of newly arrived women's hats from St. Louis in fancy boxes, he went by a woman in a gingham dress who was regarding one of the hats. She, too, glared at the newcomer who stepped to the counter. Behind it stood Matilda Greenleaf, the owner of the shop.

"How can I help you?" She stammered, looking up at the man.

"Looking for your cousin," he said quietly.

"I don't rightly know what you're talking about."

"He's on your mother's side. Goes by Dancer Dan he does."

She narrowed her eyes at him. "Why you come here?"

"You paid his bail. But he missed his court date."

"You couldn't possibly work for the court," she huffed.

"I work for bounties." He was aware two of the men from the porch had stepped inside.

Matilda Greenleaf gaped at him. "Indians can't be hunting white men." She said it as if reciting a passage from the Good Book.

He grinned lopsidedly. "They can around these parts."

"This red sumabitch botherin' you, Matilda?" The one who'd been leaning on the barrel asked.

She looked past him at the other man. "He sure is, Glenn." Then looking back at the bounty hunter she said, "I'll ask you to leave now."

"This could go a lot easier if you'd answer my question, ma'am."

"You heard the lady, now git." While he wasn't as tall as the intruder, Glenn was a husky individual with large cracked hands and meaty arms. He put one of those hands on the tall Indian's shoulder intending to spin him around.

The bounty man did turn around, knocking Glenn's hand away. "I'm just askin' a simple question."

"And you got a simple answer, redskin. You ain't welcome here."

The other man remained calm. "If you say so, pale face." He began to step past to exit the store. He was smiling, he'd read that word in a penny dreadful. The Cherokee word for white man was unega.

"What did you just call me?"

"You got too much wax in your ears?"

The third man had decided not to get involved and sat where he was outside, whitling away.

"You goddamn savage." He took a swing but the bigger man blocked the blow and countered with a blow of his own. Glenn, the barrel leaner, stumbled back into the fancy hat display, knocking several boxes and hats to the floor.

"Oh, my sweet Lord," the proprietor exclaimed.

Glenn's companion bent low and running forward, got his arms around the bounty man's waist, driving him back. They smashed into a pyramid of stacked canned goods, knocking them from a table, the cans rolling and scattering every which way across the uneven floorboards.

"Stop 'fore you all wreck my store," Greenleaf yelled. She reached below the counter for the sawed-off shotgun she kept there. She wasn't worried about putting a load of buckshot in the big Indian. But the men were now grappling with each other and she couldn't get a clear shot—yet.

As the two ganged-up on the lone man, all trading punches, at one point one of the white men was doubled over, hit hard in the stomach. The other two still standing kept going at it like bare-knuckle brawlers. The Cherokee drove the other one back. Well aware of the shotgun on him, he dove out of the way as the woman let loose. Her twin barrage blew out the picture window with the name of the shop in gold and bronze script. This also upset the man who'd been whitling. His chair slipped off the wall next to the destroyed window and he landed with it on his back. He got up shaking his head.

Wailing a string of profanities, she tossed the hog leg away in disgust. That window was going to be very expensive to replace.

Glenn was knocked to a knee, blood leaking from his nose. At that moment, he started to draw his gun. "I'll teach you," he vowed, spitting blood from his lips as the tall Indian was again engaged in fisticuffs with the other rowdy.

There was the unmistakable click of a pistol's hammer being cocked. "School's not in session today."

Glenn looked to see a black man filling the doorframe. He could also easily distinguish the barrel of the six-shooter extended toward him.

"Who the hell are you, darkie?" The man said, rising.

"You really ought to watch your mouth." The Indian bounty hunter hit Glenn flush on the side of his face bowling him over. He lay prone, moaning, the gun still in his hand. The tall man kicked the gun away, sending it pinwheeling across the floor. He then angled toward the remaining upright white man, who did not have on a gun belt. Glenn's friend was breathing hard and, along with the woman, watched Bass Reeves step inside, his gun leveled.

"Who's gonna pay for my window? The shop owner demanded.

"What brings you around here, Bass?"

"School's not in session today."

"Oh, got a little something that might be of interest, Ned. Pay's good too."

"Well then one of you is going to pay for that window." She shook a finger at the broken glass laying all around like crystalized snow.

Continuing to ignore her, Ned Christie said, "Let me get this business buttoned up and then you and I can sit a spell and palaver."

"I'll give you a hand if need be, no charge."

"You ole' snake charmer," Christie said in the Cherokee language. "Okay then."

Glenn and his friend were tied up, sitting on the floor. Reeves kept watch on them. The whittler had taken off, but he wasn't too worried about him returning with help. Like a lot of towns in the Twin Territories, formal representation of the law might be a few hours' ride away.

"I still need to find your cousin," Christie said to Greenleaf.

"And I need that window attended to, red—" She swallowed her retort. "About my window. And it's not just that. There's the sign painter I have to pay too."

It wasn't lost on Christie she'd shot at him and if he was white, he could swear out a complaint against her. But what was real was real. "Tell you what, you get your cousin to give himself up, I'll kick in an amount toward the price of that there window. When I collect on him."

"You have some nerve."

He shrugged. "You think I'm the only one that's going to come around? What about the next fella ain't as level-headed as me or Bass waltzes through your door, gun hand itchin' and not so inclined to talk it out? Plus this here shop is what you put down against the bail. You know what that means he don't come back."

She glared over at the two who were trussed up and the disarray of her shop. Sighing she said, "I'm not sure what I'm supposed to do here. He is my first cousin."

"Leave it up to Dancing Dan," Christie answered.

"Persuade him it's in his best interest," Reeves added. "And yours."

"Lordy," she muttered. "Wait here, dammit." From where she stood next to the counter, Greenleaf started toward the doorway.

"Ma'am," Reeves said to her back, "jus' 'cause we're level-headed don't mean we're pushovers."

"Of that I'm sure." Out she went.

Christie went out to his horse and unlimbered his rifle. He righted the knocked over chair on the porch and sat in it, the long gun laying across his knees. He kept watch on the street and the building in his line of sight.

Tied up Glenn said, "What about us?"

"She come back with anyone else but her cousin, we gonna strap you two to them posts out there to block any bullets headin' our way."

"You can't do that," Glenn's friend said.

"Sure I can. 'Fact, stand up and come on out with me." He shook the barrel of his gun at them.

"Look here," Glenn began to object.

"I'm not asking twice."

Their hands were tied behind their backs, their ankles free. Reeves took a step back as the two rose and he marched them outside. People passing by looked on but didn't say a word. The two made to sit down on the porch.

"Around the side," Reeves said. There was a way for someone so minded to sneak up on the shop from the rear and he intended to keep watch for that.

"I don't rightly cotton to takin' orders from no burr head," Glenn stated sharply.

Reeves poked him in the gut with the barrel of his gun causing him to grunt. "You'd do well to keep your opinions to yourself."

"Come on," Glenn's buddy advised, walking ahead of him.

Slightly hunched over, Glenn complied. They sat in the dirt on the side of the shop where there was a sort of passageway between it and where the next set of structures began. The deputy marshal pulled a crooked cheroot from his vest pocket and lit it. He got it smoked about half way down when Christie called to him from around the corner.

"You heard the man." Reeves gestured and his two temporary prisoners got to their feet again. With Glenn giving him the side-eye, they returned to the front of the store in time to see Greenleaf approaching with her cousin Dancing Dan. He was dressed like a drummer complete with a bowler hat askew on his head.

"Christie was standing on the porch, his rifle in one hand. As the two got closer he grinned at Reeves. "She persuaded him, all right."

"I guess so," Reeves said.

There was a fresh purple and black bruise under one of the wanted man's eyes. They stopped short of the porch, Dancing Dan glaring at Christie. "You got me, so what?" he snarled.

"Much obliged," Christie said to the woman as he stepped off the porch to take command of his prisoner.

"Hey, what about untying us?" Glenn complained.

Christie tossed his big knife to Reeves handle first, who used it to cut the men's bonds.

Glenn looked from the knife to the marshal. "I get it, I ain't interfering in you and the tree trunk injun's business."

"I expect you to hold up your end of our bargain," Greenleaf said to Christie.

"For sure, ma'am. Just as soon as I get the fee."

"Threw me over to a damn Indian," Dancing Dan muttered.

"You brought it on yourself," Greenleaf countered. "Jeopardizing the shop our aunties loaned me the money to open."

Dancing Dan was shamed into silence. Christie had attached shackles to the man's wrists and rope tied to those, from his horse he led him away on foot. Reeves rode beside him. They were headed for the closed outpost of the law, a town called Perseverance.

"I get to ride do I?' Dancing Dan asked.

"No but you get a swig from the canteen now and then," Chirstie said.

"I ain't had nothin' but buzzard's luck since I took off." He'd run out on a charge of swindling suckers with fake oil deeds.

"Horse come up lame did he?" Reeves asked.

"Yeah, had to shoot him 'fore I got to town. Guess I rode him too hard."

"Well, we'll take it easy on ya, Dan. We know you've been through a lot" Reeves said.

The wanted man recognized the sarcasm but had better sense than Glenn and remained mum.

Under Judge Parker and head marshal D.P. Upham, a Republican Reconstructionist, some 200 deputy marshals operated throughout the judge's jurisdiction of the Western District Court which was massive. It covered 74,000 square miles of land, rivers, inlets, mountains, deserts, forests and God knew what all else. Places where outlaws knew every crevice, every hideaway to avoid capture. Dead or alive was their mandate. Many a time Reeves had found himself on foot, a few times wounded, having to walk a hell of a lot more miles than what Dancing Dan was being forced to do.

He smiled slightly as he adjusted his hat against the glare of the sun. Ain't nobody forced him to put on the badge, he reasoned. Hardships came with the job.

It was near dusk by the time they'd turned Dancing Dan in and gotten a bite to eat before looking to talk business without being overheard. The two sat on a wooden bench at the train stop smoking and sipping on fresh lemonade. Even though there was the presence of the law, including a recent jail, there wasn't much built-up in Perseverance, still in the transition phase from being a settlement. The train stop was a raised platform with the bench and two seats upon it. There was no depot as of yet but land had been cleared behind the platform for its eventual construction. Train tickets were purchased in the saloon a block over.

Christie was a teetotaler and Reeves was fine with that. He explained the job to the taller man.

"I suppose I've heard crazier," Christie said when Reeves had finished. "But not in a while."

"From what I recall about Two Knives, this hoodoo business of his seems is in keeping with him."

Christie lifted his glass to his lips but didn't drink. "This isn't really about a score you got to settle with him is it, Bass?"

"No," he said, "I'm being straight with you like I was with O'Fergeson. We've never crossed paths. We do know some fellas in common, though."

"You figure a couple of them are running around with him now?'

Reeves stretched his legs out. "Dang if I know. But that's why I want to see if Frank Polk is interested."

"Last I heard he was on a cattle drive coming out of Amarillo."

"That was a year ago, Ned."

"Really?" he said genuinely, smiling. "You know us Cherokees and our concept of time, Bass."

"I hear tell he's over in Fenton these days."

Christie whistled. "Doin' what? They say even the pigeons in that town walk sideways."

Reeves chuckled. "Still, if'n you're in, he's the other one for this here job. Considering he'd possied with Two Knives."

Christie looked over at him, letting a silence drag for a moment then said, "Ten days, right?"

"Yes, sir." Christie had told him he planned to be attending to several repairs of his mountain cabin home over the next few days. He was rather skilled at carpentry. On the ninth day he'd take a day and a half ride into the town with the telegraph office. There would either be a telegraph waiting for him from Reeves or not.

Bass Reeves' ride to Fenton was uneventful. The town was a mixture of mostly one story buildings, though there were a few two-story structures and even a three story hotel called the Morgan Arms. This was all along the main road as off of this could be seen various tents, large and medium-sized ones. It had been a "Hell on Wheels" outpost at first, a place that sprang up quickly to cash in on an intended spur of the railroad line. That meant gamblers, sharpies and prostitutes operating out of those tents. But as these things go, the big men puffing on their big cigars decided not to bring the train through here. Yet Fenton didn't simply dry up and blow away as so often happens. The merchants stayed, a pastor arrived, and a sawmill opened on the outskirts of what was becoming a permanent town.

As Ned Christie had observed, Fenton's tawdry reputation had been derived from its early days. But Reeves knew that in the last six months or so, primarily due to the establishment of the mill, a certain stability had evolved. Still that didn't mean Fenton's rougher elements had been completely smoothed over. As Reeves slowly rode past one of the two-story buildings, containing a saloon on the ground floor called the Crystal Hook, a man in longjohns stumbled out of the swing doors onto the raised walkway. The deputy marshal halted his horse to take this in. He couldn't tell if the fellow was drunk or had been struck. He was on his elbows, butt up in the air. Out from the Crystal Hook stepped a good-sized woman in a leather riding outfit topped with a gaucho-style hat pushed back on her red curls. She had a whip with a handle ending in an orb coiled around her waist. She put the sole of her boot on the downed man's upraised rear and pushed him over onto the planks. He lay still.

"This'll learn you to understand when I say we got limits in the Hook, we got limits." She looked up at Reeves. "Well, you comin' in to wet your whistle or what?" She didn't wait for an answer and she turned around and went back inside.

He could stand a beer he reasoned, plus could ask about Polk's whereabouts. He dismounted, tied up his horse at the rail and sauntered into the bar. Making sure as he did so not to step on the man in longjohns who remained where he was, eyes open but unmoving. At this time of the day there were only a few people in the establishment, given the bulk of the potential patrons were at work. Apparently though, the bar was old enough to have regulars. Reeves looked at two older men hunched over their drinks at the curve of the fancy marble inlaid bar top. Each was unshaven and each took turns talking to the other in low tones. There were some paintings on the walls and a gambling section that included a faro table and a roulette wheel.

A few minutes later he leaned on the bar, taking a gulp of his beer. The woman in the gaucho hat reappeared and clapped a hand on his shoulder.

"You in the mood for an afternoon delight?"

He looked aghast at her and she laughed heartily. "I don't mean that, though I imagine we could make them bed springs wail." She laughed again. "Come on, I'll show you what I'm talkin' about."

Curious, Reeves followed her to a small table with two chairs opposite one another. On the table was a stack of tarot cards. They were larger than a poker deck and numerically more as well, 78 versus the 52 he knew. First O'Ferguson with his oddities and now this applesauce, he reflected. Good thing he wasn't the superstitious sort worried about omens and whatnot he reminded himself.

"What do you say?" she said, waving her hand toward the table.

"Sure, why not?" He made to sit down.

"Ever had a reading?" She sat down as well.

"Once or twice." He'd also fasted for days to take part in a spirit dance, been in a number of sweat lodges and even went through o-kee-pa, a Sioux ceremony where you were suspended by ropes attached to hooks piercing your chest muscles.

As was the custom, she shuffled the deck using her left hand and then cut the cards into three piles representing past, present and future.

"Frank Polk get his fortune read, miss?" he asked.

She was looking at the back of the cards then shifted her gaze to him, smiling. "Didn't need no deck to confirm what I figured. That gun on your hip didn't seem it was for show. The name's Josie Regert, by the way." She turned over the first card on the past pile. "Of course," she stated with finality. It was the Ace of Swords.

"Pleased to meet you, Miz Josie."

She tapped the card. The colorful image on it was of a woman, her head turned to the side. She held two swords, crossed in front of her body. "Swords are double-edged, you've been cautious and observant of what has occurred around you."

He wasn't on official business and hadn't pinned his badge to his shirt. Though often in disguise was another reason he'd not advertise his standing. Certainly what she'd said could apply to any gunman. "About Frank?"

She turned over the second card on the middle pile. This was one he hadn't seen before. It was an illustration of a bearded man in long robes and hood holding a staff. In his other hand he held a lit lantern aloft. He seemed to be searching for something.

"Frank Polk was here for about three weeks then left town day before last, a posse after him. The Hermit tells me you're given to thinking and planning." She added, nodding, meaning the second card.

"A posse?"

"Not a posse really, but it were three hombres on a mission."

"What happened?"

She put two fingers on the last card representing the future. "He was messin' around with the daughter of the owner of the sawmill. She's a grown woman and can make her own decisions, only not everybody's open-minded about race mixing even though we're in the Territories. We're a town getting civilized and that means niceties such as the way things ought to be are in effect, at least for some squareheads around these parts."

Reeves started to get up.

She turned over the third card, frowning at the result. "The Magician," she said.

"Which way did these fellas go?"

She pointed her jaw toward the east. "Toward the mountains."

"You're pretty calm about all this."

"Would you believe me if I told you when your friend took off with them other three on his heels I consulted the cards? Mindful one of the pursuers is a drunkard who relishes inflicting cruelty to others."

"Yeah, so?"

She shrugged her shoulder. "Knew somebody like you would be along to attend to this matter."

Reeves didn't have time to be vexed or confused. His next moves were clear. He was out the door before she could explain to him what the third card meant. Not that he believed any of her hogwash. It wasn't hard picking up the trail of the three after Frank Polk. There was no reason they made any effort to obscure which way they'd gone.

The following dawn he'd found one of their campsites, the embers still cooling. From there he came upon a fresh grave and was compelled to dig it up. He didn't think if it was Polk they'd given him a Christian burial but he had to make sure. Sure enough it was a white man in the ground. Reeves assumed he must be one of the three who'd been hunting Polk. He refilled the grave. Even though this man and his companions was up to no good as far as Reeves was concerned, that didn't mean he had to act accordingly. The late afternoon of the next day he was crawling through underbrush, his rifle with him. Not far up ahead he heard:

"Whowee, you sure can take it."

Laughter accompanied this. Reeves slowed his pace so as not to be detected. He inched forward till he could get a view onto an open circular patch of earth partly ringed by boulders. There was Frank Polk stripped to his waist, standing with his arms behind him, bound by barbed wire to twin stakes driven into the dirt. A sweating man held a bloody knife and had been cutting into the trapped man. The other white man present was older, heavier and sat on a nearby boulder. He calmly smoked a pipe watching the proceedings.

"You want me to cut off his privates now, Mr. Callaway?" The knife man asked gleefully.

"Not yet, Gosen. He needs to apologize to me first."

Gosen turned around. "You heard him, boy." He pressed the knife against Polk's crotch. "Say it, you black bastard."

"The only thing I'm sorry about is not being able to strangle you."

Gosen flicked the knife causing Polk to wince but he didn't cry out. "Apologize."

"Go to hell."

"That's enough."

They all looked at Reeves standing there with his rifle pointed at them.

"You best put that gun down and be on your way, nigra," Gosen said.

"Get him loose."

"You're getting yourself in deep and will regret any other action you take," Callaway said. "I'm a man of means."

"I'm the man with the rifle."

"You ain't gonna shoot no white gentleman," Gosen declared.

"Don't know why he wouldn't," Polk said. "He has plenty of times before."

"What's that?' Callaway said

Reeves came closer. "You got cotton in your ears? I said cut him loose."

"You brought this on yourself." Gosen lunged at him with the knife.

Reeves smashed him in the face with the butt of the rifle. He dropped to the ground in a flash, bleeding from his broken nose. Callaway fumbled for his holstered gun. Reeves jabbed the other end of the rifle into his soft gut. "Don't even think about it." He took the gun. "Now get busy. And any more harm befalls him, you'll see if I hesitate to send you to Kingdom Come with this Winchester."

Callaway balked but put on a pair of gloves and using pliers, got Polk untangled from the barbed wire. He sagged as he came free and wilted to the ground.

"Get him up and give him some water out of that canteen over there."

"You go too far, boy," Callaway huffed.

With no hesitation he shot a round in the dirt not two inches from the man's booted foot. "The next time I'll blow off your big toe."

Callaway got Polk up and placed him against a boulder. He retrieved the canteen and handed it to over as well. "Now what?" he said to Reeves.

"Now I tie you up."

"What sort of foolishness are you talking?"

"You should be grateful he's here, Callaway." Polk had the knife in his hand. "If it was me, I'd be carving on you like a Christmas goose. Hell, I still might."

Callaway looked at Reeves. "Keep him off me."

Polk laughed and it wasn't joyful. They used the barbed wire to wrap the two together having sat them back-to-back on the ground.

"You can't leave us like this." Blood was drying on Gosen's lower face. "A mountain lion or who-knows-what could come along." He wiggled some, the pointed barbs digging into his arms.

Polk said astride his Appaloosa. "Then I feel sorry for that mountain lion. Chewing on the both of you is gonna leave a sour taste in his mouth."

A wide-eyed Callaway looked at Reeves, also on his horse. "Mister, please."

"'Mister' now, is it?" Usually Reeves maintained his equilibrium, but something about these two got under his skin. He supposed it was the cavalier manner in their working Polk over and were going to be just as easy going when they killed him. But he was an officer of the court. True, his badge wasn't on his chest at the moment. And the good Lord knew plenty of colored folk and his Indian brethren weren't subjected equally to the law but to its capricious application. He shifted in his saddle and tossed down the pair of pliers. Reeves turned his horse around and he and Polk rode away slowly.

"Being fair is a burden you wear well, Bass," Polk told him.

"It's a hairshirt that itches mightily at times."

Polk had heard second-hand that Two Knives was holed up in an area called Edenville not far from the border. It was found off a tributary of the Red River as it flowed from Oklahoma into Texas. "Don't seem to be a town nor settlement as I understand," he told Reeves and Christie when they were on the trail. "More jus' a collection of castoffs and misfits."

Christie noted. "That's saying something considerin' a lot of people figure everybody in the Territories lives that way.

"You can't leave us like this."

"Probably an amount of the wanted in there too," Reeves speculated.

"Yes, sir," Polk agreed.

"If the three of us go in there together that might raise a few eyebrows," Reeves said. "Let alone you get seen, Frank."

"How you want to play it then?" Christie asked.

Reeves considered his next words carefully before responding.

Three days later he arrived at Edenville alone. The place was a slab of land found in something of an inlet. There was a thick forest on one side, a marsh on the other and these areas Reeves guided his horse up then over a small rise that led down to the location in a shallow valley. Here the tributary became a lake where due west the water was bordered by land and from which a low mountain rose in the near distance. Sure enough there were several structures as well as lean-tos and tents pitched here and there in no particular pattern. Hard-eyed men and women stared at Reeves while he brought his horse to a stop, watching a flat boat being unloaded with provisions at a large dock. He was pretty certain there were no families here and therefore no children. The boxes were being hauled into the only two-story structure off to one side at the end of the dock. Beyond this on a patch of open ground was a raised stone dais, five steps high.

Judging from the smells of frying fish in the air and the refrain of raucous voices, Reeves surmised the establishment was a combination bar, seafood restaurant and maybe hotel on the upper floor. He secured his horse and in he went. Inside men and a few woman of various races, sizes and shapes were eating, drinking and socializing. The décor had nets and pretend tridents tacked to the walls. Reeves had once been in such a place on a hunt that had taken him all the way to San Francisco. There was space at the bar and he leaned onto it.

"What's your pleasure?" the barkeep asked him. He was a burly man with splotchy skin.

"Beer," he said. He flipped his nickel on to the bar top when the barkeep returned with his beer.

"That'll be another nickel," the bartender said.

"Huh?"

"Damn near everything we got around here 'cept gator meat has to come by the water so there's extra overhead involved."

"Okay." Reeves added the correct amount and hooked a thumb over his shoulder. "What's with that raised platform outside?"

The bartender smiled. "It's almost that time." He removed his pocket watch to check. "In about half an hour."

"What's going to happen?"

"You'll see," he replied, an enigmatic smile animating his face.

Reeves drank slowly as more people entered the bar. In particular he recognized a face he'd seen on a wanted poster, an hombre named Butler Calicos if he recalled properly. He was a muscular man with black hair and more than one scar on his face. Several men gathered around him, clapping him on the back and buying him a drink. Calicos stripped off his shirt exposing his barrel chest and more scars. Cheers went up. One of the few good-looking women he'd seen came over and gave him a big kiss as the men roared their approval.

"And so it begins," the bartender yelled above the din. He'd come from around the bar and stood with his arms raised. "We who honor Xi-uh-te-cuht-li once again gather in his name to bring forth his glory." More cheers went up. "May the light of his sun bathe all of us in fortune and health."

Calicos went outside followed by the throng. A confused Reeves trailed them. There were more people gathered around the dais where another bare-chested man awaited.

"Interested in wagering, stranger?" A tall reedy man had sidled up to the deputy marshal. Like Dancer Dan he wore a bowler but he was in shirt sleeves rolled up past his elbows. He was holding a bundle of cash, pencil and a scrap of foolscap.

"Think I'll pass," Reeves said.

"Sure, sure." The man went off in search of other prospects.

Reeves saw at least two individuals selling small bottles of patent medicine as he worked his way through the crowd. A kettle drum had been rolled out and a dark-skinned Mexican man beat out a rhythm on it with two padded sticks.

"He's coming," someone exclaimed.

A current passed through the crowd. Reeves looked toward the end of the street to see an ornately carved wooden litter being carried by four men on their shoulders. The men, though only one was Indian, wore breech cloths and moccasins. Sitting on a chair built onto the litter was a man Reeves figured must be Two Knives. He was in his fifties and dressed not in ceremonial attire but a grey suit and open collar shirt. His graying hair was long, and he smiled and waved as the entourage got closer. People were happy to see him. The litter was set down. Two Knives stepped off the conveyance; an Aztec-styled headdress was handed to him. He put this on and addressed the inhabitants.

"My friends once again we gather in the name of Xiuhtecuhtli to honor him and do right by him so that he remains our protector as he guides us to the promise of the bright future only he can provide." He raised his arms and whoops and cheers went up.

Reeves just happened to be standing next to the man in the bowler and he turned to him. "You go for all this do you?"

He grinned. "I long ago learned not to look a gift horse in the mouth. Since this fine heathen gentleman and his bunch have arrived, they took care of the rowdies we had around here and the wimmin folk can walk at night unmolested. Not that they should be out at night, understand." He drifted off as Two Knives continued to speak. He spotted Frank Polk who'd come into town separate from Reeves as they'd planned. He hung back so as not to be spotted by Two Knives.

Soon enough Two Knives was finishing up. "And now let the contest begin so as to please he who shines down on our humble village." Headdress still on, he sat down again on the litter and the whole of it was positioned to give him a view of the raised dais. He was handed a glass of wine. As expected, the two shirtless men ascended to the raised platform. Unexpectedly it seemed this wasn't to be a bare knuckle contest as Reeves had surmised. Calicos held a short-handled hoe and the other a three-pronged cultivator tool. Its ends sharpened.

"Lordy," Reeves mumbled. Polk wandered closer, his hat pulled low on his head to block his face. As it was, no one was paying any attention to yet another stranger in town. All eyes were on the stone stage.

The combatants circled one another. Then quick as a cobra, Calicos flicked the garden tool forward in a blur. He took a nick out of the other one's arm who reacted too slowly to the assault. But he blocked the next blow with his particular tool intended for tilling the earth. They stepped back from each other, the wound on the man's arm a red smear but apparently not deep.

"I've seen all kinds of odd," Polk began, talking under his breath to Reeves. "But this beats all don't it?"

"It surely does," Reeves agreed.

The one with the rake-like tool gouged a three-lined trail in Calicos' chest. Reeves studied the crowd. The bloodlust was obvious on the sweaty faces of the men and women. Human beings eagerly anticipating the hurt fellow humans would inflict on each other. Close to the danger but not in peril themselves. He was reminded of those damnable postcards he'd seen of black men burned alive as they were lynched for what was often a lie or just because. People having a picnic as the poor bastard's feet dangled from overhead. He almost threw up as he turned away, face ashen. Polk noticed, offering a brief nod of empathy. He didn't turn away, his expression neutral.

It was getting bloodier between the two contestants. Calicos did a short stroke with the hoe, the edge cutting onto the other's leg, ripping cloth and opening a new wound. Back and forth the fight continued, alternating between who was on offense and who was defending himself. Reluctantly but resolutely, Reeves had returned his gaze to this modern-day gladiator spectacle. Until finally the hoe found purchase in the side of the other man's neck, severing a main artery. Gasps arose as blood streamed from the fatal blow and splashed a blonde woman on the side of her face. She laughed giddily and fell back, caught by a pot-bellied man behind her.

Two Knives returned to the stage and raised the reddened arm of his champion, Calicos holding his red-soaked hoe high amid cheers and applause from the crowd. The revived blonde gazed at him with decidedly wanton abandon. The dead man was taken away.

"The Old God is pleased once more," Two Knives said above the din. "For the third time in as many battles, he has smiled on Butler Calicos."

Calicos, who was bleeding from several wounds smiled and shook the hoe toward the heavens.

"Just what in the holy hell have you gotten us into, Bass?"

"Can't rightly say at this moment, Frank," the deputy marshal admitted. The crowd dispersed and the bounty men made themselves scarce. Two Knives finally removed the headdress, tucking it under his arm. He walked to a canoe tied to the dock. He got in with two of the men who'd carried him on the litter. Off they paddled upstream.

Later Ned Christie joined Reeves and Polk in the camp they'd made in the woods outside of town. Reeves puffed on a cheroot, back against a rock as he sat on the ground. He and Polk had remained in town for an hour or so more after the big contest to gather any other useful information pertinent to their task.

"Yep," Christie said, chewing on some deer jerky, "I trailed the canoe back to that mountain. I didn't want to get too close and be seen, but my guess is him and his followers, I guess you'd call them, is up there. I did see an opening to a cave off a ledge a little more than half way up.

"There's several in town seemed to be part of the group," Reeves added.

"How you mean?" Polk wondered.

"Keep the peace like what Two Knives mentioned before the fight. They don't sport any badges, but I did notice at least two of them have an 'X' tattooed here." He tapped his finger just below his right eye."

"X for Xiuhtecuhtli," Christie said.

Polk chuckled hollowly. "I did learn there's a wagon comes to town every two weeks to load up supplies to be taken back to Two Knives and his men. From what I figure, there's at least twenty of them up there at any given time." He added, "So we gonna sneak up the mountain, somehow get past a passel of hokum lovers and make off with the gold statue as bold as you please."

"When you say it like that, it sounds impossible," Reeves deadpanned.

The three went quiet for several moments. Christie finally said to Reeves, "You considering a move like what we did that time we had to smoke out the Riley twins in Okmulgee?"

"Some variation of that, yeah." Reeves flicked away his finished cheroot.

"What's that?" Polk asked.

"Create a diversion to draw off as many of them true believers as we can," Christie said.

"We'd have to set the town on fire to do that and even then it's a sure bet ole' Two Knives keeps hisself a bodyguard or two." Polk was laying on the ground, his head on his bedroll, hat over his face.

"Yep," Reeves allowed. "Problem too is we don't know how many side caves, warrens and what all else they got up there. And we'd probably wind up shooting our way in and shooting our way out. If a fella ain't wanted, well, we start shooting first, that ain't self-defense."

Ned Christie observed, "Some of us ain't all that worried about such niceties of law, Bass."

"The money got you rationalizing, Ned?"

"It's not that, not all of it anyway. But I gotta say, the challenge does get the blood up."

Reeves nodded. "I suppose it does. I wonder if there's a way to sneak in from atop that mountain. A shaft that lets in air or some such?"

"Only one way to find out," Polk said.

Christie had been sitting cross-legged on the ground. He got up and unlimbered his rifle from his horse. "I'll take first watch."

"I'll take the second shift," Polk said.

"Okay, I'm third," Reeves announced. "Before light we'll set out and start our scouting."

Not wishing to announce their presence, the men didn't start a fire and ate cold beans and biscuits. They slept and kept guard as planned and before dawn were heading toward the mountain. At one point they split off from each other, having arranged to reconnoiter later that day at a specific time. Deeper into the brush Reeves had to dismount and walk his horse in as this part of the forest was chokingly thick with undergrowth. While he presently wasn't of a mind to stop and appreciate the nature around him, Reeves noted the abundance of various types of colorful flowers and big leafy plants he hadn't seen grouped like this in any other parts of the Territories. The ground beneath him was now spongy and he came onto a small pool of water and spit of land off the Red River. He paused momentarily, letting his horse take a drink and allowing himself to breathe in the intoxicating scents of the flora. To his right he detected movement in a thicket of large mangrove-like roots. Ahead through a swath of large elephant ear leaves he also had a sense that there was someone lurking.

Rubbing his horse's head, Reeves gently turned him as he stood in shallow water. In this way he used the animal to block possible gunfire from in front of him, giving him a chance to pick off whoever it was to his right. Birds had been chirping and lizards crawling everywhere but it all went mute to him as an uneasy silence descended. Then from the purple shadows came a retort and Reeves threw himself down, blasting with his six-shooter as he did so. There was a grunt from the impact of the deputy marshal's bullets. Reeves was already up and crashing through another part of the thicket as rifle fire tore at him from where the other bushwhacker had repositioned himself so as not to be obstructed by the horse.

Reeves belly crawled forward and once he got clear of the entanglements, rose and ran after the second man who he knew was plowing through ahead of him. Onward he went, hearing but not seeing the man he pursued. Racing past a clump of trees, a trip wire laying flat on the ground was pulled and he fell forward. Bodies descended on him and his pistol was snatched from his grasp. He was hauled to his feet, a man on either side of him holding his arms. His captors were white and Indian, all of them with the 'X' tattoo. Including, he now noticed seeing him up close, Butler Calicos. The wanted man stood nearly face-to-face with Reeves.

"You getting' to be too famous these days, Marshal. More than one of us recognized you in town."

"Lucky me."

Calicos laughed and opening his fist which he'd thrust toward the other man, blew a grey-white powder into his face.

Instantly Reeves became disoriented and felt as if his brain was floating through the top of his head, his hat cocked upon it. Having experienced his share of sweat lodges, he'd known medicine men who concocted these types of substances from certain kinds of tree frogs, plants or even puffer fish. Despite wanting to remain on his feet, he blinked rapidly and became very drowsy. Soon his head was lolling at an angle on his neck and the last sensation he had before blacking out was of being tossed over a horse on his stomach, laughter echoing around him.

When consciousness returned, Reeves was on an expanse of outcropping, the flat part they'd seen on the mountain. He rose, his shirt, vest and gunbelt having been removed. Around him were several of Two Knives' men, including Butler Calicos. He glared at Reeves hungrily. Each man, of course, had a six-gun strapped on. To the other side of this area was the entrance to a cavern leading into the mountain. In this entrance was suspended Ned Christie. He was hoisted on hooks and rope, the latter tied to iron pinions above him driven into the roof of the cavern. The hooks pierced either side of his bare upper chest. The length of the rope wound around an iron spike driven in the rock wall and was tied off to an eye hook also embedded in that wall. This torture was what he'd once experienced, the Sioux rite-of-passage ritual called o-kee-pa. The pain was intense but Christie resisted crying out. Part of the ritual was to endure.

"When I came to, I was trussed up like this," Christie wheezed to Reeves. He did his best to keep his body from twisting to lessen the agony.

"I'm sorry, Ned," was Reeves' feeble reply. He prayed he'd be able to cut him down soon.

"Don't be, Bass, we're grown men, we signed on with open eyes."

Two Knives emerged from the gloomy depths of the cavern. He was wearing a robe made of buffalo hide. Underneath that he was dressed in leather pants and what was called a hair pipe breast plate. Sometimes worn for battle or ceremonial occasions.

"I see your reputation is well-earned, Bass Reeves."

"Are you just plain bed-bug crazy?"

"Watch your tongue, Reeves," Calicos warned. "The leader is not to be trifled with."

Reeves swallowed the boast he was eager to counter with. Two Knives had the upper hand and he best focus on what he suspected was coming next. "Is Frank alive?'

"Frank who?" Two Knives said.

"Polk."

Two Knives shook his head. "My men haven't seen him. But you have more important matters to see to, Bass Reeves."

"Then let's get to it."

Two Knives held his arms high once more, spreading his surprisingly long fingers wide. He said some words Reeves didn't understand. Several of his men, white and Indian, answered back in the same language.

"That Aztec is it?" Reeves asked.

"Yes, Náhuatl," he answered. "I summoned the protection of Xiuhtle-cuhtli for my champion."

"Naturally," Reeves said dryly.

Calicos also said something in Náhuatl as he took off his shirt. This time instead of a hoe he was handed a buck knife. A similar one was thrown in the dirt at Reeves' feet.

"Hold up your arm," an owlhoot ordered him.

He did so and a manacle was locked in place on his wrist. A ten-foot length of chain led from this to another manacle which was secured to Calicos' wrist. A semi-circle of the gun hands formed around them, Two Knives presiding.

"Are you ready?" their leader said.

Calicos threw his head back and bellowed enthusiastically. Even as his yell reverberated he rushed at Reeves, slashing with the knife. But Reeves hadn't been distracted by the champion's dramatics and twisting sideways, used his knife to deflect the other's blade. Calicos backed off, hunched forward, eyes zeroed in on Reeves.

"Gonna be a mighty big man when I take care of you, marshal. You done put more than one saddle pal of mine in that damnable jail in Fort Smith."

"If they're there, they deserved it."

"So you say."

Calicos moved left and Reeves did too. The trick was to keep your distance but not make the chain taut allowing your opponent to tug it quickly and pull you off-balance. The two stayed in motion, each wary and watchful. Calicos charged again and again Reeves defended. He'd once witnessed this type of death match where one of the men, cut and bleeding from several wounds and growing desperate, had thrown his knife underhanded in a last ditch effort to stay alive. His opponent had knocked the knife away and then finished off the doomed man by plunging his knife into the man's heart.

Reeves refocused. Taking the initiative, he came at Calicos, feinting a frontal attack that got him turning toward him with his knife up. Reeves suddenly changed course and coming at him at an angle, took a nick out of the bigger man's arm.

"Sneaky bastard," Calicos declared, eyes glittering with malice. Off to one side Two Knives watched, his arms folded, his face dispassionate.

Calicos got closer, the blade down low then brought it up swiftly, swiping at him. As Reeves evaded the attack, he brought his foot up and rammed it into the bounty man's chest. Down he went on his back and Calicos leaped on him, looking to plunge his blade into him. But Reeves, gritting his teeth, had managed to wind links of the chain around Calicos' wrist, halting the descent of the knife less than two inches from the tip of the blade and his throat. He rolled and now he was momentarily on top. He struck with his knife, the handle happened to be aimed toward Calicos' face. He pounded on him twice, causing bruising and then was thrown clear. Both hurried to their feet.

"Git him good, Butler," one of the gunmen said.

"Yeah, he hunted down a cousin of mine like a dog and put him in that jail," another said. At one point as Reeves back-pedalled toward him, a cut bleeding on his chest, the man tripped him. Reeves was sent to a knee but thrusting his knife at an oncoming Calicos kept him away.

Two Knives barked a reprimand at the man who cheated.

By now each man showed red marks on their arms and chests, but none of the wounds were deep. When Calicos again attacked, Reeves had kept track mentally of his usual moves. This time before the knife swept at his torso, he went low, sliding across the dirt like he'd seen a fella do in a baseball game once. Damned if he didn't upend Calicos. Crawling and scrambling like a gator about to feast on a lamb he was on his opponent. Reeves stabbed the bigger man's bicep in his knife hand and was driven off by a blow from Calicos' fist from his hand opposite. Now he pressed his assault on Reeves but as his blade took a slice of the marshal's collar bone, Reeves sunk the knife in an upward angle in his ribcage. He withdrew it, bloody to its hilt.

Calicos and several others gasped. He listed sideways but remained upright.

"We're done, cut Ned down," Reeves said to Two Knives.

"Only one walks away," he answered calmly.

"Sneaky bastard," Calicos declared.

"I don't need your two-bit pity, badge man." Calicos moved side-to-side, waving the knife back and forth. "This dance ain't over yet." He coughed, spitting red. Everybody understood his lung had been punctured and was filling up with blood. His bravado couldn't hide the reality that he was weakening. As medical attention didn't seem to be in the cards, he would soon be dead anyway.

Reeves clenched his jaw. It wasn't right to his way of thinking to keep fighting, but if he did nothing, he'd be dead and so would be Christie—and who knew what had happened to Frank Polk? In a matter of minutes it was all over. Calicos lay on his back on the ground, Reeves' knife buried deep in him. His eyes had rolled back in his head and the solemn silence of defeat gripped the onlookers.

"Now bring him down," Reeves demanded.

Two Knives nodded and Christie was lowered. He lay on the ground, the hooks still in him. Reeves went to him and knelt down. "This is gonna sting some."

"Not as much as it already has. Go on and do it, Bass."

Gently but firmly Reeves put one hand on the big man's shoulder and with the other removed the first hook and then the second one. Christie panted hard but remained conscious.

"Much appreciate your tender lovin' care, doctor."

"I got the touch don't I?" Reeves stood and faced Two Knives. "Where's Frank, staked out over a bed of vipers?"

Two Knives said, "Frank rode in with you two?"

"Yeah."

"Haven't seen him."

"Who you kiddin'?"

"You came for Xiuhtecuhtli didn't you?"

"No sense being bashful now I suppose," Reeves answered. "I did."

"For money."

"You make it sound dirty."

Two Knives snorted and started to walk toward the cavern. As he went toward Christie he pointed to him. "Somebody tend to this man. Wouldn't want to upset the marshal." On he went, Reeves and most of the others following. He picked up his shirt where it had been left lying in the dirt. He shook it off and put it back on. Soon only Reeves and Two Knives were in another chamber of the mountain. Several pieces of mis-matched furniture were there along with other homey items, including a throw rug. On a small rickety table off to one side were a chair and the remains of a lunch, a knife and fork on a plate. What light there was came from an opening above them though there was also an unlit torch stuck in a hole in the rock wall. Two Knives sat cross-legged on the rug and he motioned for Reeves to join him. He sat down cross-legged opposite him to palaver.

"I figure some rich white man sent you to steal the effigy."

"I had the impression you stole it."

"Because that's what the white man told you."

Reflecting on this, Reeves had to admit O'Ferguson had been vague on certain details. "How'd you come to acquire it?"

"I can certainly say I have more claim to it than whoever sent you here does. I made certain promises to those who safeguard the statue when they put it in my keeping. Promises I intend to keep."

Reeves was vexed. He'd allowed himself to be driven by the lure of dollars rather than be as clear-eyed going into this as he should have been.

"Aw, hell," he said.

"Don't be too hard on yourself, Bass."

Reeves and Two Knives looked over to see Frank Polk holding a burlap sack in one hand, his six shooter in the other and aimed at the two—both of them on their feet again.

"What's this about, Frank?"

"What's it always about, Bass? Money." He shook the sack. "From what you said, if O'Ferguson was willing to pay three thousand dollars, for sure there's another white man who'll pay more."

"And you won't be bothered by having to split the reward."

"I saw you and Ned get jumped but Two Knives' boys didn't see me. I tracked them taking you two back here and figured my old posseman hadn't just picked this place 'cause it looked pretty against the sky. Sniffed around and found several ways in and out of this rock palace. With everybody watching your fight, figured to find the doodad and be on my way. Took a might longer to find this trinket but looks like it's gonna work out."

"How exactly you plan on getting away from all those fellas out there?' Reeves said.

"Oh," Two Knives exclaimed.

Polk threw his head back and yelled, "Hey, get your asses in here. Hurry, hurry."

Confused Reeves soon understood as Polk took two sticks of dynamite tied together from the sack. Reeves figured he must have found the explosives poking around for the figure of gold. Damned if he hadn't cut down the fuse on one of the sticks. Footfalls and murmuring approaching, Polk kept his gun on the two. He swiped the head of a wooden match across the table top. As it flared, he lit the fuse.

"Frank!" Reeves yelled. "Dynamite!" he also yelled a warning as Polk shot at him as Reeves dove behind the table and chair, upending both as he did so. A bullet grazed his side but by this time Polk was gone and the dynamite went off where he'd tossed it into the opening into his chamber. There was a loud boom and a concussive swirl of smoke, dirt and heat. The opening ceased to be, uneven heaps of rock now blocked the passageway. Two Knives had been knocked over but otherwise seemed unhurt. He helped Reeves up then went to the blocked opening.

"Kayson? Elmore?" he called out.

"We're here," came a reply. "Tommy got it though, and Steeple's hurt."

"I'll get him," Two Knives said, turning from the pile. He stripped his shirt off revealing a sinewy body for a man his age. He started climbing up the wall, handholds having been dug into the rock toward the top and now the only way out. "You comin' or not?"

"Aw, hell," Reeves mumbled and started up as well. He kept his shirt on. But using the knife that had been on the plate, cut off a cuff and stuffed that inside the shirt on the wound. His side hurt some, the bullet having shot away a chunk of flesh but so be it. He slipped once but fortunately his foot caught purchase and up he climbed, Two Knives easily ahead of him. Finally he squeezed through the opening to see they were on another side of the mountain, about three quarters of the way up. He sat there for a few moments, winded, scrapes on his upper body. Hell of a time to start feeling his age, he reflected. Two Knives was stepping through a clump of shrubbery down a slope and he went through too. Revealed was a switchback and both men descended to level ground and a corral of horses.

"You got it all set up, don'tchu?" Reeves said admiringly.

"You take White Eye," he said, pointing at a black stallion with a streak of white across one eye. Somehow he'd acquired a gun and had it strapped on. A shooting iron hadn't been offered to Reeves.

"He the second fastest to your horse?"

"You're quick, Marshal. I'll give you that."

Reeves was in no position to argue. He didn't have time to get back to where they'd ambushed him and no doubt left his horse and gunbelt. He put a saddle on White Eye and off they rode. It wasn't hard picking up Polk's trail and anyway, they knew he'd probably be heading across the border into Texas.

"He probably has a stick or two left of your dynamite," Reeves observed as they rode.

"That did cross my mind," Two Knives replied.

Glaring at the hard-packed terrain they were covering Reeves said, "I wonder too if we're on a wild goose chase." He stopped his horse to better regard the ground. He looked behind him but even for an experienced tracker as he was, it was tough to tell if man and beast had been over this ground recently.

Two Knives dismounted and was on a knee, also studying the ground. He probed the earth with his fingers. He looked up toward the forest they'd just emerged from. "If I was a smart man," he began.

"I'd disappear in there and let my pursuers get several miles away 'fore I lit out, taking a different route to the border," Reeves finished. He too was staring into the forest.

"But that could be a bad guess and Frank could well be on his way."

"We have to split up," Reeves said.

"Sounds like the right thing to do."

They flipped a coin and Reeves won. He headed into the emerald belt. If it was him he decided, he'd hide in the densest area, then hunker down for a spell. Maybe even set a trap or two if time allowed. Once in, it was as if he were in some other place on Earth. All these plants seemed to bring with them their own weather. It was humid, yet there were pockets of cool as well. The light got tricky in places, the thick canopy overhead alternately letting in light, and in other places the going was in near gloom even though the sun was high and bright in the sky.

Reeves slowed, the ground was covered in ropy tendrils of roots and vines that crossed and re-crossed over each other and formed knots of growth hard for the beast to navigate. He got off and tethered the horse.

"Easy, boy," he said to White Eye, patting its flank. Reeves took off his hat and left it by the horse. He didn't have a gun but he had palmed the knife from the room they'd climbed out of a little while ago. Reeves eased through the underbrush, trying to go as quietly as possible, on alert for the slightest disturbance. A colorful bird burst into view from nowhere, flapping upward, the feathers brushing across his face. He nearly fell back but having latched onto a tree trunk, maintained his balance. On he crept, partly hunched over to better blend in and be less of a target. There was no tangible evidence to support his feeling, but should Polk be in the vicinity, that damn bird's reaction would have gotten his attention.

As he progressed, around him the darkness loomed and stretched, like the gloved hand of a giant closing in on him. He stepped carefully as he continued. As he entered a cone of diffused light, he halted his boot in mid-air. Something twinkled before him and bending down, he saw the tiny residue of sap that had caught the sunlight on the tip of a sharpened pine branch, the opposite blunt end impaled in the ground. Now crouched low and moving about like that, he saw more than one stake in the ground.

"Clever rascal," Reeves muttered as he straightened up. It wasn't that the miniature spears would penetrate the sole of a boot but stepping on one would crack it and alert Polk. Reeves took two of the spears out of the ground and slipped out of the near-light and into a darker area. He then snapped the two shafts in half and got ready. Though he was aware that Polk too knew how to be sneaky. The birds kept twittering and he was certain he heard a snake slithering about nearby. Eyes closed to focus his concentration, it was his perception there was movement ahead and several paces to the left. He opened his eyes, breathing shallowly. He remained still, gripping the knife tightly. A bullet singed the air, striking a tree trunk near him but Reeves didn't flinch. He noted where the muzzle flash had originated but Polk would have already repositioned himself. He had to keep believing his presence wasn't seen but felt, that Polk couldn't quite pinpoint where he was. If he were to be shaken by the gunshot or move not at the right time, Polk'd ventilate him for damn sure.

For almost longer than he could stand—though in truth it was only seconds—nothing happened. He concentrated on the dense terrain before him. A shadow drifted behind a fan of large leaves and he tensed. Then that foliage was pushed aside, the barrel of a gun suddenly very distinct. In the heartbeat it took for Polk to locate Reeves, the marshal lunged, crashing through the growth as another shot rang out. Had he not reflexively shifted his head at the same moment the trigger was squeezed, the bullet would have put a third eye in his forehead. As it was, Reeves slammed into Frank Polk and both men became entangled. Reeves plunged the small knife into the underside of the other man's upper arm. He got a blow on the jaw for his effort, bursting stars behind his eyes. Somehow the knife became lost in the dark green void. He recovered just in time to knock Polk's gun hand aside as two more shots boomed. He was on him like a second shirt, not giving him a chance to use the gun again. They grunted and grappled and fell over once more. A frog leaped on Polk's face, momentarily distracting him. Reeves pummeled him with several blows but Polk was tough and didn't succumb as he hoped. Knocked loose from him, the six-shooter came up and Reeves drove the pointed end of one of the broken stakes he'd kept into Polk's wrist, right between the twin bones. It went in deep.

"Son of a bitch," Polk yelled, involuntarily opening his fingers, the gun dropping away. He jumped on Reeves, the stake poking through his wrist. He got his hands around the other man's throat and gritting his teeth and sweating on him, squeezed with all his might. This time it was blackness spreading across Reeves' brain as he sought to breathe. Grasping the stake, he ripped it lengthwise in the wound and Polk couldn't help but loosen his stranglehold. Reeves leveraged Polk's body and rolled so that for a moment, he was on top. But he then did the unexpected and sprang off his posseman turned opponent.

Polk came after him, latching onto his upper shoulders from behind. "Not so fast, Bass," he said. "You ain't got nowhere to go."

"'Fraid I do, Frank." Reeves spun around and hit him alongside the jaw with the burlap bag he'd spied through the bush. Xiuhtecuhtli tore out of the sack, landing on the ground. The squarish figurine glittered in its glory of gold and jewels. Polk was dazed. Attempting to rise, a second blow to the top of his head by the flat of Reeves' fist sent him to a knee. Unhesitatingly he kicked him in the face. He was angry, here he'd saved him and Polk still betrayed his trust. By the time the other man was able to focus, Reeves had found the gun and had it on him.

"Well done, Marshal."

Both men looked to see Two Knives, one foot on a knot of tree roots holding a Winchester rifle.

"This is a bit of a pickle, isn't it?" he said.

"Seems to be," Reeves answered.

Polk grumbled, his sore head in his hands.

Once more Bass Reeves rode into the sugary air of the Peachdale plantation. Once more he stopped at the main house, the old retainer Portifoy waited there to greet him.

"Marshal," he said, nodding.

"How you doing today, Portifoy?" Reeves asked as he dismounted.

"Oh, fair to midlin'" He took hold of the horse's reigns. "Mr. O'Ferguson would care to take your company in the study."

Reeves looked up at the mansion. "I get to be in the big house today, do I?"

Portifoy cast his eyes downward. "If you're too busy, Marshal, I could tell him you said you'd stop by another time."

Reeves patted the older man's upper arm. "Don't you fret, Portifoy. I know what I'm walkin' into."

He looked up at him, his mouth quavering.

Reeves stepped past, a mortician's smile on his face. He went up the wide steps and through one of the double doors. Striding through the circular foyer, he once more took to the grand staircase, white marble floors and towering plush drapes. A short way down the hall with its titillating paintings, he didn't hesitate entering the open door to the study. He didn't remove his hat. O'Ferguson sat not behind his desk but on the couch, one leg over the other. Like before, he was reading a book and set it aside. His reading glasses were perched low on the bridge of his nose, and he looked up and over them at his guest. These too he set aside.

"I half expected you not to show up. Considering you failed."

He'd had a telegram sent ahead. "I don't rightly set with what Two Knives is doing but in terms of that there Aztec dodad, seems his claim to the thing is more on the up and up than your wanting it. Especially as it appears you killed a man in cold blood over this here fancy desk ornament."

"Jokes, huh?" O'Ferguson grunted. "You takin' the word of a savage over mine?"

"I checked into what he told me. On and off you'd been bird doggin' the piece, even going out to San Francisco when this sharpie you had working for you had located the, what y'all call it, relic?"

"But it turned out to be a fake, a phony," O'Ferguson said.

"You get mad did you, killing the antiques dealer when all that money and time you'd put in didn't add up to spit?"

"There a warrant out for me, marshal?"

"You know there ain't. You got friends in high places to make sure you scoot from one shady doings to the next unscathed and unbothered."

"Careful, you might be implicating your boss."

"Yeah, well, I just try to put one foot in front of the other."

"Bringing you back here."

"I'm simply telling you to leave it alone. You send others after ole' Xi-uh-te-cuht-li, you're asking for trouble."

O'Ferguson finally stood up. "You and the redman cut a deal, Reeves? He plan to melt down Xiuhtecuhtli and pluck out the jewels and sell off the pieces? Or keep it intact which I would hope and could be you helped him find a buyer to outbid me. Figured to get yourself a payday beyond all measure for a colored man. Stop having to chase cutthroats and thieves all over Creation. Who-wee." He started toward the desk.

"Careful," Reeves began, "some of your open-mindedness is slippin'."

O'Ferguson chuckled. He opened a drawer and removed a pistol.

"You best set that down."

The master of Peachdale waved the gun slightly. "Or what? You can't shoot me. Remember, I have friends in high places? You muss my hair and I'll not only have you drawn and quartered, but get that ranch of yours taken away. Your wife and them snot-nosed kids of your living in rags, begging for food and shelter. You resting in a cold, unmarked grave."

Keeping his eyes on the gun Reeves said, "Did you hear what you just said? I got too much to lose if I don't defend myself."

"Self defense plea for a black man with a fast gun? When the all-white jury condemns you in court, you'll learn the limits of the law you so heartily operate under, Reeves. Not to forget that advance you owe me as well."

Reeves had taken back what he'd laid on Frank Polk and gave that over to Ned Chirstie. The big man though wasn't holding a grudge against him.

O'Ferguson was still talking. "What you need to do is come to your senses and march outside where I'll shackle you to the stock and have Portifoy whip you within an inch of your miserable life for your temerity. You'll take this whipping because you can't shoot me without suffering severe consequences. Not the least of which is you being strung up."

Reeves's gun was suddenly in his fist, causing O'Ferguson to blanch. He also produced the stick of dynamite he'd gotten off of Frank Polk. Eyes steady on the other man; he lit the fuse and clicked the hammer back on his gun. He tossed the explosive onto the rug.

"Have you gone simple?" O'Ferguson worried. He started to back up and Reeves blasted a bullet past his ear. Fearful, he threw the gun down and put up his hands.

"Don't think 'cause I respect the badge I won't come back here one night and slip inside and slit your self-righteous throat. You ever threaten my wife or my children again you better see to it I'm in the ground for damn sure. Because I'll happily die killing you to make sure they are unharmed."

"You've made your point."

Reeves let the fuse burn a bit lower then stamped it out. He picked up the dynamite and backing out, left the study. Elmira and Portify were in the foyer. He tipped his hat to their smiling faces and left the Peachdale plantation. Riding steady, but in no hurry.

THE END

THE WAGES OF WRITING

As I write this it's the 80th anniversary of the debut of the noir film *The Maltese Falcon* which premiered on October 3, 1941. It was the third and best version of the novel of the same name by Dashiell Hammett. There's an apocryphal story that the film's writer-director John Houston on a Friday gave the book to his secretary on his way out the door at lunch time for a weekend of drinking and carousing. Supposedly he told her to convert the whole of it into screenplay format and he'd be back on Monday to do his edits and whatnot. Like the Falcon, that's probably the stuff of dreams but it is the case that damn near line for line, the dialogue in the movie is lifted from Hammett's sparkling prose. I could go on, but the point is the Black Bird was on my mind as I finally got in gear to pen my second Bass Reeves adventure.

Too, the idea was to incorporate some of those elements we want in a western. In this case our main character is a stalwart type who often finds himself working with certain individuals who walk a more crooked path. Yet circumstances occur that put them into motion as the plot unfolds and, hopefully if I'm doing my job, character is revealed as well. I could have Bass working alone but I enjoyed playing him off another historic black cowboy, the antihero Deadwood Dick, in his previous outing, I decided to team Bass up with two others this time around. Which also meant the job he took on would have to be of a certain magnitude requiring more than just him to pull it off.

This then sent me to do a bit of research in a couple of the books on my shelf about Bass' time period, *The Black West* by William Loren Katz and *Black, Red, and Deadly* by Art Burton (whose *Black Gun, Silver Star* about the deputy marshal is a "bible" used by us Reeves writers). Eventually my decision was to use First Nation's outlaw Ned Christie and the obscure Frank Polk. In Burton's book there's this intriguing passage, "Frank (Becky) Polk, a tall black man, was selected by Deputy U.S. Marshal Paden Tolbert to serve as cook with the posse that killed Cherokee Ned Christie. Polk had served with Tolbert on many such missions and was

125

not only an excellent cook but also could handle a pistol and rifle as well as any man." In my version Christie and Polk would be reinvented as fellow bounty men. Those who had proven themselves able and therefore the type of hombres Bass would recruit for this story. It wouldn't be a usual manhunt but, circling back to the Falcon, a task about retrieving a lusted for thing that as Sam Spade icily observed about its pursuit, "And I know the value in human life you people put on it." Admittedly, there's also a touch of *Heart of Darkness-Apocalypse Now* in the guise of the Two Knives character and his reprobate followers glomming onto him and his possessing the Aztec bejeweled statuette, interpreted as a mystical symbol of the deity Xiuhtecuhtli.

Had a lot of fun writing this and I hope you enjoyed reading "Wages of Gold."

GARY PHILLIPS – Is an L.A. based writer. In addition to writing Bass Reeves, he created Jimmie Flint, Secret Agent X-11 for a linked anthology he edited entitled *Day of the Destroyers*. His new pulp character Decimator Smith was in *Black Pulp* I & II, set in 1930s Los Angeles. You can find his works in bookstores and online via Amazon, Bookshop.org and others.

THE DEAD OF NIGHT

By Mel Odom

"You know what all this rain and these dark woods remind me of?" A cold feeling that wasn't associated with the rain ran across United States Marshal Bass Reeves's neck. He might have even shivered a little at the question because he dreaded what was to come.

Restless, cold and tired, he glared out at the surrounding dark woods, then he glared at Alfred Tubby, his posseman, who rode slightly behind and to the left a good ten feet so they both couldn't get picked off at once by a disciplined sharpshooter. They'd been riding together for a long time in dangerous places and had faced sharpshooters and other killers.

Alfred had posed the question and Bass didn't want to answer because he knew it would only push the unwanted conversation further along.

The old man was somewhere in his seventies, not really vain about it, but he hadn't pinned down the actual number since Bass had taken him on. Alfred was mostly Cherokee, but he carried some white blood too, courtesy of an unwelcome ancestor.

The posseman was thin and rangy, and he sat his horse well despite his years. Rain dappled his dark skin and slid down his sharp cheekbones. Scars showed on his face, and there were others that didn't show that he'd earned over the years.

Even though they'd ridden hard trails together over the years, Bass didn't know the stories behind all those marks of past violence. Bass hadn't shared stories about all the scars he carried. Some things were just a man's own business.

Under his wide brimmed flat top hat, Alfred wore his salt and pepper hair in a neat braid that ran down his back. An oilskin slicker covered his brown button up shirt and beaded turquoise necklace. The necklace was new, a gift from one of the old posseman's many nieces and nephews. Like Bass, Alfred's dungarees hung over his boots to keep the rain from filling them.

"I don't care to hear what you're reminded of," Bass said irritably.

"Especially if it has to do with haints an' flesh-eatin' monsters. I've about had my fill hearing about those this past few hours."

The deputy marshal was six feet two inches tall and broad-shouldered by nature and from working on his horse ranch over in Fort Smith, Arkansas. He lived there with his wife and eleven children. He worked in the Indian Territories and other places Judge Parker sent him. He'd even been out as far as California a few times.

"I know you don't want to hear it," Alfred said. "You already told me that a few times, and I am not deaf. But these things are on my mind because of this investigation we've been assigned to by the judge. I figure if I have to think about it, I should tell you about it. We are partners after all."

"You're my posseman." Bass just wanted to draw a line and thought that might help.

"Partners, like I said. Maybe something I've heard will help us figure out how Bud Hundey got killed. The way he got murdered was peculiar. You said so yourself."

"I did, and I said I'd rather see his house my ownself instead guessing before we get there."

"I'm not guessing. I'm just collecting information. Giving us something to think about while we ride."

"I'd just as soon not go over your stories again."

"I've got a whole passel of stories you haven't heard."

"And I'd just as soon not hear them."

Alfred chuckled. "It's strange, big as you are and everything that you have seen, that you believe in ghosts and other monsters."

Sometimes it was what a man *didn't* see that got him killed. That was in Bass's mind too.

"I don't believe in ghosts and monsters," the deputy marshal said.

He was sure he sounded confident of that. He might not have been completely confident about it on the outside, but he figured he could act the part. When the time called for it, he was good at being just about anybody he needed to be at the time he needed to be that person. That particular skill was part of why he was such a good lawman.

"Then why does talking about those things bother you so much?" Alfred asked. He was just pestering now and both of them knew it. When the posseman got bored, Bass usually suffered for it.

"It doesn't bother me. You just keep talking about it. Over and over. That's about wore out its welcome."

"That's because all these woods remind me of those times when I was a boy and we sat around with the Elders while they told their stories about the Little People, Uktena, evil spirits, and creatures with a taste for human flesh. Those were some exciting times because my friends and I believed what the Elders told us. Those old men—"

"Any of them older than you are now?" Bass asked just to be ornery his ownself. "Because right now you're reminding me of them a lot."

Alfred ignored him. "They would finish those stories, get us good and scared, and they'd make us go out into the dark woods to fetch firewood. Sometimes they'd sneak out after us and jump out from behind trees to scare us. It worked every time. They thought that was about the funniest thing they'd ever seen. Never got tired of it. When they did that, Boyd Emoche always screamed like a trapped rabbit, and he even loaded his drawers a couple times. Everybody called him Stinky Boyd after that. That's a hard name to come back from."

"Filling a boy's head with that kind of foolishness ain't no way to raise him."

"I don't know," Alfred said. "The Elders told us those stories so we'd look for and appreciate the things the spirits did for us, and to know there were more things in the world than we could know. Which, if you think about it, is most days. Those tales kept us open to possibilities."

"Of getting ate by monsters?"

"Sometimes men eat men. Those stories warned about that too. It helps to remember that. You and I worked that murder of James Walking Deer a few years back. You remember that one, right?"

Bass did, and he wished he didn't—especially out here in the dark like he was. The things a United States deputy marshal saw while keeping the peace burdened a man something fierce.

"I try not to remember," Bass said.

"When we found what was left of James Walking Deer," Alfred went on, "Horace Kilkenny had eaten almost half of that man's body."

Lightning seared the dark sky, and for a moment Bass again saw what was left of James Walking Deer hanging from the rafter in Kilkenny's smokehouse. Only now it was hanging in the woods and looking at him with accusing dead eyes.

The smell of cooked human flesh, so close to that of fried pork, had taken a long time to fade. Some days Bass remembered the stench well enough that the memory put Bass off his feed. Despite the heavy rain, that scent filled his nose now.

Knowing he was tired, Bass blinked his eyes, and when he looked into the woods again, the hanging piece of a man and the smell was gone.

"Why, if we'd arrived a week later," Alfred said, "Kilkenny would probably have gobbled that man up and we wouldn't have been able to pin that murder on him. We wouldn't have had a habeas corpus. Luckily we only needed *half* of a habeas corpus."

"We didn't pin that murder on Kilkenny," Bass insisted. "We caught him red-handed—"

"Mighty red-handed," Alfred agreed.

Bass ignored that. "—and Judge Parker hanged him."

"Yeah, that is so. Did you ever wonder what Kilkenny asked for a last meal?" Alfred slipped that in innocently, like he'd only then thought of it.

Bass was pretty sure Alfred had brought the topic up before on a cold and miserable night just like this one. The question sounded familiar.

"No," Bass stated coldly, "I did not, and I don't want to think about it tonight."

"It appears to me you've gotten a little worrisome about things that don't exist."

"I'm not worried."

"I can see how you would be since the details of this investigation are so strange."

"I'm *not* worried," Bass growled. "If you've got to talk—"

"I thought I was breaking up this long, lonesome ride. I'm doing my best to make the time not so monotonous. I'm bored. I figured you might be too. I've been thinking about rain, too, but I've about had enough of rain. I can't wait to find a fireplace and a warm bed. Instead, I got all those stories that the Elders told me running around in my head."

"Find something else to talk about."

"I would. I've tried. It's just that being out here in the woods, so far from a town, I get to thinking about things like monsters sometimes. You know as well as I do that they're not all made up. Kilkenny was proof of that. Him and his half of a habeas corpus."

"Thinking's usually a private concern," Bass pointed out. "That's how I favor it. You might try thinking to yourself about such things."

"I think about things, strange and not so strange, to myself a lot. It's only now and again I think about them out loud. I'm thinking out loud tonight. Maybe this time I'm thinking about ghost stories and monsters on account of how Bud Hundey was supposedly locked in a room all by himself and ended up tore to pieces by something that left without unlocking that cabin door."

A chill stole across the back of Bass's neck. *That* was something that had been worrying at his mind like a mouse feeding on grain. The murder didn't consume his thoughts, but that question kept nibbling away. He wished Alfred hadn't been the one to read the telegram from the judge. If he'd known, he'd have kept the details to himself. But Alfred was the only one of them who could read.

"We don't know if that story's true," Bass said. "That's what Judge Parker was told, and it's what he told me. Could be a lie that was told to the judge, and he just passed it on without knowing."

"You believe a man would lie to Judge Parker?"

A man facing a rope would. That was a fact. Judge Isaac Parker was known as the Hanging Judge for a reason.

"And that's what that telegram said," Alfred continued. "That right there put a lot of thoughts in my head. The judge's story is responsible for all this thinking that's filling my head. If you want to be disagreeable with someone, be disagreeable with the judge. He's the reason we're out here looking into this."

The horses trudged up a hill and the wet ground sucked at their hooves the whole way. The mud squelched and popped like the mouths of greedy calves suckling their mommas, like those mouths would open right up and—

That thought didn't sit well with Bass, and he pushed it right on out of his mind. He pulled his oilskin slicker tighter around himself and concentrated on thinking about the new foal that had just been born on his ranch. He'd hated leaving it because he took a lot of pride in his horses.

But he kept wondering about Bud Hundey and the way the man had been killed. About how that cabin had gotten locked up.

"You're thinking about it, aren't you?" Alfred asked. "About how Bud Hundey was killed?"

"No. I'll think about that later."

Alfred chuckled.

Thankfully, when the horses crested the hill, the lights of Goodland shined in the distance. The town was small, no more than a few streets with a dozen buildings and a few houses. They cut trees and took lumber in Goodland. They built houses and barns and fences, and they shipped the rest out to Albion on freight wagons where it was used there or loaded onto a Saint Louis-San Francisco railroad car.

Lightning flashed across the sky, fat and thick, like a parasitic worm laying just under the skin from one of Alfred's stories. Bass was pretty sure that one couldn't be true. Thunder rumbled and cascaded through the woods.

Despite the quiet little fear lodged in the back of his mind, Bass kept his horse to a cautious pace. He didn't want to have to walk all that way in the rain if it broke a leg, and he sure didn't want to be afoot in case some *thing* out of Alfred's stories broke from the woods.

Not that anything ever would. Still, Bass liked to stay prepared. It was how he'd stayed alive so long in a dangerous career.

Almost an hour later, Bass and Alfred reached Goodland and rode through the muddy streets. Rainwater filled deep ruts left by wagon wheels. A dozen shops sat quiet and empty on either side of Main Street. When the lightning flared, blurred reflections of Bass and Alfred and the horses slowly crossed the darkened store window. The flickering images were disconcerting, almost like the haints the old people he'd grown up around had warned him about, and he tried not to pay those stories any mind either.

At least Alfred had stopped talking about monsters and ghosts. Maybe the old man was spooking himself.

Bass was glad to be back in Goodland. He had nice memories of the town and some of the folks who lived there, but the last time he'd been through Goodland had been over a year ago. He'd chased a gang of rustlers who had been cutting cows out of the local herds and running them on down to Texas.

That assignment hadn't involved anybody getting torn to pieces in a locked room.

Reining his horse in, Bass stopped in front of the two-story High Hill Hotel and peered through the rain dripping from his hat brim. The building was sandwiched between the town's dry goods store and the Hot Griddle, the small restaurant that was only open from breakfast through late afternoon except on Saturdays. Respectable folks were expected to eat at home.

When the lightning wasn't flashing, full dark fogged the few muddy streets of downtown Goodland. The light from the lantern hanging by the hotel door gave a brief shine to the rain pelting Bass's oilskin slicker.

A shadow moved on the other side of the window to the left and Bass's hand strayed to the Winchester rifle in his saddle scabbard because this wasn't a night he was willing to just set caution aside. When no threat emerged, he released a tense breath and relaxed.

"Jumpy?" Alfred asked, and the posseman's tone held humor.

"No," Bass growled.

He had stayed at the hotel in the past and had enjoyed those infrequent visits. The desk clerk had a small office and could usually be found there till eight p.m.

It was only a handful of minutes after seven p.m., so the shadow probably belonged to Kurt Emerson or Quick Fox. Emerson was German-born, came across with his parents, and moved into Indian Territory fifteen years ago. He owned the hotel with Quick Fox, his Choctaw brother-in-law.

Emerson had worked as a carpenter, and he'd fallen in love with Josephine Many Stars, a young Choctaw maiden. Her people had allowed Emerson to make a home among them. When Josephine was a girl, train robbers had killed her parents. She'd been left with a young brother to care for. Emerson had married the woman, taken the brother as his own family, and had built the hotel at Josephine's request. She'd wanted a business she could operate while her husband and brother worked as sawyers and carpenters.

Under Josephine's management, guests at the High Hill Hotel had received clean sheets and hot breakfasts. The hotel had eight rooms on the second floor and four on the first. The rest of the first-floor space had been kept for Josephine's office and modest living quarters for the family.

When the High Hill Hotel had first opened, the structure had been one of the largest and finest buildings in town. Emerson, Quick Fox, and Josephine had built it to last. The hotel was still one of the biggest, but age hung heavy on it.

Josephine had died a few years back and her absence showed in the baskets along the boardwalk that had once held flowers but now only held withered stems. Emerson and Quick Fox had lacked the heart to get rid of the hotel and had taken over the running of the business, but Josephine's attention and care was gone, and the place was sadder for it.

When peacekeeping business in the service of Judge Isaac Parker in Fort Smith, Arkansas, brought Bass to the Kiamichi Mountains in the southeast corner of the Indian Territories, he had sometimes found a reason to stop by the hotel for a brief visit. Josephine always set a fine table, and her apple pie was among the best Bass had ever had.

Bass missed the woman and her witty banter and sass. He missed a lot of people these days. That came with getting older, and there was nothing to be done for it.

A lantern flared on the other side of the window, curtains parted, and Kurt Emerson peered through the dark glass. A lightning bolt zigzagged across the sky and revealed his round face and ruddy tan. He raised a hand in greeting.

Bass waved back and winced because lifting his arm caused rain to run into the slicker's sleeve and trailed a chill all the way to his elbow. As the cold water ran along his arm, he blew out an angry breath. He wanted to be dry and warm.

"You ride out in the rain," Alfred Tubby said, "you're going to get wet. Squalling about it like a two-year-old won't do any good."

"I wasn't squalling about the rain," Bass groused.

"Sounded like you were."

"Maybe you've been listening to the rain too long. We've been riding in it for hours."

"That's just another complaint," Alfred said. "I think you're getting soft."

Bass wanted to argue, but he didn't because some days he thought about how much harder deputying was. He'd spent a lot of miles in the saddle, a lot of time sleeping outside on the hard ground, and enduring harsh weather while chasing murderers and thieves all over the Territories.

Taking up his reins again, Bass rode his mare around the hotel to the small livery behind the building. The alley between the hotel and the dry goods store next door was narrow and the ground was mushy. The horses' hooves slapped through small puddles.

The hotel's back door popped open and yellow light spilled out through the rain and across the muddy ground.

Out of habit because it was night and the movement was sudden, Bass's right hand slipped under his slicker and dropped to the Colt Model P .44 leathered butt forward on his right hip. He wouldn't have admitted it had anything to do with the stories his posseman had told.

"Marshal Bass," a man yelled. He raised a lantern. "It's Fox. Don't shoot. Thought you might like some light while you put your horses away."

"Come ahead," Bass said and took his hand from the pistol. "The light will be appreciated."

Holding the lantern up to one side, Quick Fox trotted to the livery with his free hand shading his eyes.

Bass dismounted and led the mare into the shelter. Fox's lantern lit up the interior. A half-dozen horses in paddocks stamped and snorted at the intrusion. The storm had them spooked too. Another half-dozen paddocks sat empty. Not many travelers were staying at the High Hill Hotel tonight.

Bass left the first paddock for Alfred's horse and took the next in line.

Bass stripped his saddle from the mare and carried it to the tack posts near the entrance. "Is Mrs. Hundey here?"

"Yeah. Her an' the Lighthorseman rode in a couple days ago. The Lighthorseman got a telegram that said they were supposed to wait for you. Me an' Emerson put them up in rooms." Quick Fox was slim and rangy and in his thirties. He'd been ten years younger than Josephine, who was a handful of years younger than Emerson.

Bass grabbed a towel from a peg on the wall and wiped down his saddle. "Is Mrs. Hundey doing okay?"

"Looks scared as a long-tailed cat in a room full of rockers." Quick Fox held his lantern up high enough that it shined over the paddocks where Bass and Alfred tended their mounts.

The lantern light revealed the tension stamped onto the young Choctaw man's face. He'd left his long black hair loose and it had gotten wet. It hung over his shoulders. He wore bib-and-brace denim dungarees that showed wear and tear from the carpentry work he and Emerson still did. He held the lantern in his left hand and the light revealed the blackened thumbnail on that hand.

"That woman got reason to be so scared?" Fox asked.

"Maybe."

"I know her husband got tore apart. If I was her, that would be enough to scare me."

"Seen him?"

Fox shook his head. "I don't want to see anything like that. A couple other Lighthorsemen brought the body in about an hour after the missus arrived with the first one. It's over to the undertaker's."

"The body was in pieces?"

"That's what they said. I got to admit, that was more than I wanted to know."

Alfred placed his saddle on the tack wall and grabbed another towel.

"Way I hear it," Fox said, "afore Bud Hundey got killed, somebody done put a hex on him."

Alfred paused in toweling his horse down. The old man frowned. Bass figured maybe those stories the posseman had taken such delight in were working against him now.

"We didn't hear about a hex," Alfred said. "Who told you there was a hex involved in all this?

"The Lighthorsemen who brought in Hundey's body said there was hexes writ in blood all over the walls of that house."

"They know about hexes?"

"One of 'em is Lighthorseman named Fieldstone. He said he knew hexes."

Bass knew Fieldstone enough to say hello in passing.

Alfred gazed at Bass. "Seems like that would have been something worth mentioning in the judge's telegram."

"It was a telegram," Bass said. Irritation bothered his stomach. "Not a book."

"Hexes can be troubling things," the posseman mused. "I once knew a Seminole medicine man who could take away warts and raise blood blisters in a man's eyes."

"Blood blisters in a man's eyes?" Fox's eyes were wide, and he dropped his hand to the belt knife he wore.

"That's what I was told," Alfred said. "I never saw it. They said after a few days, his eyeballs just exploded and ran out of his head."

Fox drew back a little. "Somethin' like that is real?"

"As real as a lot of other things I've seen. I suppose it would do a man good to watch out for such things."

"Ain't no such thing as a hex," Bass growled.

Alfred was having fun at the younger man's expense. At least, he hoped the posseman was. That was a story he would have remembered if Alfred had told it.

"Those hexes was writ on that man's walls," Fox insisted. "Everybody in town was talkin' about them. An' how Bud Hundey was killed in a locked room where nobody could have done it."

The story about the hexes was an aspect about the current assignment that Bass was leery of. He wasn't a big believer of the supernatural, but, when he could, he fought shy of any of it that might come his way. There was no sense in taking chances when he didn't have to.

"Don't be talking about hexes to the deputy marshal," Alfred admonished Fox in mock seriousness.

"Is it a secret?" Fox asked. "Because that Lighthorseman said plenty about it."

"It isn't a secret," Alfred said. "Not exactly. We didn't even know about it. But the deputy marshal doesn't much care for the subject."

"That's because I've seen some things now an' again," Bass grumbled. He shot Alfred a glance. "Probably stuff the like of which you've never seen."

"I don't know about that," the posseman said. "I had a cousin who kept a headless chicken for months."

"A headless chicken?" Fox asked. "What happened to its head?"

"Got chopped off one day when the family was going to put him in a pot," Alfred said. "It was my cousin's favorite chicken. It got picked for Sunday dinner by mistake. His granny was getting on in years and was losing some of her vision. It was a simple mistake. My cousin found the chicken after it lost its head, but it was still breathing through that hole in its neck, so he took care of it. He figured it would die, but it didn't."

"Don't that beat all? How did it eat?"

"He put food and water into that hole."

"That kept the chicken alive?"

Alfred nodded. "It did. For months. Times got hard and they put it in a pot anyway."

"I've never heard of anything like that," Fox said. "When we were younger, me an' Emerson went down to New Orleans. Josephine wanted to go shoppin' as part of her honeymoon. Me an' Emerson just wanted to see everythin' we could. We went to a voodoo show an' watched a young woman fine as could be sittin' on a chair in a tent. She was bitin' the heads off snakes."

Bass had seen things like that too. Some of the folks in the mountain country here kept old ways that had followed them out of Louisiana and Florida. And there were granny women who'd come out of the Appalachian Mountains of Kentucky and Tennessee who held similar practices and herbal remedies. All of them had stories that had scared Bass as a young boy, and that left him uncomfortable as a full-grown man.

Quick Fox held up his lantern and peered into Bass's face. "Do you think there's anythin' to this hex business, Marshal?"

"I reckon we're gonna see." Bass slid his Winchester rifle and ten-gauge Greener shotgun free of the saddle scabbards and draped his saddlebags over one shoulder. He adjusted his hat, gazed at the downpour on the other side of the stable doorway, and regretted having to step out into the hard rain.

Next to him, Alfred yanked his own long guns from their scabbards. Evidently the old man wasn't taking any chances with hexes either.

"That shotgun ain't gonna cut much hay against a ghost," Bass pointed out.

"I believe the spirits of our ancestors still walk among us," Alfred said, "but I don't believe in ghosts. I've never seen one and, old as I am, I would

"Do you think there's anythin' to this hex business, Marshal?"

have before now."

"Thought your head was filled up with them notions your Elders fed you."

Alfred's eyes narrowed. "Hex or not, somebody out there has killed a man. These guns will handle whoever did that."

Following Quick Fox, Bass stepped out of the livery. Driven by the rain, the chill sank into him,. He hadn't thought he could get any wetter, but he was soaked, and rain ran down his slicker.

A sudden stitch of lightning threaded the black cloth of the stormy sky. Thunder followed and shook the earth.

Hexed or not, Mrs. Hundey wasn't going anywhere tonight. None of them were. That thought didn't sit well with Bass. He'd never thought of the High Hill Hotel as a trap before, but the thought occurred to him now.

"Evenin', Marshal," Kurt Emerson greeted.

Short and powerful, clad in dungarees and a flannel shirt, the man stood in the doorway of the small office to the left side of the building beyond the entrance. He wore a red beard with gray sprinkled in that hung to his chest.

"Evenin', Kurt," Bass said. "Hope we didn't keep you up."

"Hard to sleep in a storm like this," Emerson said. "An' when you an' Alfred got in, I wanted to be up to get you squared away. Been a while since we seen you. Me an' Fox was readin' some of Edgar Allan Poe's short stories around the potbelly stove in here. This here's the weather for it." He jerked a thumb over his shoulder at the stove and two chairs near the small desk. "We've only just started 'The Fall of the House of Usher,' so you two can grab a cup of coffee an' join us if you've a mind to."

"Poe?" Bass frowned. "He's that horror writer from back East."

"Yes." Emerson reached back and picked up a pipe from the desk. A fat book lay on the desktop beside it. "Interestin' story about them Usher folks. Me an' Fox have read it lots of times."

"Picked a strange night to be revistin' somethin' like that," Bass said.

Emerson grinned and breathed out a cloud of smoke. "Only if you believe the dead can get up walk around. Me an' Fox don't, but we've heard some stories tonight from the Lighthorsemen that kind of rekindled the interest."

"So I've heard. You got two rooms?"

"You can have rooms two and five on the second floor. You know the way."

"I do," Bass said. "Where is Mrs. Hundey?"

"Room three. I put Robert Tall Bear in room four. He's the Lighthorseman stayin' on till you an' Alfred got here to take over. Your rooms are in the middle of the second floor so you an' Alfred bookend her. Thought maybe that would suit you."

"I know Bob Tall Bear," Bass said. The Lighthorseman was a solid police officer and had been around for years. "Are the two of them still up?"

"Probably. Tall Bear is sittin' with Mrs. Hundey. She's takin' her husband's death mighty hard. I took a fresh pot of coffee up to them not quite an hour ago."

"Can me an' Alfred get a pot of coffee? I need somethin' to push the chill out of my bones."

"I don't need it," Alfred said. "I'm still tough as leather, but I do like the taste of coffee, so if you have it, I'll drink it."

"You surely can have a pot," Emerson said. "I'll brew a fresh pot an' bring it up to you. Need anything else?"

"You got bread and meat? When we got the judge's telegram a few hours ago, me an' Alfred lit out. Too wet out for most of the trip to even eat jerky. My stomach's shakin' hands with my backbone."

"I can do better than bread and meat. When me an' Fox heard you was comin', we put on a large pot of stew. It's Josie's recipe."

"She always made good stew," Bass said.

"That she did." Emerson's eyes misted a little. "On some nights, I swear I can still feel her here. Like all I gotta do is turn the corner quick enough an' I'll see her." He shook his head. "Ain't that somethin'?"

"Yeah," Bass said, "that's somethin' all right." He hoped he didn't run into Josephine Many Stars now that she was dead, and he blamed Alfred for putting such a notion in his head.

"I'll bring up the coffee," Emerson said. "Won't be any time at all. After you're finished talkin' with Mrs. Hundey, you an' Alfred can eat all the stew you want. I'll fry up some fresh cornbread to go with it."

"Me an' Alfred are gonna take a minute to get into some dry clothes. Can I get the coffee after that?"

"I'll listen for you."

"Thanks, Kurt."

Long guns in hand, Bass climbed the narrow stairs to the hotel's second floor. His boots thudded on the steps and the noise emphasized how empty the hotel was.

He took the corner at the top of the stairs where a large window on the back wall overlooked the town behind the hotel. He walked a little slower than usual. Just in case Josephine Many Stars was checking on things.

"I went into the room, Marshal," Elleanor Hundey said. "When I saw Bud laying there, I had to get into the room to him to see if I could help. I had to break a window to get in because the door was locked. It does that sometimes. My husband put a latch on it so we could keep the animals out. They tend to try to crowd in."

"The latch closed by itself?" Bass asked.

"Sometimes when the door hits just right, it happens. I had to break the latch to get inside."

That was one mystery solved, and it took away some of the supernatural aspects of the murder. "You tried to help your husband?"

"I did." Elleanor shook her head. "I couldn't, of course. Help him, I mean. I could see that I couldn't help him. I just couldn't accept it."

She sat in a straight-backed chair next to the room's potbelly stove. The metal coffee pot Emerson had brought up sat on the stove so it could stay warm. The scent of coffee filled the room and warmed it a little.

A lantern on the wall threw yellow light over the room that contained a bed and four chairs. Emerson and Fox had brought up the chairs for the meeting. With the woman, Bob Tall Bear, Alfred, and Bass occupying the chairs in a loose circle, the room was full to bursting. Bass was grateful for the potbelly stove, though, because it was still raining and cold outside.

Elleanor Hundey was in her late twenties, a thin birdlike woman with claw like hands made rough from plowing and caring for livestock alongside her husband. Her brunette hair was pulled back under a scarf. The dark green dress she wore was a little large on her, but not much.

Bass suspected the woman wasn't wearing her own clothing, probably because her own clothing was wet, and maybe covered in her husband's blood. The dress might have been one Josephine Many Stars had worn.

He was glad the woman hadn't been walking the hallway. If he'd seen her, he might have thought she was Josephine Many Stars because the two women favored one another. After all of Alfred's stories, he wasn't wishful of that experience. Even after learning the door latch probably closed on its own.

"I'm sorry, ma'am." Bass looked at the woman and pushed away the guilt that threatened to flay him. He adjusted his grip on the tin cup of coffee in his hands and soaked up the warmth it afforded. "I'm going to have to ask you some uncomfortable questions. I apologize for that."

"That's fine. You go ahead on and ask." Heat gleamed in Elleanor Hundey's dark eyes above the tears. "I want you to catch whoever murdered my husband. He didn't have that coming, and I'm not some shrinking Violet to shy from talking about what happened to him. I helped my husband butcher hogs when it was time. If I can help you now, I will. I'm not a weak woman. I never have been."

"Yes, ma'am. Was your husband still alive when you found him?"

Elleanor hesitated a moment. She fixed the deputy marshal with a hard stare. "No. How could he be alive in that kind of shape? Have you seen him?"

Bass shook his head. "No, ma'am, I have not. I've still got that to do."

The woman's body shook and tears streamed down her face. "You'll know as soon as you do that there was no chance of him being alive. No man torn up like that could survive. When I found him, he was already gone. I knew that. Even after I saw him, after I saw what had been done, I just didn't want to accept it. I couldn't."

The woman's features were familiar to Bass, and the certainty that they'd met nagged at him. He'd seen her before, but he just couldn't remember where. He was good with faces, but maybe this woman had changed since he'd last seen her.

Or maybe she wasn't the woman he was trying to remember.

"No one was around the house?" Bass asked.

"No. It was just Bud and me. It's only been Bud and me since we got hitched three years ago."

Alfred made a note of that in the journal he carried. He was the notetaker of the two of them, but Bass knew between them, the old man and he remembered most everything that was said in an interview with folks—even if it was years later. Remembering was a skill that came natural to him, and he'd had to shine it up to work in Judge Parker's courts where he offered testimony on a regular basis.

"When your husband was killed, where were you?" Bass asked.

"I was over to the neighbors. Isabel Folsom had a baby boy a few months ago. He was colicky. I know how that can wear down a new mother. I took her some food and watched over the baby for a few hours so she could sleep." Elleanor's breath hitched. "Bud and I never were lucky enough to have children. We kept hoping."

Bass sipped his coffee and let that regret sit for a moment. It would haunt the woman for a time. Those things always did.

"Did your husband have any enemies?" Bass asked.

Elleanor shook her head and stifled a sob. "No. Why would he? Bud was a good man. A simple man. He loved me and I loved him. When he hadn't any reason to do it, he loved me, brought me out here, and gave me a good life." Her voice broke and pierced Bass's heart. "He didn't have to do that, but he did. That's why I loved him so much."

Bass waited and gave her a moment to collect herself. "Any strangers around the farm lately?"

"No. Nobody. The way we are out in the woods off to ourselves, someone has to ride out that way deliberately. They had to know we were there. And if they knew that, they also knew Bud and I didn't have much."

"Was anythin' taken?"

"Not that I could see. I didn't look around much. I was concerned with Bud. When I saw that he was gone, I just didn't—" Elleanor dropped her gaze, took a breath, and clasped her hands more tightly. She looked up again. "Marshal, I don't even remember getting here, and Lighthorseman Tall Bear tells me we've been here two days."

Bass gazed out the room's window where the rain still fell in sheets. Looking for tracks out around the Hundey home would be a waste of time. He lamented that because he and Alfred were good trackers.

The house and those hexes were still there to see, though, but that could wait till morning.

"Marshal," Elleanor said.

He looked at her. "Ma'am?"

"Promise me that you'll get that monster that killed Bud."

Bass nodded. "Yes, ma'am, I'll surely promise you that."

After Bass finished the interview with Elleanor Hundey, he wished her good night and took the coffeepot with him. The coffee was almost gone, but there was enough left for a couple cups for Alfred and him to have with their meal.

Bob Tall Bear followed Alfred out of the room and joined them at the end of the hallway where the stairs ended. They stood at the landing just in front of a large window that overlooked the town behind the hotel.

The Lighthorseman was just short of six feet tall and in his mid-thirties. He was compact and rawboned. He wore his hair long and pulled back in a queue. His features were sharp edges, tight flesh over bone. His mouth looked small on him, but his eyes saw everything. The red ribbon in his slouch hat looked fresh and clean. Tall Bear took a lot of pride in his job and himself.

"That woman was lucky," Tall Bear said.

"How's that?" Bass asked. He didn't see any kind of luck for Elleanor Hundey in what had happened.

"When her husband was killed, she wasn't there. If she had been, she wouldn't be here now."

"And no one would have known what happened," Alfred said.

"Did she go for help?" Bass asked.

"No," Tall Bear answered. "After Mrs. Hundey left the Folsom house, Nick Folsom, the husband, sent one of his boys over to help Bud Hundey lay in some wood. They helped each other like that."

"So the boy was with her?"

Tall Bear nodded.

"Tell me about him."

"He's fourteen, seems like he has a good head on his shoulders."

"You talked to him?"

"I did. Briefly. He didn't see anything that Mrs. Hundey wouldn't let him see."

"Did he go in the house?" Bass asked.

"No. She wouldn't allow it. She didn't want him to see anything that bad. But he peeked through the window. He was pretty shook up."

"Where's he now?"

"Back with his parents. At his father's direction, he rode for the Lighthorsemen over to Albion and brought us back. The department contacted Judge Parker."

Bass sipped his coffee. "They did. And the judge sent me to get to the bottom of this. You've been here two days with the missus?"

"I have."

"You still good to stand watch over her?"

"I am."

"Does she have any family around here?"

"She hasn't said."

"In the morning, try to find out."

"I will."

"I appreciate it, Bob."

"Of course." Tall Bear jerked a thumb over his shoulder. "I'm going to get on back to her. She doesn't sleep so well at night. I can't do anything for her but sit there."

"Sometimes that's all that's needed," Alfred said.

Bass shook hands with the Lighthorseman and Tall Bear went back to Elleanor Hundey's room. The deputy and the posseman headed down the stairs.

"You got that look," Alfred said.

"What look?"

"The one that says something's on your mind."

"I'm thinking about that stew we were promised."

"That's not all you're thinking about."

Bass sighed. "I want to go to bed before I have to go look at that dead man."

"Me too," the posseman said, "but that's not what we're going to do, is it?"

Bass shook his head. "Nope, it ain't. You reckon that rain has let up any?"

Outside, lightning flashed and lit the window at the end of the hallway. Thunder shook the hotel.

"Nope," Alfred said.

The undertaker's small establishment stood between the town church and the blacksmith's shop across the street and down the block from the hotel. The arrangement with the three businesses made sense. Folks could get their dead prayed over if they were of a mind to, then buried in a coffin made by the undertaker that sported ironwork forged by the blacksmith.

Judging by the names on the undertaker's and blacksmith's shops, Quentin Teaberry—Undertaker and Marvin Teaberry—Blacksmith, both were family businesses. That was probably convenient too. Bass wasn't familiar with the Teaberry names in Goodland, but he'd crossed paths with Teaberrys before.

When the wind changed and brought the rain in from another direction, Bass dipped his hat to block it and rapped his knuckles against the undertaker's door. The thudding echoed inside the building. Images of caskets, some empty and some not, filled Bass's head.

He gripped the Winchester in his left hand a little more tightly.

Alfred stood behind him and watched the empty street. Rainwater eddied in the overflowed wagon wheel ruts. Water gurgled and ran all around them. The town looked like it was drowning.

"Who is it?" a man yelled from the other side of the door.

"United States Marshal Deputy Bass Reeves," Bass said. "Came to see Bud Hundey's body."

The door opened with a screech and revealed a big man wearing brown saddle pants and scuffed mule ear boots that were mostly clean of fresh mud. He held a Colt Single Action .44 in his right hand. A younger man dressed in the same manner stood a little to one side of the door and held a shotgun canted on his right hip.

"Evening, Bass," the big Lighthorseman greeted.

"Evening, Koi," Bass said. "Is it all right if we step in?"

"Come ahead," Koi Fieldstone said. He stepped back and opened the door wider. "That's a real toad strangler coming down out there. Wouldn't wish it on my mother-in-law. I spotted rats in back of the building who were building an ark."

"There are *no* rats in this building," an irate man declared.

Carrying a lantern, the man stepped from the back of the undertaker's shop. He wore a dressing gown over pajamas. He looked clean and fastidious even this late in the evening. His tall stovepipe boots didn't match his outfit.

The lantern light glowed brightly and lifted the shadows from the six coffins that almost filled the big room. A potbelly stove created a small pool of light in the back of the room, and the smell of old coffee warred with the scent of lilacs, alcohol, and other medicines Bass couldn't identify.

Two of the coffins were open and empty. Bass hoped the four that were closed were empty too, but he wasn't interested in having a look. Bud Hundey might not be the only customer in the undertaker's shop at the moment.

"It's bad enough that I have you two louts in here," the man declared, "without you besmirching my business by mentioning rats. I'll have you know I keep the premises very clean."

Fieldstone nodded in the man's direction. "That's Quentin Teaberry, the undertaker. He's been complaining about me and Obediah being here since we arrived two days ago. After a while, you don't even hear him any more."

Teaberry strode over to Bass and only halted when the deputy marshal shifted the Winchester into the space between them. The move wasn't threatening, it was just remindful.

"You're the reason I've got that bloody jigsaw puzzle in my back room," Teaberry accused.

Relieved that he knew where the body was and he wouldn't have to open caskets, Bass relaxed a little.

"That body's evidence," he declared in his marshal's voice, and it was big enough to fill the small shop, "and it's here because Judge Isaac Parker wanted it to be here. You want to argue that point, you take it up with the judge."

Teaberry swallowed and took a step back. "I wasn't told about Judge Parker. I was only given your name."

"I work for Judge Parker," Bass said.

"I told him that," Fieldstone said. "Problem is, Mr. Teaberry doesn't much hear anything he doesn't want to hear."

"This is my place of business," Teaberry accused. "I don't just allow anyone to drop off a body here." He flicked his glance to the two Lighthorsemen. "And this sure isn't a hotel."

Fieldstone ignored the man. "Me and Obediah got a room over to the High Hill. We've been sleeping in shifts. We knew you were coming in tonight. Figured you might want to talk to both of us, so we stayed here to see you if you came on over."

"Tomorrow would have been more convenient," Teaberry stated.

"Bud Hundey's not gonna worry about convenience no more," Bass growled. "His widow, on the other hand, she wants to know who killed her man. So we're gonna look into that."

Teaberry took a cautious step back.

"I told him he could have gone on home," Fieldstone said. "The problem is, he sleeps upstairs."

"Now that's something I wouldn't do," Alfred said.

Bass silently agreed. He'd done his share of sitting up with the dead, but doing that on a regular basis wasn't appealing in any way whatsoever.

"I'd have probably got him up anyway," Bass said. "Especially when I heard how cantankerous and unwelcoming he's been to you all."

"You're not in a position to tell me what to do," Teaberry said, and he almost had a spine in the words.

"Tell that to Judge Parker. He's probably gonna frown on your treatment of lawmen representing his interests too. Could be you'll get a summons to visit his court in Fort Smith."

Teaberry swallowed, turned pale, and his antagonism and tinhorn view of himself evaporated. His shoulders slumped. "I'd rather not deal with that."

Bass waved the Winchester to the back of the building. "You said the body's back there?"

The undertaker swallowed hard and nodded. "It is."

"Let's go have a look."

Reluctantly, Teaberry took the lead.

"I'll do the best job I can with the body when the time comes," Teaberry said. "Mrs. Hundey is a fine woman and deserves the best."

Judge Parker's court was footing the bill and would oversee the work too, so the undertakers promise didn't much impress Bass. The body, on the other hand, left quite the impression.

Over his years as a lawman, Bass Reeves had seen all manner of evil men could do to others. He'd seen horrible deaths of men, women, and children, and none of those poor unfortunates ever quite left his mind. Some nights he woke up in a cold sweat. At times in those small hours right before the dawn, when she found him like that, his wife fussed over him and asked him what the problem was, but there were some things a lawman couldn't share with the woman he loved.

Partially covered by chunks of ice to preserve the body, Bud Hundey lay in pieces on a slanted wooden table in the small back room of the undertaker's shop, and it wasn't the worst thing Bass Reeves had ever seen. The corpses that were left out in the wilderness for days were the worst.

But this body came close.

Water, still carrying a tint of reddish brown two days later, ran from the body and the ice and dripped into two large tin pails at the bottom of the table. The chill from the ice leached away the warmth Bass had struggled to hang onto after crossing the rain-swept street.

Bud Hundey had been tortured for some time, then killed. He'd been decapitated, had his hands, feet, legs, and arms hacked off by something sharp and heavy. The joints had been cut through, but not with any care. They'd been bludgeoned with what looked like a cleaver.

In life, Hundey had been a broad-shouldered man with thick brown hair and a little heavier than he should have been. His hands, laid together instead of at the ends of his arms as they should have been, were rough and callused from hard years of managing a farm. His feet were still in his boots.

Whoever had killed Bud Hundey had also covered him in sigils and symbols the like of which seemed familiar to Bass.

The deputy marshal took the lantern from Teaberry and leaned in closer over the body. On the other side of the table, Alfred leaned in too. Bass steeled himself and raked a fingernail over one of the small pictures. The line he touched broke and scraped off.

"Wrote on him in charcoal." Bass wiped his finger on his handkerchief, and he was glad it was wet with the rain. He put the handkerchief back in the pocket of his slicker.

"Somebody spent some time at it," Alfred said.

"You ever seen anything like this?" Bass asked.

The posseman hesitated for a moment. "Maybe. Might have been in New Orleans or in Mexico City."

Bass gazed at his posseman in surprise. "You've been to those places?"

"There was a time," Alfred said, "when you and I didn't ride together. I rode a lot of places. You think I sat home waiting for some deputy marshal to ride by and offer me a job as his posseman?"

"Well...no." Bass didn't know what he'd thought. He and Alfred kept busy enough that he didn't have much time for such wondering. He'd just figured he'd known everything there was to know about the man. *Most* of the important things anyway.

Alfred took out his journal and sketched some of the marks on Bud Hundey's scattered body.

"What do you think they are?" Bass asked.

"Important to somebody," Alfred replied.

Bass frowned. "I meant—"

"I know what you meant," Alfred said impatiently. "Have you seen anything like these symbols?"

Bass scratched his stubbled jaw. "Could be. I was down in Texas chasing an outlaw and ended up riding on into Juarez."

"A man can see a lot of things in Juarez."

"Saw a couple of things that almost got me killed. But there was a woman

"Wrote on him in charcoal."

there who read fortunes. Offered to tell me my future. Said sometimes she could see the day when a man was gonna die."

"Did you take her up on that?"

"No. I want to be surprised."

"Me too," Alfred agreed. "Surprised, and a lot older."

"That woman was giving a bed to the man I was chasing. I caught him there. Some of the marks I saw in that backroom that woman worked out of put me in the mind of these marks." Bass nodded at the dead man.

"Did you find out what the woman was?"

Bass thought it was strange Alfred asked about *what*, not *who*, but *what* was actually more to the point. "Man I arrested said she was a witch, that she was gonna put a curse on me for fetching him."

"Did she?"

"She pulled a knife on me. Maybe she figured it would do more good. I punched her and left her laying there. Got on back to Fort Smith quick as I could."

"Have you ever met a witch?" Alfred asked.

Bass narrowed his gaze. "You believe in witches?"

Alfred shrugged. "The Elders talked about them. The Elders always said witches were some of the worst things a man could ever run across."

"Met some who claimed to be witches. Met some other folks claimed was witches. Granny women from back in the hills have tended me now and again with salves and potions that worked mighty fine. I've heard them called witches."

"Then you haven't met a witch. Granny women know root magic and how to heal. A true witch knows how to kill a man with magic."

Bass waited for a moment, thinking Alfred was just poking fun at him. Only the posseman remained deathly serious. Bass asked, "Have you ever met one?"

Before Alfred could reply, if he was going to answer the question, thunder pealed outside, and the front door of the undertaker's shop blew open and banged against the wall. Rain swept in and dappled the floor.

"You didn't shut the door properly!" Teaberry squalled.

Before his words died away, a gunshot shattered the hammering rain. Two more followed. Two bullets struck the wall that separated the front of the shop from the back room. The third bullet hammered a casket and sent wood chips flying.

A man wearing a hood stepped inside the undertaker's shop with a rifle at his shoulder. Two more hooded men standing out on the boardwalk flanked him with rifles. They stepped forward as well. The lead man fired, and the muzzle flash, trapped inside the front of the shop, banished the darkness in the room for an instant.

The bullet whizzed by Bass's ear and slammed into the wall somewhere behind him.

Near the door, Teaberry yelped and hunkered in on himself.

Alfred stepped in front of the man and dropped his Greener into position before him. Both barrels pointed at the entrance. The man at the shop door levered the action on his rifle.

Bass grabbed the undertaker by the scruff of the neck and hauled him back and to the side out of the way. Teaberry fell to his butt and scooted backward into one of the tin pails collecting water and blood from the melting ice and Bud Hundey's body.

Alfred touched off one of the shotgun's barrels and the large pellets blew the rifleman back through the door. A heartbeat later, Alfred fired the second barrel and dropped another gunman half on the boardwalk and half in the street.

Stepping back to one side of the door to the back room, Alfred broke the shotgun open. He plucked the two spent cartridges from the barrels and reached for fresh ones from his pocket.

"Give me a minute," Alfred said.

The third man sprinted out into the street and Bass sighted on him through the shop's window. He squeezed the trigger and the man sprawled face first into the street.

"Catch up," Bass said, and he levered a fresh cartridge into the rifle.

Winchester in hand, Bass ran for the front door. More gunshots split the night air and echoed inside the undertaker's shop. Three saddled horses strained at the hitching post out front.

Out on the street, at least two dozen men on horses fired rifles and shotguns at the High Hill Hotel. The bright muzzle flashes tore slashes through the darkness and briefly illuminated the gunmen. Like the men who had attacked the undertaker's shop, hoods covered their faces. Their horses milled around nervously.

Overhead, the dark clouds swirled, and the wind changed directions in a heartbeat. The hair on the back of Bass's neck stood because he could guess what was coming with the shifting winds. Weather in the Territories was an uncertain thing and often altered as quick as grease shot through a goose.

Emerson and Fox fired from the hotel's office window and their muzzle flashes lit up the small room. One of them doused the lantern and plunged the space into darkness.

Bob Tall Bear fired from the upstairs hallway window. At least, that's who the gunman had to be.

Standing in the middle of the muddy street that was loose and slippery under his boots, Bass pulled his Winchester to his shoulder, sighted along the barrel through the rain, and slid his finger over the trigger.

"United States Deputy Marshal!" Bass announced. Shooting a man without warning didn't set well with him. "Throw down your—"

A handful of the men turned their weapons on Bass. Bullets slammed into the mud around him and splashed water into his face and eyes. Half-blinded from grit, Bass freed the reins of one of the horses in front of the undertaker's shop. Moving quickly, he pulled the horse along beside him so it created a wall of flesh between the gunmen and himself.

He ran for the dark hulk of the general store on the other side of the street. Staying bunched up with Alfred at the undertaker's wasn't smart. His boots took on more mud with every stride and threatened to slide out from under him. Bullets chopped quick craters in the street and tore through posts holding up the small eaves in front of the general store.

At least one round struck the horse and the animal stumbled and tried to bolt. Bass held onto the reins and ran faster, but he didn't let his moving cover get away.

Tucked into the undertaker's building, Alfred fired his shotgun from the alley between that structure and the blacksmith's.

One of the men yelled in surprised pain, lost his rifle, and desperately gripped his saddle horn. He reined his horse around and spurred for the edge of town.

Alfred fired again and another man dropped into the street. The other horses stepped on a fallen rider and stumbled. One horse dropped to its knees for just a moment, then pushed back to its feet. Bullets chased Alfred back into the alley. He leaned against the structure and plucked the empty cartridges from the shotgun.

Blood jumped from the horse's neck and splashed hotly against Bass's face. He resisted the impulse to sleeve the blood away and concentrated on maintaining control of the horse and crossing the street. Ten feet from the general store, the horse stumbled again and went down. Abandoning the horse, Bass threw himself forward and reached the building. Bullets hammered the front of the general store only a few feet from his position.

Braced against the general store, Bass turned his face up into the rain and let it wash the grit from his eyes. Blinking his eyes clear, ignoring the stinging sensation, he wheeled around the edge of the building, lined up the rifle's sights, and shot into the crowd. One of the men slumped forward and bleated in pain.

Fieldstone and Obediah fired from the alley on the other side of the undertaker's building. Two of the riders tried to hang onto their horses, but they went down into the street. A hail of bullets from the riders tore splinters from the corner of the undertaker's building and sent the Lighthorsemen ducking for cover.

"*Vamanos!*" a woman yelled above the noise of the gunfire and the storm.

Like a swarm of bees, the men attacking the High Hill Hotel turned and galloped toward Bass. The deputy marshal stared into the approaching mass and tried to spot the woman giving orders, but he saw no such woman. Her presence caught him by surprise, but it also stirred some memories.

The riders and horses with empty saddles blended in the lightning, the gunfire, and the rising winds. They were a mass of shifting shadows where muzzle flashes bloomed brightly and bloomed again.

Bass held his ground. Bullets chipped the corner of the building and splintered the wooden sides. He levered a new cartridge into the Winchester. Around him, Alfred and the two Lighthorsemen fired again and again. Blood jumped from wounds the riders received, but only one more rider fell.

Sights settled on one of the lead riders, Bass squeezed the rifle's trigger and watched the man's head snap back. During the brief lull in the gunfire, Bass ran for the front of the small general store and hoped to find a better position. If they caught him in the alley, he'd be a sitting duck. When the retreating riders rode past him, his position would be exposed.

Bass threw himself onto the wooden boardwalk in front of the mercantile and took cover behind a rocking chair and a small keg that was probably used as a table. Another fusillade of bullets shattered the rocking chair and the store windows. Broken slats and glass spilled across Bass. He covered his head with his arms to keep the glass from his face and neck.

Muzzle flashes flamed out of the alleys on the other side of the street.

After taking a quick moment to make sure he hadn't been hit, which surprised him to no small degree, Bass sat up and levered another cartridge into the rifle. He peered through the sights at the retreating riders melting into the darkness. He didn't shoot because he couldn't be certain of the shot at the distance in the darkness. A heartbeat later and the riders disappeared into the stormy night.

"Hey!" Alfred yelled. "You still alive over there?"

The old man stepped out of the alley.

"Yeah." Bass pushed himself to his feet and stood. His mud-caked boots felt like anvils.

"You hit?"

Bass shook his head, then realized Alfred probably couldn't see him in the darkness. "Don't see how, but they missed me. You?"

"We're good," Alfred said. "Obediah caught a bullet through his side. Looks like it bounced off a rib though. He's going to be all right."

"See if Doc Raeborn's still in town."

"He is. When Mrs. Hundey arrived, Raeborn looked in on her. I already sent Fieldstone to fetch him. I'll get Obediah to the hotel. I told Fieldstone to have Raeborn meet us there. We can hold those riders off if they come back."

"Watch yourself in case they decide to come back before you get there. I'm going to look at these men in the street. See if I know any of them." Bass slogged out into the street and remained watchful. He had no idea why the group had attacked the High Hill Hotel.

Alfred lurched across the street with one of the young Lighthorseman's arms pulled over his shoulder.

The first hooded man lay facedown in a wagon rut filled with water. Bass squatted, ignored the way his dungarees sopped up the water, and grabbed the man by the shoulder. Since the man's face was in the water and he wasn't bubbling, he had to be dead.

Bass flipped the man over onto his back, then reached for the hood and tugged it off.

The dead man stared blankly up at the sky. He hadn't shaved in a few days, but the bushy mustache beneath his broken nose had been there for some time. An old scar halfway closed his left eye.

Bass recognized the man as Stanley Gull. He'd arrested the man once for a train robbery he'd committed with his twin brother, Earl.

"What are you doing here, Gull?" Bass mused. "Last I heard, you and your brother were out in Arizona Territory raising hell."

Despite the rain and the feeling that tonight's danger wasn't yet passed, Bass turned over three more men and removed their hoods. He didn't know two of them, but when lantern light fell over the third man, he recognized him easily enough.

"That's Les Gruber," Alfred said. He walked out into the rain and joined Bass in the street. He rested his Greener over one shoulder and carried a lantern in his free hand.

"It is," Bass agreed.

"With a big chunk of his nose missing like that, he's pretty easy to remember. After he slapped a saloon girl up in Dodge, she took it off him with a pocketknife."

"Yeah. That's the story I got too." Bass stood and strode to the next man. "Gruber dipped down into the Territories every now and again, but he fought shy of here for the most part."

"Because he liked saloons and there aren't any here."

"Everybody okay at the hotel?"

"Bob Tall Bear caught two in the leg. He'll be okay, but he won't be worth much in a stand-up fight for a while. He's having a hard time getting around. Emerson and Fox are fit to be tied after all the hotel's windows were shot out. They're keeping watch."

"What about Mrs. Hundey?"

"She's up there taking care of Bob Tall Bear till Doctor Raeborn gets here. She's one to ride the river with. She's not panicking and is taking care of Bob."

Bass walked toward another downed rider, but when he rolled the dead man over, he didn't know him. The man was awful young, but the owlhoot trail used up young men fast.

Alfred split off from Bass and rolled over another dead man. "This one is Chuck Locke. I've arrested him a few times."

"Locke was wanted for a couple stage holdups over in Alamosa, Colorado. He was running with Tupelo Nowlan."

"Here's Nowlan." Alfred held the lantern close to the latest dead man.

Nowlan had caught a bullet in one eye, but enough of his face remained that he was recognizable.

"How many men did you count in that group attacking the hotel?" Bass asked.

"Counting the men we shot in front of the undertaker's?"

"Yeah."

"Twenty-seven."

"I figured there were close to two dozen men."

"It was hard to keep count with all the bullets cutting through the air and them milling around like they were," Alfred admitted. "I might have counted a couple of them twice."

"And I might have missed a couple," Bass said. "They rode off pretty fast."

"We caught them on all sides, and all of us could shoot. Especially with them packed as tight as they were. They couldn't hold that position and whoever was in charge knew that."

"A woman," Bass said. "It was a woman in charge. I heard her."

He tried to recall her, but he couldn't. He didn't even know if she was wearing a hood. She had just been one of the riders.

But she had been leading them. A woman leading a pack of outlaws was a rarity. Bass should have known her. If he laid eyes on her again, he was confident he would recognize her.

Alfred knelt beside a man. "I've got one here that's still breathing."

Bass joined the posseman and together they carefully rolled the man over.

Alfred took the pistol from the man's holster and slipped it into the pocket of his slicker.

Bass pulled the hood from the man's head and Alfred leaned in closer with the lantern to reveal the man's features. He was young, Hispanic, and good looking. Blood wept from a pair of chest wounds that bracketed his heart. His breathing came in hoarse rasps and he blinked against the rain.

"You know him?" Bass asked.

Alfred shook his head. He picked up one of the man's hands and turned it over. "Does this help?"

A tattoo of five roses crossed into a star stood out on the back of the man's hand.

Tiny rodent's feet crept up Bass's spine, and the back of his neck turned hot despite the cold rain and blowing wind.

"Yeah," Bass said. The answer came out hoarse and strained. "It ain't help, exactly, because that there is a bad sign. I've only seen it once, but I know who came out here tonight, and I know what she wants. And she ain't gonna go away till she gets it."

Even though it was still raining hard, the wounded man opened his eyes and looked at Bass.

"Bass Reeves," the man rasped. He grinned dazedly. "The *bruja* is gonna get you. She raised a demon to come for you. An' when it's done, it's gonna drag you to Hell."

He laughed, then his eyes rolled back up into his head so only the whites showed and his body went limp.

"Is he dead?" Alfred asked.

Bass stared at the thready beat in the side of the man's neck. "He's not dead. Not yet. Let's get him inside and see if we can get him to talk some more."

Lightning flared and lifted the darkness from the street. Bass and Alfred carried the wounded man into the hotel. He knew where he'd met Mrs. Hundey, and how they'd come to meet.

Her name hadn't been Elleanor Hundey then, and she'd been in a whole lot of trouble at the time.

"Mrs. Hundey." Bass Reeves stood in the doorway of the hotel's dining room.

Located centrally in the building, the dining room only had one window that was now covered by heavy shutters used during storm seasons. A thick blanket had been thrown over the window to block the light of the lantern sitting on a side table.

The main table held Bob Tall Bear lying prone and in pain. His broad face was creased in agony and his eyes held dulled reflections of the light. His right dungarees leg had been crudely cut away to reveal two bullet wounds that were mostly covered by bandages. Blood stained his leg, his dungarees, the table, and the floor beside him.

Elleanor Hundey glanced up from her patient, but she never stopped tearing white sheets for bandages. "Yes, Marshal."

"Your name isn't Elleanor," Bass said.

The woman's eyes narrowed, and she pursed her lips. She tore another strip from the sheet she held in her fists.

"Forgive me, ma'am," Bass said. "I'm still running ragged from that gunfight and that came out wrong. Your name is Elleanor now, but it wasn't always. I met you a couple years ago, after that bank robbery in Haileyville. You were Rosalee Kickingbird then."

Elleanor took a breath and tied the new strip around Tall Bear's thigh. The big Lighthorseman grimaced a little, but he didn't make a sound.

"I left that name behind a long time ago," Elleanor stated coldly. "I met Bud and got married. We came out here and none of what happened then and there matters anymore."

"I'm afraid it does," Bass said.

The woman glared at him. "How?"

"Because of those men out there," Bass pointed toward the covered window with his hat. Water dripped from the hat to the floor. Not much of the dining room floor was dry at the moment. "I think they're following a woman named Rafaela Orozco."

"That name means nothing to me."

"Let me try another one. Francisco Calderón."

Elleanor blinked but remained silent.

"I remember him," Tall Bear said. His voice came out a little strained and thick. "Frisco Frank. He called himself that because at the start of his outlaw career he robbed a handful of Saint Louis-San Francisco Railway trains in Missouri. The Pinkertons started gunning for him and put a price on his head. He and his gang headed on down to the Territories and swapped over to robbing banks and stages."

Bass nodded. "That's him. You remember him now, Mrs. Hundey?"

The woman tore another strip from the sheet. "I do."

"Calderón and his men robbed the bank in Haileyville. You were there visiting your sister. You were living in Dallas at the time."

"I was living in Haileyville." Elleanor tied another strip of bandage to Tall Bear's leg and the room was so quiet the rustle of cloth was heard over the patter of rain against the side of the hotel. "I worked as a saloon girl in Dallas. I wasn't proud of the work, and it got me by, but I give it up. My sister had taken sick and needed help with her children. While I was there, I met Bud Hundey. He was working as a coal miner, but that wasn't what he wanted to do. Like with me being a saloon girl. We stayed there long enough to put some money together and came out here."

"That was after Calderón's trial," Bass said. "After you identified Calderón as the man who gunned down three people, a Lighthorseman and two innocents, in the street."

"It was. Calderón's mask slipped off and I saw his face plain as day. His face was hard and cruel. I doubt a smile ever lightened it. With that tattoo on his cheek—" Elleanor touched her face.

"A rose," Bass said.

"That's right. A rose." The woman shivered. "Well, I wasn't going to forget something like that."

"No, ma'am, I reckon not. You testified to that very fact in Judge Parker's court."

"When it happened, I was out in the street with my nieces and nephews. I was afraid we were going to be killed. Something like that sticks with you."

"Judge Parker ordered Calderón hanged for those murders because of your testimony and identification."

Elleanor swallowed. "Calderón was an evil man."

"Yes, ma'am, he was. I arrested Calderón and put him in Judge Parker's court. I was there the day Calderón was hanged. You did a good thing by testifying."

"What does that have to do with tonight? With what happened to Bud?"

"Frisco Frank had a woman," Bass said.

"Some said she was in league with the Devil himself," Tall Bear said. "She did all manner of dark spells and hexes against folks over in Louisiana, and even a few things here across the Kiamichi Mountains. I tracked her a few times, but I never caught her. I heard that after Frisco Frank was hanged and buried, she dug up his body and rode off with him in the dead of night."

Elleanor turned to the Lighthorseman. "She dug up his body?"

"Yes, ma'am," Tall Bear said.

"That's not been confirmed," Bass said.

The young gunman's words echoed in Bass's mind. *The* bruja *is gonna get you. She raised a demon to come for you. An' when it's done, it's gonna drag you to Hell.* Bass craned his neck against the sudden chill that crept across his shoulders.

"So she didn't dig him up?" Elleanor asked.

"Somebody dug that body up," Bass said. "Nobody saw who. Just the next morning, the new grave was found empty."

Thunder boomed outside.

"What does that have to do with me and Bud?" Elleanor whispered.

"When you identified Calderón in court that day," Bass said, "do you remember what he did?"

Elleanor didn't speak.

"He swore he'd get revenge on everybody." Bass spoke flatly. "I remember that. Promised he was going to kill Judge Parker, me, and you. Everybody that was involved with hanging him."

"I know. I didn't feel safe after that trial. When Bud and I came to Goodland, I changed my name because that man scared me something awful that day." Elleanor smoothed the sheet on her lap with trembling hands. "And I wanted to put my past in Dallas behind me. I didn't want anything of it clinging to me."

"Yes, ma'am. I can understand that, but I think what's going on now has something to do with that court trial."

"You think Calderón's out there? Is that what you're saying, Marshal?"

"No, ma'am," Bass answered. "I think that Calderón's woman is out there aiming to get revenge for her man. And I mean to put a stop to it."

"You aren't going to do it alone," Bob Tall Bear said. He gestured to Bass. "Give me a hand up."

"You think you're up to it?" Bass asked.

"I can stand," Tall Bear declared. "Now that I am not bleeding to death. And if I can stand, I can shoot."

Bass took hold of the man's hand and helped him to his feet. "Keep watch over Mrs. Hundey."

"We'll keep watch over each other," Elleanor said.

"Yes, ma'am, that would be fine. I'm going to see if I can find out anything more from our prisoner about that woman."

"He's awake," Doc Raeborn said quietly to Bass.

Stocky and powerful, gray around the temples now, and his eyes slightly magnified by his round-lensed glasses, Raeborn washed his bloody hands in a basin in the bedroom where the wounded outlaw lay gasping for breath on the narrow bed under Alfred's watch. Raeborn was in his late forties, fastidious and always dressed in trousers and a wool vest, even late at night.

"But I don't know how long you're going to have him," Raeborn continued. "That young man isn't going to survive his wounds. All I can do is make him comfortable."

"I appreciate it, Doc," Bass said.

Raeborn picked up his black medical bag. "I'm going to go have a look at those two wounded Lighthorsemen now."

Bass stepped aside so the man could walk through the door. Bass waited a beat, looked at the dying man lying handcuffed on the bed, and marshaled his thoughts. The laudanum Raeborn had given the man would help loosen the outlaw's tongue, but there was no telling what he would say.

Or if it would make sense.

Bass crossed over to the bed and glanced at Alfred.

"His name's Gilberto Orozco," the posseman said quietly.

Bass lifted an eyebrow.

"Rafaela's kid brother," Alfred said.

Grim certainty filled Bass and roiled in his stomach. "Then she ain't done with this," he said.

"I don't think so either." Alfred picked up his Greener from where it leaned against the wall behind him. "I'm going to go find a perch on the second floor to keep watch. Koi Fieldstone is already up there, but it wouldn't hurt to have another set of eyes."

Bass nodded.

Alfred left.

"Gilberto," Bass said in a louder voice.

Weakly, the wounded man turned his head toward Bass. A loopy grin filled his face and offset the pain and fear glittering in his eyes.

"Bass Reeves," Gilberto wheezed.

"Tell me about your sister, Rafaela."

The grin got bigger. "My sister's gonna kill you. Her an' Frisco. They're comin' for you."

"What is she doing here?"

Gilberto tried to reach his nose, but the handcuffs prevented him from achieving his goal. "My nose itches."

"Tell me about Rafaela. What's she doing in Goodland?"

Gilberto sighed in annoyance and gave up trying to reach his nose. "Came to kill that woman who testified against Frisco. Only she wasn't home. But her husband was." The prisoner laughed for a moment. "Ol' Frisco, he had himself a high time choppin' that man up. Never seen the like. Just kept choppin' an' choppin'. Rafaela had to make him stop. He sure didn't want to. That woman not bein' there made him mad."

"Why didn't Rafaela wait for Mrs. Hundey to get back?"

"On account of us not knowin' when she'd be back." Gilberto gurgled and fought for breath.

Guilt stung Bass because the young man was dying, and he couldn't give him peace. Dying should be something a man did under good circumstances.

"Then Rafaela," Gilberto said, "she got a new idea. Figured killin' Bud Hundey might draw you out. Especially once you figured out who the wife was. She said we was to leave that woman as bait."

"For what?"

"You, of course." Gilberto wheezed again, and the rasp was wet with desperation. "She knew you was supposed to be in Albion. We couldn't get to you there as easy as here, it bein' a bigger town an' all, so she said we

"Rafaela's kid brother."

would bring you here. Figured Judge Parker would send you to see what was goin' on. An' he did, didn't he? She had that figured right."

"How did Rafaela know Mrs. Hundey was here?"

"A few days back, one of Frisco's old crew saw that woman in town. He was coolin' off from a stage job he did over in Texas. He was from here as a boy, so he comes back every now an' again to lay low." Gilberto sucked in a breath and didn't get as much of it as he had the last time. "He knowed it was her an' he got word to Rafaela an' Frisco, an' here we come."

Just bad luck. Just like Mrs. Hundey seeing that bank robbery.

Bass drew in a breath. A lot of life was due to bad luck. A man had to work hard to change that. His own beginnings had been difficult, and he strove hard every day to keep his life right.

"Hell's comin' for you, Marshal. Frisco's gonna snatch you on up an' take you there screamin' the whole way." Gilberto tried to sing-song the threat, but with his wind failing, he couldn't quite pull it off. There was too much gurgling.

Then the gurgling ended, and the young outlaw breathed his last. His body relaxed and he stared at the ceiling with unseeing eyes.

Bass stared at the dead man. Cold emptiness swirled within him. He wanted to sleep, to be rested up before the fight continued.

"Hey Bass."

The marshal turned toward the voice. Emerson leaned through the doorway.

"Alfred said to come get you. Those gunmen are back."

Bass reseated his hat, took a firmer grip on his Winchester, and followed Emerson.

Goodland's streets remained dark. Thunder cascaded and lightning flashed farther to the east, on toward Missouri. The storm was passing.

But the killing was headed on back into the town from the west, like it followed as a second wave of storm.

The darkness allowed the arriving riders to be glimpsed only now and again. Bass stood to one side of the window overlooking Main Street and peered out. He tried to keep count of the horses and men, but he was sure he wasn't seeing everything.

"How many?" he asked.

"I don't know," Alfred answered. He stood on the other side of the window. The posseman held a Winchester and his Greener hung from a strap over his shoulder. "I see less than before, but I think that's a lie. I think they split up and we're only seeing maybe half of how many is really out there."

Bass blew out an angry breath. "So do I."

"It's what we would do. We've done it before. Only makes sense."

"I know."

"Rafaela and her men still have to take the hotel," Alfred said. "That's not going to be easy. Emerson and Fox built this place to last."

"I know, but we're going to be spread awful thin." Bass watched the riders that only showed up occasionally in their approach to the hotel. "We'll hold them outside the hotel as long as we can. When we have to, we'll surrender the ground floor and set ourselves up on the second floor. We can cover the stairs and some of the lower floor from the second-floor landing. Catch them in a crossfire."

"Maybe," Alfred said. "It's the best chance we have until they decide to set fire to the building."

"We'll have to stop that as long as we can. If that happens, we escape the hotel and try to get to the barn and the horses."

Alfred nodded. "We have you and me, the three Lighthorsemen, and Emerson and Fox."

"And me," Doc Raeborn declared.

The man stood in the doorway behind Bass and Alfred. He had two pistols thrust through his belt and a Winchester canted at his hip.

"Thought you'd gone, Doc," Bass said.

"And leave you men, some of you wounded, up here alone?" Raeborn shook his head fiercely. "I haven't been in a gunfight since the War Between the States, but I still know how it's done."

"All right then," Bass said. "Why don't you go on up to the second floor and find you a spot. If we get fresh wounded, that's where we'll be taking them."

Raeborn nodded and pulled back into the hallway.

Waiting for violence was tense business. Bass had done it many times, and it never got any easier. He bided his time, though, and watched Main

Street from Emerson's office window.

Bullets already scarred the walls, and there would be more. Josephine Many Stars would hate to see what had happened to her hotel, and she would hate what was about to happen.

With grim deliberation, he pushed that thought out of his mind and concentrated on surviving over the next few minutes.

A man out in the street called out, "Bass Reeves! We know you're in there!"

"What do you want?" Bass yelled.

"We're gonna kill you," the man said. "Don't nobody else in that buildin' have to die."

Bass glanced to the other side of the window where Alfred was hunkered down.

"Well, there it is then," Bass said.

"That was stated pretty clear," Alfred replied.

"You hear me, Marshal?" the man yelled.

"I think I'll mosey out there for a minute," Bass said to Alfred. "It'll buy us a little time. Maybe we can see where more of them are. Maybe I can convince some of them they need to be somewhere else."

Alfred adjusted his hat. "I'll follow you as far as the door."

When Bass reached the hotel's front door, he took a breath, set himself, and opened the door. All the lights were off in the hotel, so when he stepped out onto the boardwalk, he wasn't backlit. He kept the Winchester at his side mostly hidden in the folds of his slicker.

Six men stood spread out across Main Street. Two of them were on the same side of the street and hidden in the alley on the other side of the general store where Bass had taken shelter earlier. He ignored them for the moment, but he kept them in mind.

One stood across the street in front of the barber shop. The other three stood brazenly in the middle of the street.

"Get on out here," one of the men in the street said. Even in the shadows, his eyes stood out: bright and maniacal.

He's on something. The look was familiar to Bass. Alcohol was forbidden in the Territories, though some got in every now and again, but peyote, hemp, and laudanum flowed pretty freely.

"A lot of men want to see you die," the speaker went on, "an' plenty of 'em is here tonight."

Bass pulled his Winchester to his shoulder with practiced ease and squeezed the trigger. As the rifle recoiled, the speaker fell backward into the street with a bullet through his head.

Bass shot the man on the speaker's left in the chest and he stumbled back in a half-turn. The man in the street on the speaker's right wheeled to his left and headed for the general store. Bass picked him off before he managed his second step.

The man across the street fired his rifle and the bullet ripped through Bass's slicker. Alfred's rifle roared and the outlaw across the street jerked backward and went down.

Bass retreated into the hotel, took rounds for the rifle from his gun belt, and fed them into the Winchester.

"Get ready!" he yelled loud enough to be heard throughout the hotel. "They'll come now!"

The marshal set up at the open door because it gave him more of a view of the street. Bullets whacked into the boardwalk, the front of the hotel, and the doorframe. The detonations of the weapons fired inside the hotel filled the building with deafening thunder.

More gunshots came from above where Emerson, Fox, and Raeborn were posted, and from the back of the hotel where the Lighthorsemen were set up to cover the rear and the sides of the building.

"They're coming," Alfred stated calmly. His rifle boomed and banged against his shoulder.

One of the shadows out in the street dropped, but a half-dozen bullets bracketed the door and dug divots from the wood.

Bass fired at one of the shadows and it spun away. He levered the action, sighted on another, and fired again.

Still, the outlaws came, powered by blood lust and fear, and maybe some "medicine" Rafaela Orozco had given them from her witch's bag of tricks. If they broke their charge, the outlaws would have a hard time getting their nerve up to try it again.

And there definitely wouldn't be as many of them. The shadows dropped into the street and along the boardwalk and became dead and dying men.

"Get him!" The woman's shout carried over the gunfire. Hatred and determination echoed in her words. "Drag him out so Frisco can have his revenge!"

Frisco?

The dead outlaw's name rolled around inside Bass's mind. That couldn't be true, but if the outlaws were drugged the way he believed, maybe they thought Frisco was alive.

One of the men slid across the boardwalk unseen and whirled around the door with his pistol extended into the hotel. The man's face was covered with rain, but his flesh held gray death pallor that would have looked at home on a corpse.

Knowing he might already be too late, Bass ducked and tried to get his rifle up.

The outlaw pulled the pistol's trigger again and again, but the hammer fell on spent cartridges. Crazed laughter ripped from the man's throat, and he lifted his eyebrows in what might have been fear or surprise or expectation.

His face jerked to the side and a bloody crater erupted where his nose had once been. Bass shoved his rifle into the man's chest and pushed his opponent back before either of them realized he was dead.

"She's drugged them," Bass said hoarsely.

"I saw that," Alfred said. He levered a fresh cartridge into his rifle and fired again.

A wave of outlaws appeared out of the dark and ran toward the hotel in a line that looked like it had no end. Bullets thudded constantly into the hotel despite the fact that the building's defenders cut down their number.

"Time to go," Bass said. He fired into the crazed shadows, and still they ran toward the hotel.

Alfred turned and headed for the stairs. "Coming up!" he yelled.

"Come ahead!" Emerson yelled. "Bass, you too!"

Bass fired a last time, then ran for the stairs. Alfred was already halfway to the second floor.

Outlaws flooded through the door after Bass, but Emerson, Fox, and Raeborn covered them with withering fire. Men died and fell and became a barrier of flesh and blood for those who followed.

At the top of the stairs, nearly blind because of the darkness, Bass reached the second floor.

Josephine Many Stars stood there waiting for him.

Although she'd been dead for years, Josephine looked the same. Her long, dark hair was pulled back. She wore one of her favorite dresses that she'd made herself. Moccasins covered her feet. She held a wooden spoon in one hand, the way she had several times in the hotel's kitchen when she'd talked to Bass over breakfast or supper.

Moonlight speared through the window at the back of the landing and turned Josephine pale, like she was made from fog.

A shadow darkened the window and fell across the woman. Then the glass exploded and flew inward.

Josephine struck Bass on the head with the wooden spoon, knocked his hat off, and yelled, "Move!"

Gathering himself, Bass stepped to the right. A muzzle flash lit the landing briefly and a bullet burned through the spot Bass had been standing. The round tore through his slicker.

Bass raised his rifle and pointed it at the large man who stood before him. Blown by the wind, the shredded curtains danced around the man like ropy, dripping tendrils. The moonlight outlined the broad figure, but it didn't highlight the man's features—except for the thorned rose tattooed on one of the man's stubbly cheeks. The man stepped forward and light from a lantern carried in by one of the dead men below revealed the gnarled features and pallid skin.

In his life before he'd been hanged, Frank "Frisco" Calderón had been a large, strong man. His head had resembled a stone block atop a mountain. His features had been blunt and fierce. Now the lips were curled in a horrifying grimace that revealed broken, yellowed teeth and purple gums that looked withered and diseased. His head no longer sat properly on his shoulders but now leaned to one side and was tilted back to the left. His nose was broken and no longer centered.

His hair had gone gray in places, and patchy, like he had mange, or like parts of his scalp had died.

Calderón wore dungarees, boots, a shirt, and a slicker. All of it looked ill-fitting, but new. The stench of a fresh grave clung to the man.

Or whatever he was.

Bass's finger slid over the rifle trigger, but before he could squeeze it, Calderón grabbed the barrel in one big hand. Bass fired, but the bullet buried into the wall beside Calderón.

The big man roared in inarticulate rage like an animal and yanked the rifle from Bass's hands.

Around them, the three Lighthorsemen appeared from the rooms where they'd been exchanging fire with attacking outlaws. Bob Tall Bear limped into the hallway only to get hit by Bass's rifle gripped by Calderón. Tall Bear dropped immediately.

Fieldstone raised his weapon, but Calderón fired his pistol first. The bullet knocked Fieldstone back into Obediah and both of them crashed to the floor.

Only a few feet away, Alfred raised his rifle, but he didn't have a clear shot because Bass was in the way.

Bass drew both his pistols, but before he could take aim, Calderón hurled himself at the marshal and knocked them both back down the stairs. Falling and banging on the steps, Bass tried to keep his wits about him. His right hand struck the balusters, and he lost the pistol he was holding. He couldn't bring the pistol in his left hand around.

Calderón latched onto Bass's throat with one big hand and closed off his air. Black spots danced in Bass's vision and his throat burned. Calderón howled again, more like a thing than a man.

When they hit the floor, Bass was on bottom and Calderón sat astride him. The big man looked dazed. The smell of death clung even more fiercely to him. Bass tried to bring his pistol around, but two outlaws with crazed eyes entered the hotel's main door and focused on him. Bass rolled the hammer back on the .44 Model P and fired twice in quick succession.

The rounds drove the men backward. Calderón shifted atop Bass. Thankfully, the man had lost his pistol somewhere down the steps as well. Calderón gripped his hands together and slammed them down. Bass rolled his head to the side and the blow caromed off his head and struck the floor.

Senses reeling, feeling half-sick because of the sudden dizziness that exploded inside his head, Bass braced his feet against the floor and heaved his stomach up. Calderón tilted to one side and fell over. Bass rolled the other way in a desperate bid to escape. He slammed his pistol into Calderón's misshapen face and the big man staggered away.

Guns thundered overhead. Some of the shooting struck the outlaws at the hotel's entrance.

Breath rasping through his bruised throat, still dazed, Bass forced himself to his feet. Before he could get his true balance and face Calderón in front of him, before he could raise his pistol, something struck him from behind.

He stumbled to the side and his shoulder crashed into the wall.

Standing in Emerson's office, with the broken window behind her offering mute testimony as to how she'd gotten into the hotel, Rafaela held a scattergun aimed at Bass's midsection.

She was small and dark and fierce. A rose tattoo marred one of her cheeks. Her long black hair was tied back with a yellow ribbon, but her hair was wet and bedraggled. Her dark eyes held the same crazed fires of the outlaws who followed her.

"Put down the pistol, Marshal," Rafaela ordered.

Knowing if he didn't, he'd probably be dead, Bass dropped the pistol to the floor.

"Frisco," Rafaela said. "Are you all right?"

Calderón growled and shook his head.

"He understands you?" Bass asked in disbelief.

"Yes," Rafaela said. "He's not what he was before you and your judge hanged him and had him buried, but he is mine." Fierce pride blazed in her eyes. "You didn't succeed in killing him completely. I dug him up. I brought him back to life with the potions my *abuela* taught me. He still loves me, and I love him. We both want you dead. You and that woman upstairs. And we'll have that too."

The woman was crazy. She had to be.

Calderón strode toward Bass and knotted his hands into blocky fists. He threw a hard right punch straight at Bass's head. Bass blocked the blow but still got rocked back. He drove his own right hand into Calderón's face and snapped the man's head back, but Calderón only growled and readied himself for another attack.

Bass drove two left jabs into the bigger man's stomach, but it was like hitting a tree trunk. If Calderón felt the blows, he didn't show it. The big man came at him again and his head was still twisted and tilted. Now, in the light of the lantern that had been lit in Emerson's office, the rope scars on Calderón's neck were visible. Some of them were still scabbed over, like those wounds never quite healed.

Desperate, Bass punched Calderón in the face twice, then hit him with an uppercut to the chin that drove him back a half-step. Calderón growled again, but this time there was pain mixed in with the malevolence.

His neck's weak. Bass hung onto that thought. Goliath had a weakness and the marshal intended to exploit that weakness.

"Stop!" Rafaela screamed. She pointed the shotgun with more deliberation. "Stop!"

Calderón threw a wide, looping punch at Bass's head. The marshal ducked under the blow, slipped around to Calderón's side, and threw himself across the big man's broad back. Bass wrapped his arms around Calderón's head and his legs around the man's thighs. He tucked his face in tight against his opponent's body so he couldn't grab it and pull him away.

Saddled with extra weight, Calderón stumbled among the dead bodies on the floor and went down to his knees. Rafaela had a clear shot and Bass didn't want to let go of his opponent because, with the way his senses still spun, he might not get the upper hand again.

Still, the woman hesitated because if she fired, she would hit Calderón with the buckshot too. A gunshot rang out, and for the first time Bass realized most of the shooting had stopped.

A hole appeared in Rafaela's forehead. Her knees buckled, she dropped the shotgun, and her body hit the floor.

Calderón roared again and grabbed Bass's left arm with both hands. Bracing himself, Bass grabbed Calderón's chin and hauled it sideways as hard as he could. The marshal was big and strong from handling horses and other livestock.

The big man's spine snapped with a crack like dead wood splitting. He stood for just a moment longer, swayed, and dropped. Bass kicked himself loose and landed on his feet. He scooped up his pistol, eased the hammer back, and surveyed the hotel for anyone still gunning for him.

Only dead and dying men littered the floor.

"We killed most of them." Alfred walked down the stairs with a pistol in each hand. "Those we didn't kill ran away. I suppose they'd gotten a bellyful of killing."

Bass took a deep breath and nodded. Two dozen dead men lay at his feet.

"There was sure enough of it."

The next morning dawned bright, a hard shift from the stormy night. Birdsong filled the air back in the woods that weren't far from town, and Main Street was quiet enough for their happy tunes to carry over the High Hill Hotel.

The horses hooked up to the three wagons full of dead men and one woman snorted and stomped their feet to show their displeasure at having been pressed into service so early.

Before they drove out of Goodland, Bass intended to feed them all well.

Alfred carried two cups of steaming coffee out of the hotel, walked over to Bass, and handed one cup to him.

Bass accepted the cup gratefully. The morning might be filled with bright sunshine, but it still carried a chill left over from the night.

"Any more of them in there?" Bass asked.

Alfred nodded toward the three wagons. "That's all of them. Emerson and Fox have got a lot of cleaning and repairing to do though."

As he drank his coffee, Bass stared at the hotel's bullet-riddled front wall. "Josephine sure would be unhappy to see this place."

"Emerson and Fox will have it back to rights quick enough," Alfred said. He was silent for a moment and sipped his coffee. "Emerson told me what you said to him—about Josephine being there last night."

Bass shook his head. "I shouldn't have said anything, and I was probably imagining it anyway. Things got pretty confusing there for a while, what with dead men climbing up the back of the hotel and breaking in windows. And owlhoots jumped up on whatever Rafaela Orozco was giving them."

"It was confusing," Alfred said. "I'll give you that." He looked Bass in the eyes. "But I'll tell you what I think."

Bass sighed. There was no way to stop Alfred from telling him what he thought.

"I think Josephine was there," the posseman said. "She protected you, and she probably did her best to protect all of us. This was her place, and that means she has power here. When she needed to warn you, she was able to reach out to you."

Bass wasn't going to argue because he didn't have any way of supporting an argument. And he knew Alfred was going to hang onto this one.

"That's a thing the Elders always made sure we knew: that the ancestors and the spirits were still around to look after us whenever they can," Alfred said. "I believe Josephine Many Stars was there last night, and I believe she saved your life."

"While all the shooting was going on, it's just as likely I got hit by a slow-moving ricochet or a piece of wood."

"You go ahead and tell yourself that," the posseman suggested. "We'll see if you believe it later on."

Elleanor Hundey walked out of the hotel and joined Bass and Alfred. "Mr. Emerson suggested I go over to the Hot Griddle next door and have breakfast. Bud and I ate there a couple times. The food was always good. Perhaps you'd like to join me."

"We can't, ma'am," Bass said.

The idea of eating after carrying out enough dead men, and one woman, to fill three wagons killed whatever appetite he might have had. Bedding down next to them while traveling on back to Albion to deal with them would not be something he wished for either. But he had to do it because some of those men were known to him and were wanted by Judge Parker. So a proper accounting of the dead would have to be done. Albion had enough gravediggers to get the bodies buried once that was done, and those bodies would be in bad shape after that trip.

"We've got to get these bodies on over to Albion," Bass said. "I suspect folks around here can't be shut of them soon enough. They might not like the idea of us waiting to have breakfast."

Several of the townsfolk gawked at the bodies, but none of them stopped by to ask questions. That would come. Bass didn't want to be around for that either.

"I want to thank you both for getting Bud's killers," Elleanor said.

"Yes, ma'am," Bass replied. "You go on and get your breakfast while it's hot."

The woman walked away.

"She's going to have a hard go of trying to take care of that farm by herself," Alfred said.

"She'll do it," Bass said. "She'll do it, or she'll sell it and build herself another life. When something bad happens, something that changes our lives, that's what we all have to do." He took a breath. "You think about it, most of the folks in the Territories got chased out of somewhere else to make new lives here. All of us. Or our parents and grandparents. They're building towns like this one. Good towns where a man and woman can plan for the future and raise a family."

"Not all of them do," Alfred said. "Not when they're faced with folks like Frank Calderón and Rafaela Orozco."

"No," Bass agreed. "Not all of them do. That's why, when things go bad, Judge Parker sends men like you and me out here to balance the scales. I like the work and I'm good at it, so that suits me." He smiled. "After all those hardships I've been through, this is how I built my new life, and I'm glad of it."

THE END

Hair-Raising Stories

While growing up in rural Oklahoma, I was exposed to stories of the macabre and frightful on a regular basis. As a kid, I watched television on days when the "skip" was good. For those of you who don't know what that is, it was back in the days when everybody had to use a television antenna of some sort to pull in a television signal from the ether.

A television signal. Meaning one.

In those small towns I grew up in, all you ever got was one television station—if you could turn the antenna just right, the cloud cover didn't interfere, and if there was anything on television worth watching. I saw a lot of things I didn't believe in. Big cities like New York and San Francisco weren't real to me. How could so many people live in one place and not kill each other? (The sad truth is that a lot of the times they can't.)

I also saw a lot of things I wanted to believe in. Like the old Flash Gordon serials, *Lost in Space*, and *The Voyage to the Bottom of the Sea*. There were a lot of other things I believed in automatically. Ghosts, hexes, witches, bad luck caused by breaking mirrors, birds in the house signaling a death in the family. My father grew up with those things in the even smaller town (and outside of that!) he grew up in.

Back in the days when there were no cell phones and folks sometimes got stranded on the roadside in the middle of nowhere and had to walk to somewhere to borrow a phone, many of us would stop and offer rides. I did that a few times because I'd sometimes found myself stranded and in need of a phone. I stopped and offered rides just to keep that goodwill out in the world. However, I *always* made sure whoever I gave a ride to wasn't a ghost. Tales of the lost dead wandering the highways and byways filled my imagination. "You can let me off just up the road a piece. There's a stop I gotta make."

That never happened to me, and I don't stop as much as I used to because everyone has a cell phone these days, but that thought of "women in white" and "ghostly hitchhikers" still crosses my mind. As I grew up, I found out a lot of those haints, stories about witches, and skinwalkers

175

weren't true. At least, I've never crossed paths with those otherworldly folks. Haven't found any aliens either, and not once have I been abducted. So I put away those superstitions my father handed down to me. I didn't forget them though. They're still a part of me, still right within reach when I want them—and when I could least use them.

While putting together a story idea for my latest Bass Reeves story in this volume you hold, thanks to Captain Ron's indulgence because life has been chaotic for us all of late, and I got caught up in much of it, I remembered *Night of the Living Dead*. I can't remember when I first caught that movie. I was too young to go to the movie theater to see it when it first came out, but I distinctly remember watching it on a black-and-white television, which means I was still living with my parents. As soon as I got married at nineteen and moved out, one of the first things I purchased was a color television set. They'd been out for years, but my parents didn't see the need for one.

That image of the zombies flooding that house near the end has stayed with me for years. I knew I wanted to do something with witches. Almost every culture I've read about has its belief in witches. I don't believe in the creepy ones that live in the woods in gingerbread houses and want to eat children—at least, most of the time I don't. I never let my kids go out into the woods by themselves although I wandered everywhere in them. I grew up in the "unsupervised" generation. "Y'all go out and play. I'll honk when supper's on the stove." I'm pretty sure I was more worried about snakes and spiders and deep ponds, but critters that lived out in the woods crossed my mind too. I wanted to do a story about a witch. Native Americans believe in them, and they believe some are good and some are bad, just like everyone else in the world. I even had a discussion with a fellow professor at Gaylord College at the University of Oklahoma about witches in his native Malawi and the surrounding African countries. It was all fascinating stuff about human organs being used in spells, especially organs harvested from albino children. Maybe one day I'll write a story about that.

I chose a *bruja*, a woman of Hispanic origins, because that made her seem more mysterious and dangerous. But that image of zombies attacking that house in *Night of the Living Dead* stayed in the back of my mind. I wanted to roll that in too. Also, since witches in some cultures (I'm looking at you voodoo), I knew I wanted a "zombie" too. After all, who else would be so fierce to a man like Bass Reeves, a legendary lawman who saw everything during his time serving the Hanging Judge?

I had a *bruja* and, after a fashion, I had a zombie for my tale. The story came together pretty quickly after that, although there was some fitful stops and bumps along the way. Times lately do get difficult for all of us, and it's hard to focus on things when more wrongness occurs in the world. This Bass Reeves story takes place in a matter of hours, not days like I normally spin them. I wanted that compression of time. I wanted action and mystery and atmosphere to drive the story. I think maybe I delivered that. I put Bass Reeves in more danger than I ever have before, and he almost doesn't get out of it.

Of course, he does. His story continued on for years after this little tale of witches and almost-zombies concludes. But for one night in the small town of Goodland in the Kiamichi Mountains, in a place called the High Hill Hotel, Bass Reeves, Alfred his posseman, and three Choctaw Lighthorsemen are up against a horde of outlaws.

And dawn is a long way off.

Enjoy.

MEL ODOM - grew up in southeastern Oklahoma, where diehard country boys still eat possums and soft-shelled turtles, but now lives in Moore, Oklahoma, a wonderful town that unfortunately attracts Pecos Bill riding a twister on a regular basis. He's lived through hog raising and F-5 tornados, surely two of the most dangerous things in the world.

Over the last twenty-plus years, he's written dozens of novels in many different genres, including some based on television shows like *Buffy the Vampire Slayer* and novelizations of *Blade, Tomb Raider,* and xXx. He's trekked through deadly forests and braved the Sword Coast in the Forgotten Realms, and written adventures of bioroid detectives in Fantasy Flight's Android game.

He teaches in the Professional Writing program at the University of Oklahoma and writes all the time. He can be reached at mel@melodom.net, www.melodom.blogspot.com, @melodom on Twitter, and on Facebook.

His current military science fiction trilogy, *The Makaum War,* has been hitting bestseller lists.

BASS REEVES
FRONTIER MARSHAL

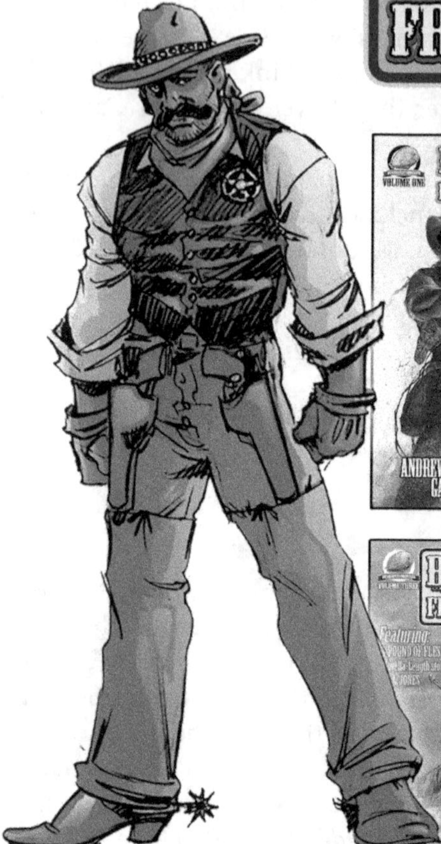

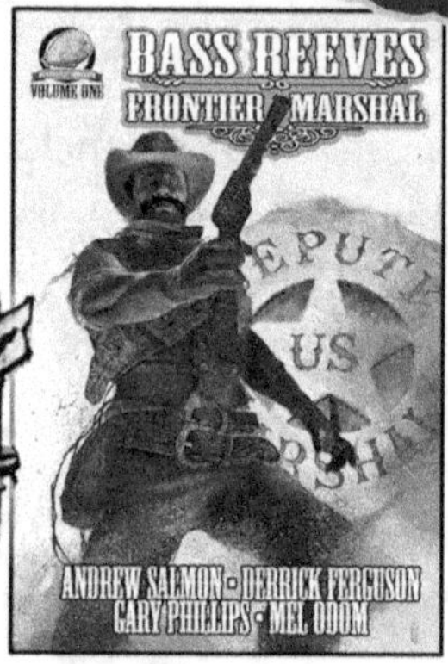

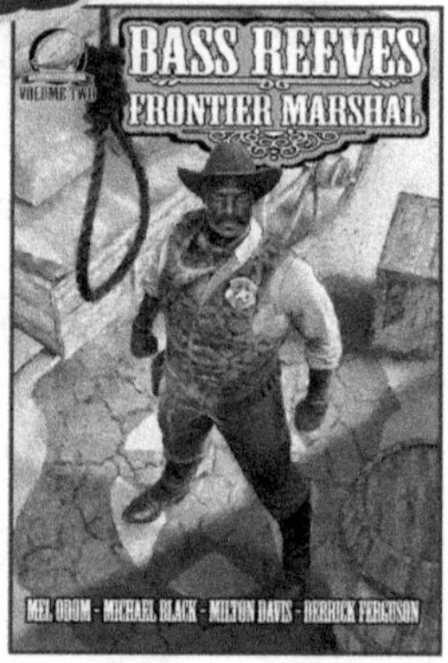

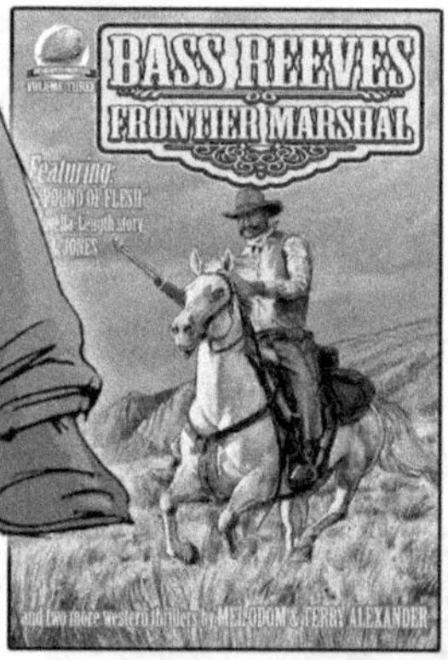

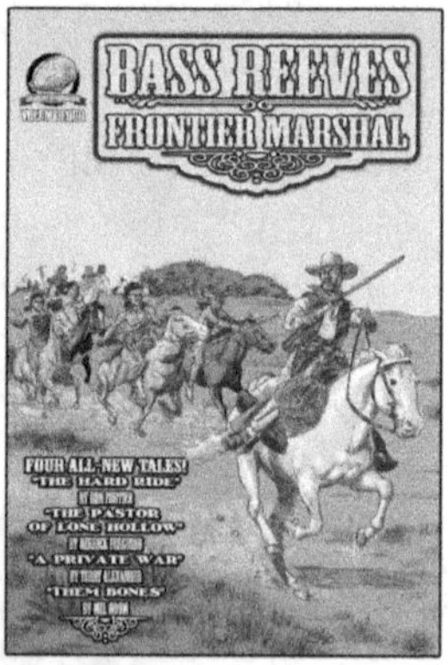

IN THE FIRST FOUR VOLUMES FROM AIRSHIP 27

A WESTERN LEGEND COMES TO LIFE

FEATURING RIP-ROARING, WILD-WEST STORIES BY SOME OF THE BEST WESTERN WRITERS OF TODAY!

AN AIRSHIP 27 PRODUCTION

PULP FICTION FOR A NEW GENERATION!

FOR AVAILABILITY: AIRSHIP27HANGAR.COM

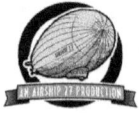

LIKE YOUR WESTERNS A LITTLE "WEIRD?" WE'VE GOT JUST THE THING:

Richard O'Malley is a hard working Boston reporter in the years following the Civil War. He is fascinated by tales of the wild west and the colorful frontiersmen who are taming it. None captivate him more than the stories of the Dead Sheriff; a dedicated lawman who had risen from the grave to continue his mission. Taking his life savings, O'Mally embarks on a personal quest to find this mythical figure and chronicle his exploits. What he finds will make them both legends.

MARK JUSTICE'S
The Dead SHERIFF

PULP FICTION FOR A NEW GENERATION!

For availability of these and other fine pulp style publications visit: airship27hangar.com

AN AIRSHIP 27 PRODUCTION

During the Civil War, young Jason Mankiller had a tattoo painted on his left check; that of blood drops falling from the corner of his eyes. Since that time, earning his reputation as a bounty hunter, he is known on the Texas frontier as *The Man Who Cries Blood*.

In this second tale, Mankiller is on the trail of three vicious Comancheros who have been stirring up trouble between the Comanche and the white settlers of Fort Rogers. Even though the skilled hunter has the friendship of the notorious half-breed Comanche Chief, Quanah Parker, it is still left to him to find the renegades and prevent more bloodshed.

Once again writer R.A. Jones weaves a thrilling adventure set against the backdrop of post-Civil War Texas, bringing to life the pioneer men and women who crossed a vast wilderness to create a new chapter in American history. Comanche Blood is a part of their story.

GUN GLORY

HE RODE A GUNFIGHTER'S TRAIL

R.A. Jones

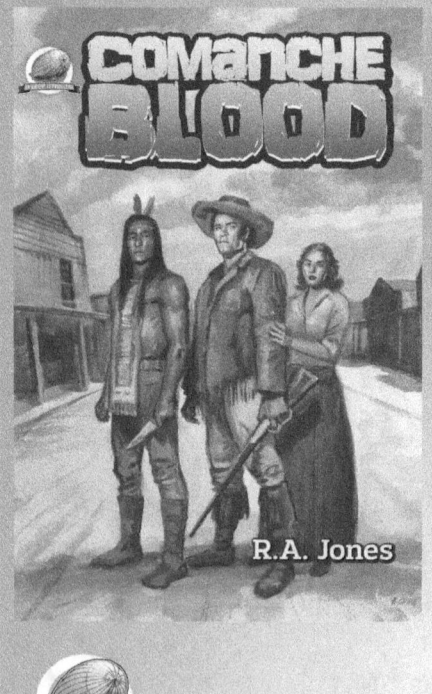

COMANCHE BLOOD

R.A. Jones

Young Jason Mankiller never believed his surname was an omen of his future until the Civil War broke out and he joined the Union Army. Fate took him to the fields of Gettysburg. By the time the battle ended, he was sitting atop a small rise surrounded by the bodies of dozens of Confederate troopers. Days later, while drunk, his fellow soldiers had tears of blood tattooed onto his face. From that day forward, the Man Who Cried Blood's reputation spread far and wide.

Ten years later, Jason Mankiller is in Ft. Rogers, Texas, hoping to find a job and bury his past. But the blood tattoo won't let him escape the gunfighter's trail. Writer R.A. Jones delivers an old fashioned western adventure in the grand tradition of Max Brand and Louis L'Amour. Here are pioneering men and women facing the birth of a new American destiny that will demand their blood, sweat, tears and sacrifice. For Jason Mankiller, that promise of a better life will be claimed at the end of a smoking gun.

Airship27Hangar.com
NEW PULP

Pulp Fiction for a New Generation!